Lunch with Her Idol

Dedicated to Matthew Richard Enos.
I believe in you. You believe in me.

Prologue

Chicago-1980

"I love you," Katya said. "I love you too," he whispered as quietly as he could, his sweaty hand grasping the handset of his black rotary phone.

"What's going on? We just talked an hour ago." Dr. Loering responded, trying to hide the rising irritation in his voice.

"I know, but I really need you today." Katya said with a hint of playful desperation in her voice. "Why don't you come by? Let's have some fun and we can talk about that new method you want to explore for the writing program."

"Tonight?" he said, twisting the black phone cord around his index finger. "I don't know, I have a lot of reading and an exam tomorrow. Some other time?"

"No," she said with the authority that had initially excited him. "I want you here tonight. It's been too long."

"It's been a week Katya. I can come tomorrow." There was a pause, a lapse that stretched long enough that he thought she hung up or got disconnected.

Abruptly she said, "Either you come tonight, or you don't come at all. Ever."

"What's wrong with you? This isn't like you" he said, the agitation building, the softness of his words spoiling. Sharpening into linguistic knives.

"You need to come over tonight. Tonight, Henry. Be here or don't count on my money for your ideas again," she angrily said to him.

"But I can't tonight, listen, I love you..." came out his mouth just as Gloria stepped back into his dorm room.

He quickly hung up the phone, forcing himself to the present, with Gloria. Gloria in her white blouse, red skirt, and high white boots that clicked on the hard floor as she approached him. She looked stunning that evening, her usual curly hair straightened and held back with a headband the color of a sparkling red jolly rancher candy.

"The bathrooms here are disgusting. You boys are dirty," she said sitting down next to him on his twin sized bed. She glanced at his once white sheets, now a stained cream color lying in a tangled pile.

He knew she didn't care.

"Who was that?" she asked as she brushed his arm gently with her hand, moving closer to him.

"Oh, my sister," he said nonchalantly, trying to hide the lingering agitation.

As Gloria moved closer to him, Henry caught the scent of her perfume. She smelled faintly of peonies and the scent shaved off a sliver of his anxiety. Women could always unarm him with their scents, their softness.

"Your sister?" Gloria questioned as she began to kiss his neck. "I didn't think you talked to your sister."

Receptive to her kisses, he alerted to her charms. He hoped the subject would go away, go away like Katya's attitude. And on that note, all the angry women he dealt with. Their problems, their need for attention... He responded to her charms with his hands gliding over her body,

"Did I say that?"

"You did. You said you hadn't spoken to her in years after she stole work from you."

His kissing accelerated as her kissing abruptly stopped.

"I did say that didn't I?" he said, slipping his now hungry hand into her shirt. Rubbing the knotted tension out of her long, smooth, elegant neck.

"You did. You said she was horrible to you when you were younger and you wouldn't talk to her again," she said pulling away. "What did she want? I heard you say, "I love you" like you meant it."

"So many questions," he said with a little laugh, struggling to unclip her bra. He felt her body stiffen.

"Yes, and lots of excuses." she said standing and stepping away from him. "You're always busy always tired. You have a paper due. You're working on your new writing self-help method, or whatever the hell it is. You never have time for me, only occasionally when you want sex. And even that's sporadic. What college boy doesn't want sex all the time? And in the beginning of a relationship?" She started to pace in front of him as she continued… "You get this blank look on your face. Anytime I mention our relationship, it's the same fucking look. We've slept together and been dating for over a year and a half. I get the same blank look, the same excuses. Always."

Sighing, he searched for a pack of cigarettes on his nightstand. "I have time right now. What do you want to talk about?" Calmly, he sifted through several empty packs to find one single Parliament. He sighed, rolling up the sleeves of his blue linen shirt, straightening his slightly off-balance glasses before he lit up. Taking a long drag, he exhaled, blowing a big puff of smoke, blowing it in her face. In a tone laced with condescension he said, "Let's hear it, what do you want?"

Gloria was visibly angry, and it made her even more beautiful than she already was. He always had a thing for brunettes, especially ones that were as curvy and vivacious as Gloria.

Tapping the ashes of his cigarette in an empty Coke can sitting on his desk, he turned towards Gloria, grabbing her by the shoulders and gently pushed her to the bed.

"What does anger mean to you Gloria? How can you infuse it into your art?" He stood over her, feeling the advantage of being substantially taller when she was sitting down.

He took another long drag feeling satisfied with himself in the moment. It didn't matter to him what Gloria did, he thought to himself. Only to the extent that he liked curvy, vivacious brunettes.

"Perhaps you could apply the 8th step, to how you're feeling," knowing the words would ignite her.

"I don't need your steps. It's phony bullshit Henry." She stood, looking around for what he supposed was her jacket and purse.

"You're scared." He said in the calm neutral tone he had honed over the past two years in his workshops.

Emotions heightened sometimes, especially after the first critiques attendees received.

"You know, you're responsible for your own feelings," he tried a softer tone. He laid the hand that wasn't smoking his cigarette on her shoulder. He was trying another subtle phrase he had come up with to diffuse tension.

"That's a scary feeling in itself," he said with empathy, knowing it usually worked.

She took his hand off her shoulder and fumbled to put her jacket on. Good, he observed, he unnerved her. She would second guess herself now. Just as she had several times since they had been "dating", or whatever it was she called it.

She stopped and intensely stared at him head on. He stared back thinking she would be back. He was certain of it. That gaze, the posture, the affect, said it all. She might be upset. Yet, when she realizes he's the only guy on campus she can have an enlightening conversation with about writing *and* fuck, she'll be back, he thought taking another drag and exhaling right as she said,

"I don't have proof, but I know you're fooling around on me."

An exaggerated laugh burst out of him. The kind of reaction that suggested the accusation was ludicrous.

"I'm going to hang out with Arthur now," she said as she walked to the door.

His laughter came to a halt. "What is it with you and that Arthur anyway?" He called after her as she left, slamming the door behind her.

"He's old. You're sleeping with him because he's a professor," he said to his empty dorm room.

He finished his cigarette and sat for a moment, practicing withholding emotion. Leaders need to be strong. Without strength, nobody would trust or follow him. He was convinced his methods were golden. He knew his workshops were effective. The feelings of raw disappointment and worry of being found out were trying to overtake him. He wouldn't let the feelings win.

Gloria would be back. Besides, Dr. Loering didn't want to be in a long-term relationship with her. And that's what she wanted. Her high-pitched voice endlessly asking him for more. Every other word out of her mouth, "Commitment this, commitment that". He did his best to derail the conversation when she brought it up.

Yes, he missed out on sleeping with her. He got caught talking to one of his other girls, his top one, Katya. He had to take her call it even though it meant risking Gloria finding out. He needed Katya more than all the others. She had money, power, connections in the city. She believed in what he was doing with his writing and was a knockout beauty. He had a feeling that she also was becoming suspicious of Henry's extra activities.

Recently at one of his promotional events, she caught him directing a writee to call him Dr. Loering instead of Henry. She brought it up later that evening.

"Dr. Loering? Really? You haven't even been accepted into a master's program yet. Why'd you tell that writee to call you Doctor? I didn't know English majors got to call themselves doctor," she said laughing.

He hated her at that moment. Hated that she caught him. Hated she'd seen him lying. Hated, she was making fun of him. His power ceased. She'd angered his mind blank. His emotional reaction was almost as humiliating as getting caught using PhD credentials.

"They take me serious that way," He responded.

What's worse, is later he later realized, was the awareness he later had. He could have played her taunting off in a million ways to make what he was doing seem inconsequential. Now the seeds were planted and there was no way to stop them from growing. She knew who he really was. He had to keep Katya happy. Exercise extreme caution with her. That meant putting his other relationships with women at risk, like taking the call when Gloria was around.

It wasn't easy juggling women, and this wasn't the first time he ran into issues, but it was unusual of Katya. She'd gone out of her way to make him feel nothing but special. Happy to see him when she did. Of course, she wanted to see him more, but she didn't complain like a lot of the others, especially like Gloria. He glanced at his clock. She hadn't given him a specific time to come over, but it was already 7 in the evening. He grabbed his jacket and left his room.

It was a cold, damp, and dark evening. The leaves had fallen off the trees exposing a grey, muted sky. Katya was a five-minute walk from his dorm. She'd poke fun at him for living in the dorms as a senior. He chose to because he got access to new girls, prospects for his workshops. Of course, he told Katya and the others that it was to stay focused.

The blaring of horns and heavy traffic blurred his surroundings as he briskly walked down Fullerton approaching Lincoln Ave. He spotted her building on the corner and quickly ran up to ring her doorbell.

"Come to the back," she said before he could respond.

Annoyed but trying to maintain his emotion he walked around the back of her building, which required going through a dark, dank alleyway bound to have rats running around. Katya lived on the third floor of a building and had the entire floor to herself. When he tired of his dorm, he would stay with her for a week here or there. As he walked up the steep, dark, back steps he thought about Katya's world of privilege.

She'd no understanding of what it was like to not get what she wanted. That is why she is so kind, he thought. He also suspected she was messing with other people. It was impossible for him to accuse her given the fact he was doing the same. As he neared the top of the stairs and caught his breath, he noticed a pile of clothing outside her door. It took him a moment to realize, these were his things.

"What the hell?" he said as Katya opened the back door.

"I know," she said hanging halfway out of the door, wearing a dress that suggested she had other plans that evening.

"What do you mean?" he asked, adjusting his glasses from falling down the bridge of his nose.

"I know that you're with Gloria. And Amanda, Lacy, Stephanie, shall I keep listing them off?"

He stood stunned, for a moment.

With as much passion as he could muster, "They're lying. How could I possibly pull off being with that many women? You know how busy I am trying to write and build my workshops."

"There's no use in trying to me you are lying. Amanda found out first, then she told Lacy, it snowballed from there. The women you supposedly try to help through your lame workshop, they're nothing but your toys. I can't believe I fell for this," she said eyeing him up and down.

"Your writing was never that great anyway." The words slipped out before he could stop them, but he knew it was over.

"That's interesting you say that because I'm the one who wrote most of your framework, "she shot back.

"Regardless, I don't care what you think about my writing, I have more important things to worry about. Take your shit and get the fuck out of here," she said pointing to his pile of belongings and slamming the door.

He stood motionless as he heard the door lock, then unlock, and door fly open again,

"You're sick" she said and before he could respond she slammed the door in his face and locked it.

Katya closed the door, backed up against the cold wooden frame and sighed. She pulled out the pregnancy test from her back pocket and looked again: positive. She counted to ten and, despite herself, practiced withholding emotion.

Chapter 1

Method 1.) A writee is someone who isn't yet a writer but wants more than anything to see their name in print.

Dancing in the wind is the answer to where you should go. Stand still and release words until they flow. Sometimes it's alright to stay where you are and realize how reality can take you far. Even though there are more obstacles on the way the sunset is still beautiful at the end of the day. Grasping the moment is the real test...

Chicago-2009

Hailey sighed as she stopped typing. She had spent the weekend sitting near Lake Michigan, writing about wind. It was mandatory to write at least 1000 words a day, but Hailey always found herself writing at least 3000 words. Even though she loved writing, there was extra incentive to write more words. More words equaled less of Writer Marie's demands and domestic tasks. Today was special, throwing her typical morning routine off, forcing her to rush through her morning writing exercises. Today she'd scrambled to finish 500 subpar words. The blistering cold wind off Lake Michigan had more to say than she could ever write.

She'd wanted to create a poetic tribute to the lake. Even though Writer Marie had wanted her to focus on another essay, Hailey insisted that she work on her poem. She needed to write for herself. That was the only way she could get her word count and progress in the workshops. Yet, choosing the right outfit for Dr. Loering's event tonight was entirely consuming her attention this morning. Now she was rushed and out of sorts as she made her way to the drugstore.

Since Hailey graduated from college almost a year ago, she lived in Chicago. So far it had been a lonely existence, minus her job and the monthly obligatory dinners she had at her parents'. Dr. Loering's writing workshops felt the closest to a home she had found so far.

Dr. Loering's newest issue of "Writer's World" was coming out today. It was imperative, according to workshop rules, that she have the latest copy. She had to pick up a copy before her commute, even if it meant facing the wrath of Kevin for being late for work. It would be better than facing the wrath of Writer Marie if she was asked to discuss any of the articles. Writer Marie spit when she was angry. Hailey was certain she'd gotten a cold from her spit the last time she was angry.

As she rushed through the drugstore, she eagerly grabbed a copy and approached the checkout, the usual hope stirring within her that Fritz Malort, the salesclerk, would recognize her. A well-known poet in Wicker Park, Fritz was a trailblazer of performative art with the use of ketchup and chickens in his one-man show. Hailey dreamt of giving him a sample of her writing that he would swoon over. He'd beg her to write his next show, citing her creative genius as his new muse to his fanbase of all the up-and-coming writers in Chicago.

Hailey noted that Fritz worked as a salesclerk almost every morning, besides weekends. A job he clearly didn't enjoy. Part of his act includes telling tales of his job. He played it off as research rather than necessity. People ate it up. Tall, brown curly hair, with dreamy hazel eyes, she'd been going through his line for months hoping to gain his attention. Hailey knew that she was plain in the eyes of Fritz. As he rang up diapers, six packs of Bud-Light, toilet paper, and other odds and ends, Hailey noted the way his hair fell into his face, giving him the disheveled look of a starving artist.

Occasionally, his intense gaze locked onto her in a way that electrified her body. She pictured all the doors that would open if he saw her genius. When it was her turn, she walked to the counter, carefully setting down her copy of "Writer's World". She tried to lock eyes with him, hoping he'd comment.

He rang her up in silence, with no visible reaction on his perfectly chiseled cheeks. She inched over to the pick-up area, lingering for a moment near the register, hoping he would recognize her. "It's me," she said internally, as she bore her gaze into him. "The writer you wish you had for your shows."

Hailey barely noticed when he said declined.

"Miss, your card is declined, do you have another way to pay?"

She didn't. She must have spent the rest of her money on the errands she ran for Writer Marie last night and forgotten to get reimbursed.

"I must have forgotten my other card..." She mumbled.

"Next," Fritz called without giving her another glance.

She pushed away the disappointment sinking in and thought of all the future opportunities for him to notice her.

Burning red from shame, she turned around to exit an older man bumped into her, spilling his scalding hot Chai on her jacket.

"Sorry Tootz, I didn't see you standing there." His tone made it hard to believe he was sorry or that he hadn't seen her there.

"You didn't see me either, so I guess we're even," he continued.

"Oh, that's ok," Hailey mumbled as she looked around for anything to wipe her jacket with, boiling up inside. An image of her mom before Sunday church flashed in her mind. Carefully steaming her dark purple suit, with the pleated skirt. "Rudeness begets rudeness," she'd offer as her weekly tidbit of wisdom.

The old man, dressed in the kind of slacks that suggested retirement, chuckled at her. "You're off to quite a start there, can only get better, right?"

"I suppose I am off to some kind of start, if you'll now excuse me, I'm late." She said, trying her best to keep the annoyance out of her voice, she walked away. She heard a low throated chuckle escape him as she stepped out into the brittle, November morning.

The smell of asphalt and train tracks overcame her as she took a deep breath, trying to exhale the annoyance. Why was it so hard to be noticed by Fritz? She rubbed out the spot of Chai the best she could with her hand.

She glanced over, noticing a couple sloppily making out on the corner. She was 25 and had never experienced love. Or even a kiss a person could describe as passionate.

A puff of steam exited her as she exhaled. Checking her watch, she realized she needed to hurry to make it to the office on time. She needed to be early so she could leave on time that day. She hadn't been able to reschedule dinner with her parents, and if she didn't go, she wouldn't hear the end of it. Lately it seemed like they were looking for ways to cut her off.

It would be tough to leave on time with her workload. Her boss, Kevin, didn't believe in breaks and pushed his workers to follow his lead. Hailey heard him bragging numerous times to customers as he gave them office tours. Sometimes Hailey would mouth along with one of his favorite boasts,

"I'd use my boat more often, but I'm a workaholic, I just can't seem to stop, 7 days a week, 10-hour days at least..."

He always found a way to mention his boat.

"Oh Frank, you know, since you know so much about motors, I'd love for you to come out with me on my boat sometime, I have an engine with 1050 pure horsepower..."

Hailey rushed into the Damen station. She sprinted through the turnstile and up to the platform in time to hear the train doors open. Jumping on the first car she could, she headed to an open seat in the back as the train lurched forward. She'd have twelve minutes. Twelve uninterrupted minutes to look up "Writer's World" online, it was better than nothing.

Then, tonight she'd see Dr. Loering speak at his event and tomorrow have lunch all alone with him. It was hard to believe. She wanted to make an announcement to all the morning commuters. " Excuse me everyone, it doesn't matter that Fritz thinks I'm invisible. I'm going to see Dr. Loering in person, one-on-one, and he's going to change my life!"

Instead, she closed her eyes, relieved to be on the train. Relieved she would be on time and smiled, letting her morning annoyance dissipate. She'd anticipated this day for six months now since she bought her ticket.

One Sunday morning, shortly after Hailey moved to Chicago, she felt listless. She worked up the courage to check out a sketchy looking Occult Bookstore near her apartment. The dark and gloomy storefront didn't extend a friendly invitation to the passersby. It was that fateful day, in the Occult Bookstore, where she discovered Dr. Loering. She'd seen his face on billboards promoting events and knew of him. As did most people. He was good looking, like a model or actor. While she was browsing in the Tarot section, she overheard two middle aged women talking about him.

"I used to put spells on my roommate," one woman said as she picked up one of his hardcover books on display. "She was such a slob. Prize pig that woman. I swear, I've never seen such a mess. When she cooked a meal, no matter what, she used every single dish in the kitchen. She didn't want to throw paper towels out so she would keep the same ones bunched up all over the counter for months. One time I went to the bathroom and almost threw up because of the smell of her tampon in the trash. It was laying on top, not wrapped in anything, like it was a piece of tissue or an unused Q-Tip. It was only after I started applying Dr. Loering's methods, things changed. I noticed it especially with the 8th step, "Poised Responses to Writer's Block".

Hailey observed the ambiguous nature of the women's relationship. They didn't seem interested in what the other one was saying. Her companion asked in a flat, uninterested tone, "What was the 8th step about?"

"Poised Responses is all about controlling the feeling you want to feel. The 8th step explains how to express feelings in a way that encourages creating. Dr. Loering talks about how you can apply this to anything, but of course he is trying to influence us writers. It's getting to that root cause of what your emotion is and expressing it. So, I expressed my anger and disgust. I left notes all over the bathroom, "You disgust me. You're smelly, your hair is all over our shower, the food you eat smells, the way you do things angers me to the core."

"How did she react?"

"She cried. But once she stopped crying, we had a chat.

"Wasn't she pissed off at the stuff you wrote?"

"I don't think so. After I expressed myself, she started cleaning the entire kitchen, even my dishes. She doesn't leave her trash lying all over the place anymore. She still leaves her dirty socks by the armchair but for the most part she's a changed woman. I swear by his book. I swear by his methods. He's unbelievable. Every word of his contains keys. And the weekly groups hold me accountable. Have you read his older material?"

As her companion leafed through a spell book she droned, "Yeah, I've read all his stuff."

"He's so hot sometimes I find myself imagining what he'd be like in bed," her friend loudly whispered, and they both erupted in giddy giggles.

Curious, Hailey walked over and picked up one of the books on display. "How to Write: Doing Is More Important Than What You Think". The cover pictured Dr. Loering, cradling his book in his right arm like a baby. He was muscular, wearing a light brown suit with a baby blue shirt, unique color contrasting.

Hailey didn't think he was handsome, too clean cut. But there was something special about him. Short, thick blonde, hair, cut neatly.

He wore thick, black framed glasses. They were his trademark and became fashionable for young impressionable fans like herself.

After reading several of his books and watching his talks, she too wanted to see the world through those thick, black lenses, just like Dr. Loering. He had something, something special in the way he could captivate an audience. His million-dollar smile could win anyone over. The charisma oozed from his teeth and his biceps. Additionally, there were profiles of writees getting their name in print. Especially after attending his top tier workshops.

His facial expression on the book cover was stoic. His gaze bore into Hailey, like he had all the answers to life's secrets. She immediately fell for him, the intensity of him. The power it was to be him, radiant, inviting you in. Inviting you to be something more, and there was an anchor of safety in his confidence. She bought every book of his that day and devoured them one by one. His work had opened her eyes to even more possibilities. His methods gave Hailey a framework to get out of her current situation. Begged her to dream not just of being a writer, but to dream of a life where she could have adventure. A writer's life. Hailey had dreamed about being a writer since she was a little girl. Dr. Loering's methods were the reason she began to fantasize about being a famous writer. His methods made anything seem tangible.

– – –

The train jolted, then jerked her out of her daydream. The lights went out. Shortly after, John Murphy, the old crotchety wizard that Hailey imagined as the Chicago Transit Authority voice, started to give orders. "The train has stopped everyone remain seated. Do not move from your car. The train has stopped everyone remain seated. Do not move from your car". John Murphy liked to hear himself talk. Now, Hailey was stuffed into the corner of her row. A larger man had plopped down next to her two stops ago. She glanced at her watch, anxious to be on time.

Hailey's gaze remained focused on her digital "Writer's World." "*Dr. Loering returns to U.S. after a tour in Italy*" one headline read. "Writer's World" chronicled his travels around the world speaking to his loyal, almost manic seeming fans. Tonight, he'd be in Chicago talking about his newest book. She'd anticipated the event and planned to buy a ticket months before they went on sale. Tickets sold out in a flash for the "What You Don't Know" Tour. Hailey had taken an entire day off to buy her ticket. She spent hours clicking refresh on the screen of his homepage before the tickets went on sale. Miraculously, she got one. And after all the waiting, the anxiety, she was going to see him today.

Even more exciting than seeing Dr. Loering speak tonight was that she had won lunch with him. She'd paid more for a special, limited ticket that was put in a lottery to have lunch with him. To her utter surprise, she'd won the lottery.

It was her chance to meet him in person and hopefully impress him. Nothing, nor nobody could ruin her excitement for the next two days. Not Fritz Malorts' ignorance of her genius, nor the old man who spilled coffee on her jacket. Nor the large man who had no sense of the space he was taking up or John Murphy, the CTA wizard. She was walking on air. With nothing but the feeling you have when anything seems possible, and your dream is within reach. No matter what happened today, no matter how awful, dread would not prevail. Even the dinner she'd have with her parents after work wouldn't sap her positive energy. Her wildest desires were within reach.

Thankfully the train lurched forward. The train was packed like sardines smelling freshly showered and wearing too much cologne. Hailey was glad for the seat she secured, even though she could barely breath with the large man resting on her.

To be a writer was all Hailey ever wanted, a successful writer. Now, she had several short stories she was looking to publish. Dr. Loering was famous for his preaching, inspiring people to write. He developed workshops and texts that aimed to help combat writer's block. His methods helped explore a writer's resistance in creating. Hailey attended workshops for about a year. She was working up to the final workshop. The workshop that was supposed to entirely transform you.

Hailey hoped that she would be able to give Dr. Loering a story of hers during lunch. She hoped he would fall in love with her story, the one she considered her best. She scrolled through "Writers

World" considering her writing from the morning. She was developing short stories in a collection, and something was missing. Passion, she thought. Life experience. I don't have experience. Her lack of experience haunted the stories she imagined. Speaking of haunting, she remembered that she'd have to submit her writing for the week to Writer Marie this weekend.

The thought then trailed off to thinking of meeting Dr. Loering as her stop came up. She nudged the mammoth of a man next to her who had fallen asleep.

"Sir," she said quietly, nudging his leaden arm, "I need to get off, can you move?"

She hated to raise her voice. She glanced around looking for help. A more boisterous person to holler at him, but most people's eyes remained fixed to their phones or papers. The train stopped. There was no choice but to push past the now, stooped over frumpy man.

As she got up and attempted to crawl over him, he awoke with a snort and yelled, "What are you doing woman? If you would have just tapped me, I could get out of the way for you." His voice rang in her ears.

Hailey didn't have time to explain to him that as she pushed through the entire expanse of people standing in her way to the exit. She sneezed. Her oversensitive nose was overwhelmed by the fog of perfumes and deodorants.

"Cover your mouth, you ever hear of germs" she heard a man say as she exited the train right in time to miss the doors closing.

As she entered her office building, she saw the elevator door opening. She sprinted to catch it, thankful that nobody else was inside. She pushed the button to the 17th floor and breathed a sigh of relief as the elevator began to move.

The office had a sterile feel. Rows of fluorescent lights and grey carpet. Each wall displayed backlit stock photos of smiling workers. Every object in the office screamed "desk life efficiency". Hailey made her way through the maze of cubicles hoping to avoid small talk. Thankfully, most people hadn't arrived yet. She settled into her centrally located desk. While starting up her computer she felt an assertive tap on her shoulder.

"Hailey are we early today? Aren't we a bunch of workaholics?' Her boss, Kevin, loomed over her. He was wearing the usual grey or black suit that he always wore. Hailey often wondered how many suits he were in his closet.

Hailey responded with a fake chuckle. "I have lots of work, and, um, you know I have that weekly dinner with my parents tonight." She offered enough information in hopes he would give her a break when she left early. Kevin knew Hailey's dad well from his prior job. Enough to give her a job when she'd been desperate enough to take it.

"Ah, good ol' Frank, tell him I say hi and I hope to see him out on the course this weekend, he needs to work on that speed grip." He disappeared for a moment, coming back with a stack of papers. "Since you're here Hailey, I have a pile of invoices." He slammed down a foot high stack of unorganized papers onto her small, crowded desk, knocking over her pen holder. As she picked up pens off the floor he continued, "I need these processed. Would you mind?"

Hailey knew it wasn't a question and was annoyed. Invoices were not her job; invoices were Gwyneth's job. It was going to be challenging enough to get the work finished if she wanted to leave on time. This happened every day. If Kevin approached Hailey, it usually meant that he would give her more work. Or comment on the lack of work she was doing.

Hailey reminded herself that without this job she'd have to move back home with her parents. That was enough motivation to put up with Kevin and this dead-end job. Everyone held captive at that office knew this was the last stop before rock-bottom. Nobody had a passion for plastic shipping logistics, except for Brock.

"There now, that will keep you busy. When you're finished you can hand them to Gwyneth to be checked. What I like," he said with a strained look on his face, "What I like about your work is that you get it done. What I don't like is the mistakes you make. It's simple work to do. So double check, Brock will check in on you and help if you need it," He winked at her.

Brock, his secondhand man.

"Yes sir." Hailey mustered as much composure in her answer as she could without giving away her annoyance. Kevin walked away and left Hailey for what seemed an impossible amount of work.

"You only get one chance to get your name in print. One," he said as a matter of fact.

Dr. Loering stood on stage, peering out like a hawk looking for its prey. He was wearing a tight black turtleneck with jeans and black tennis shoes. He looked sharp, approachable, and strikingly confident all at once.

Hailey was on Dr. Loering's website contemplating buying a ticket to the final workshop. The one that was thought to push writees into becoming writers in one year within completion. She couldn't afford it right now. But she could if she ended up getting the promotion at work. Plus, she wanted to be able to say she was attending one at their lunch the following day.

After a pause he continued, "If you miss that chance to find your name in print, some people might say, "Don't worry, it will happen."

He took a drink from a plain white coffee mug on a small stool standing next to his lectern.

"People will say," his voice rising, "don't worry, you'll have another chance to publish, keep going," the crescendo rising in volume.

The audience, full of anxious women, were now in the palm of his hand, yearning for the climax. Some looked terrified, everyone was on the edge of their seats. They were ready, they wanted this.

Hailey glanced around the office to make sure Brock or Kevin weren't nearby.

"People will say, keep writing," Dr. Loering bellowed so loud several women jolted and jostled in their small wooden folding chairs.

One woman gasped loudly. Another knocked over her water bottle. Several people giggled as it slowly rolled a few rows in front of her before someone intercepted it and handed it back through the rows of anxious women. There was a pause, and the silence rang for a moment, almost eliciting doubt in his audience.

But then, in the most jarring of gestures, he slammed his hand on the lectern. The sound echoed throughout the small auditorium. He paused, scanning the audience left to right, looking for a challenge.

The words tumbled out softly, “The truth is you don’t get more than one chance as a writee. Don't waste your time doing the thing you hate. Do what you are charged to do. Do what inspires you. Write what moves you into action."

Hailey clicked to buy the ticket. She was sold. Plus, this would only enhance her writing so why not do it? As she confirmed the date and filled in her mom's credit card info (saved on her computer), she felt a twinge of guilt. I’ll pay her back after my promotion, she thought. The video continued.

"You, you over there.” He pointed to a random woman in the audience, “The blonde writee in the pink sweater, you only get one chance to get your name in print. You, writee, over there,” he said pointing to another woman, “With the brown curly hair in the purple dress. You only get one chance to have your name in print.

“You,” he shouted at a beautiful woman in a sleek black dress. He paused, most likely scanning to see her writee badge. He locked eyes with her and began to speak in now a menacing tone,

“If you blow it, that chance is gone for good. You're done. Your dream of becoming a writer is dead.”

Something always stuck out to her at the end of this video. The beautiful woman who often heckled Dr. Loering. Hailey felt a deep recognition, like they’d met before, but couldn’t place where.

Her ticket confirmed, she decided on one night instead of two because it was so expensive. Maybe her mom wouldn't notice the charge on her card. Taking a deep breath she glanced at her watch, 3:37 PM. Clicking out of the video she pulled up her work email. Due to the location of her cubicle, it wasn’t easy to hide her screen, or anything for that matter. Kevin warned the employees twice about watching YouTube. Hailey needed the promotion he had recently broadcasted with the enthusiasm of someone announcing a lottery winner.

As she clicked on an email with the subject line "Update Requested on Order", she could see the first line, "We want a full refund and provide us with an update..." She was interrupted from reading further as Brock approached her.

Chapter 2

Method 2.) Writees need to understand where they are in the food chain and how they can get to the top. The shortcut to finding your way to the top can be found in Dr. Loering's writing method workshops.

As he closed in, she dreaded the feeling of his long cold fingers firmly tapping her.

“Ahem, Hailey,” he said quietly but loudly enough that everyone else around could hear. She could smell his lunch of tuna when he spoke. "Was that video you were watching work related?”

She sputtered out, “Yes," surprised. How did he see her? She looked several times to make sure nobody was watching.

Brock's beer belly brushed against the back of her seat; a snug fitting V-neck argyle sweater exposed a tuft of chest hair. He wore a soft sneer on his face with dark beady eyes that darted around her body. Like she was juicy piece of meat on his plate soon to be stabbed with his fork. Brock was Kevin's un-appointed right hand man, the ears and eyes of the office, and a constant annoyance.

"You know, if you get caught by Kevin..." He stood tapping his fingers and long fingernails on her cubicle wall. ..." You’re just giving him another excuse to give that promotion to Gwyneth." Hailey knew he intentionally spoke loud enough for the entire office to hear.

"Don't worry though," He whispered, “Your secret is safe with me." He slipped a note in her hand and laughed as he walked away. Hailey took the piece of paper, knowing it was probably another attempt to ask her out on a date and stuffed it in her pocket.

She exited the email. It was not the moment to spoil her mood. Her phone buzzed, and she picked it up, welcoming the distraction.

MOM: SEE YOU TONIGHT AT 6, DON'T BE LATE AND BE SAFE ON THE TRAIN

Hailey blankly stared at the screen. She needed to go to the bathroom, but she feared running into Brock. She tentatively opened the note he passed her, not wanting to know what was in it but needing the intel.

Written all in caps on greasy stained paper: WHY DON'T YOU LET ME SHOW YOU THE BEST DEEP DISH IN CHICAGO?

Hailey pictured eating with Brock. A big floppy slice of deep-dish pizza, in his hands, cheese dripping onto his goatee. Grease stains on his V-neck argyle sweater.

She briskly walked down the hallway to the bathroom. In addition to avoiding Brock, she would pass Gwyneth. Gwyneth, who was the main reason her work doubled on a regular basis. Gwyneth held the same position as Hailey at their firm. They were both going for the same promotion, yet Gwyneth was treated differently. Kevin loved Gwyneth.

Nobody at the company liked Gwyneth, except Kevin. Hailey walked by them multiple times while they were laughing. Flirting, or whatever it was. Gwyneth spent a lot of time in his office with the doors shut. Hailey had a feeling that Brock was jealous of all the love Kevin gave Gwyneth.

Hailey ate lunch by herself in the breakroom and often overheard conversations about whether she wanted to or not.

"She is such a slut Donna."

"I know, Kevin just adores her. Barbara, I tell you what, it drives me up the wall."

Taking a big bite of egg salad, "You heard she's going for that promotion, right?"

"Unbelievable, just like that egg salad you have today, it looks so yummy…" The gossip between Donna and Barbara would continue for the duration of lunch. In between sloppy bites of egg salad.

– – –

"Hailey! How are you?" Gwyneth called out, as Hailey passed by her desk making it impossible to pretend she hadn't noticed her.

"Good, headed to the bathroom.

"Oh, of course. Do you have any plans tonight? I heard Dr. Loering is doing some big event? Are you going? I know you're a huge fan."

“Yeah Gwyneth. I’m going," Annoyed that Gwyneth was holding her up, increasing the chance of Brock appearing Hailey responded, "I got the special ticket, you know, where I get to have lunch with him...”

Gwyneth interrupted, “And go to lunch with him? How did you pull that off? That's crazy! Paying your way to the top, huh. I would love to grill him on some of his...methods are they called? I bet you're super excited.”

As Hailey paused to think of an answer, she took in the outfit Gwyneth was wearing. Her outfit was loud. Too loud for the plain, sterile office environment they worked in. Too extravagant for their horrifically boring jobs. Today she was wearing a lime green swing dress. A cute white collar matched it with tan high heeled Mary Janes. Her hair was done in soft curls, and one side was pinned back, allowing her bright red lipstick to pop. Her smile was pure friendliness. It was difficult to snub her regardless of what Brock, Donna or Barbara’s opinions were.

“I paid for the ticket, anybody could”. Hailey responded in a curt tone, trying to end the conversation.

“They were expensive, weren’t they?” Gwyneth said, shifting her stance, putting her hands in the pockets of her dress. She was either unaware of or ignoring Hailey's need for the bathroom. “I glanced but it looked like it was in the range of $1,700.00, she continued on, That’s like a whole month’s rent!” She exclaimed, taking her hands out of her pockets, and stepping closer to Hailey. Her voice was nice, sweet, and smooth. A liquid honey tone.

Hailey took one step back. “I saved for it. I have to go; Lots to finish before I leave. Kevin loaded me with a bunch of invoices today. See you later,” she said quickly walking away.

“The invoices I was supposed to do? I'll have to speak with Kevin about that. Tell me how it goes," Gwyneth called as Hailey walked away.

Hailey walked into the bathroom and locked the door. She stood a moment with her back to the door, relieved as she always was to be alone in her thoughts. It was the only place in the office where she found solitude. She walked to the white porcelain sink and looked in the mirror. Her face, bright enough from sleeping well the evening before. No puffiness under the eyes. Hailey knew she was plain, but she did have a nice jawline and thick full lips. Her mom constantly gave her grief about her short hair.

"You look like a boy," she'd say, "Is that what you want?"

"No mom, I want to be a writer."

Her outfit was a little wrinkled despite being ironed before work. She smoothed her light pink blouse and black pants. Her figure, slim and petite, was the opposite of Gwyneth. And men certainly didn't pay attention to her. The few dates she'd been on were tragically awkward. She brought hot pink heels for the event and would slip those on after dinner with her parents that evening. She wanted to look classy and put-together, to have an appearance of togetherness. A confident, powerful woman whose work was important for the event that evening.

That is what she wanted to exude when she met Dr. Loering the following day. Her life felt the opposite of being together. Hailey read articles by Dr. Loering about the importance of organization in art. That was one of his top tips to get your name in print. Hailey hoped to please him with her appearance, knowing he wouldn't be interested in her. He just needed to take her seriously. Hailey quickly tried to ignore the vision of her fridge filled with groceries from Walgreens. All her clothes strewn over the floor she was too lazy to sweep or vacuum since she moved in.

She finished using the toilet, taking care not to get drops of water on her blouse, she washed her hands. One last glance in the mirror. For months she'd been planning what to say and how she would slip in the fact that she was a writer to Dr. Loering. She smiled to make sure there was no leftover lunch in her teeth. All good. She looked alright. Mission accomplished. She hesitated to leave, slowly walking out. Outside awaited the likes of Gwyneth, Brock, and Kevin.

Gwyneth was at her desk, watching Hailey as she walked by.

"Wow, looking good! You freshen up for Dr. Loering and the big event?"

Hailey felt Gwyneth's intense gaze on her, and it made her uncomfortable. "No, I'm freshening up because I have dinner with my parents...

“You know,” she said, interrupting Hailey, taking a sip of Diet Coke from her straw, "He’s a womanizer?"

Hailey stared at the red stained straw, trying not to react.

“He has like five different women in his life at any one time. He's a god to them. They worship him so it doesn’t matter what he does.”

“That’s speculation, Gwyneth.” Hailey shot back with venom.

Kevin exited his office which was right next to Gwyneth's desk. Hailey took the interruption to escape Gwyneth.

"Gwyneth, I'm going to need you to help me out with a few things. Can you come to my office please?" He glanced at Hailey, "Hailey, thanks for doing those invoices. Make sure to let your old man know I want to hit the green with him soon."

What green? Hailey almost called out but caught herself. She was pretty sure Kevin and her dad toked it up in the garage while listening to Kenny Loggins.

“I’m only saying it to help you,” Gwyneth called after her.

"Help Hailey?" He laughed. "Hailey doesn't need your help," Hailey heard Kevin say as Gwyneth walked into his office and the door shut.

She walked back to her desk steaming and annoyed. The last thing Gwyneth wanted to do was help Hailey. Maybe she was jealous that Hailey was having lunch with Dr. Loering. That she had access to one of the most profound men of all time. A quote of Dr. Loering’s floated through her mind, “Don’t waste your time on people who are small. They only like small things.” She put the thoughts of annoyance to the side. Taking deep breaths to will her flushed cheeks back to normal. Tonight, was what she wanted to focus on.

It was a little before 4. Usually, she worked until seven. The event began at 8 and she needed to attend a mandatory dinner at her parents' prior. She glanced at her inbox again. Nothing changed since the last time she looked. Then she looked at her personal email. Junk mail, a lot, the usual invitations to yoga events and Groupons she would never end up using. Then she saw it. Five or six emails past all the junk was his name, *Dr. Loering*.

Butterflies began to flutter violently in her stomach. She wasn't sure if she wanted to open it. Her expectations of him falling in love with her *and* her writing was her only lifeline for the past 6 months. For a moment she thought about the idea of not opening it at all. What if she never opened the email? What if she skipped lunch? Then the only disappointment would be not knowing. The hope that he would make her a famous author would still be there.

She stared at the name, savoring the last moments before knowing the truth. There was a never a choice; she was going to open it. It was predestined. Dr. Loering, the name stared back at her as intensely as she was staring at it. *His name*, a man who had all his books adapted into screenplays. *His name* made box office hits starring Tom Cruise. *His name* was in her inbox. She finally worked up the nerve to open the email. The subject was, *"Lunch"* with a timestamp of 4:40. It was recent.

Dear Hali,

I heard you are my lunch date. That is great news. I wanted to reach out to you to tell you that I do not talk about any of my past work. I only focus on future projects.

I look forward to meeting you.

-Dr. Loering

Hailey read it over and over. She wanted to find something that wasn't there. This email deserved proper absorption. But first, she needed to skim several times to make sure she hadn't missed anything. Although there was scant to miss. He misspelled what was an easy name. Maybe the person who relayed her information to Dr. Loering did that on purpose. A jealous assistant. An assistant that wanted Dr. Loering all to themselves. Of course, in Hailey's imagination this assistant was also fighting to be a published writer.

The information began to settle in after several reads.

The lunch was going to happen. Her imagination created a bunch of different scenarios in which Dr. Loering would cancel. Bad airplane food, flight delays due to weather (not unlikely at this time of year in Chicago). The flu, a family emergency, etc. She also imagined all the ways in which she wouldn't be able to go to lunch. Getting hit by a car, having to work (with the threat of being fired), a family death, terrorist attacks, or being too downright scared to follow through. But despite her imagination, it seemed like she was going to have lunch with a man she completely idolized.

After soaking in the reality of the impending lunch, a second thought occurred to her. He didn't want to talk about any of his past work. She didn't know what to make of it, but it stunned her. No matter though, she thought. The initial feeling of getting to meet him trumped the fact he didn't want to talk about what obviously would be the subject of interest to her. Then the added fear that this lunch wouldn't ever happen started to come back.

He hadn't listed where they would meet or what time. Those details were missing, even after she purchased the ticket. It was another piece of anxiety. The next wave of anxiety to hit was the idea of responding. She glanced at her watch. She'd spent 15 minutes reading a two-line email. If she was going to catch her train and get to her parents on time for dinner she needed to leave in a few minutes. She felt she should respond in a prompt manner. But if she didn't, would it give him the feeling that she was so busy that she didn't have time for the man she idolized?

She decided that she should quickly respond. She hit reply and began typing,

Dear Dr. Loering,

Thank you...

Panic rushed in. There were a million ways she could respond. This was a task that shouldn't be rushed. What if she said something he hated? She couldn't take the risk. She'd respond on the train. More time to wisely pick her words then.

With that she started to close what she counted as seventeen tabs on her computer and shut it down. She glanced around to spot Brock who she desperately wanted to avoid.

Her computer finally shut down. As she grabbed her jacket to leave towards the elevator, she saw Brock glance up and lock his eyes on hers. He started to jog over.

Chapter 3

As a writee you must never say no to anything someone suggests if it helps you become a writer.

She put her head down and walked as quickly as she could to the elevator, terrified to look back. She arrived at the elevator and by a stroke of luck it stopped on their floor. Several people waited to get on. Hailey shoved herself through them, hoping to use them as a blockade if necessary. She turned around to see Brock's disappointed face through the slits of the elevator.

_

It took Hailey 25 minutes to get to her parents from the city. Crowded and stuffed on the train from afternoon commuters. Hailey already felt stressed when she arrived at her parents. She flipped open "Writer's World." She stopped at an article "When you are stuck being a Writee…Top Tips to Writer Freedom". Hailey often pondered the vernacular from Dr. Loering's "Dictionary of What it Takes to See Your Name in Print."

Writees were people who wanted more than anything to be writers, to live the life of a writer. There were rules to follow as a writee. Rules that, if followed, lead to seeing their name in print. The goal was to transform from writee to writer. Writees were expected to run errands for Writers. It was part of their growth. Any errand was on the table. Even picking up Writer Marie's kids from school, which Hailey periodically did.

"Writer Marie, if I have to stay to put your children to bed, I won't have time to write." Hailey tried to put her foot down several times to no avail.

"Writee Hailey," Writer Marie would say as she sat in her red velvet armchair. That armchair was her pride. "Until you understand how to juggle and complete every task, you aren't ready. You want to be a Writer, don't you?"

"Yes, Writer Marie." In addition to putting Writer Marie's hyper children to bed, Hailey ended up making the kids' lunches for the next day before she left. She didn't come home until midnight.

But Dr. Loering's methods worked for so many people Hailey put those thoughts away. Anyway, if she said no, she'd be kicked out of the workshop without a second thought.

Writers were only those who succeeded in getting published. Or reached a certain level in Dr. Loering's program. Some of the Writers were secretive about how their name ended up in print. When she attended her first workshop, she was given a neon purple badge with green lettering "Writee". Writers wore a black badge with white lettering.

Hailey longed to be part of the writer group, with their special badges. She hadn't managed to publish it yet. The workshops were expensive, and she could only take one a month. A feeling of guilt crept over her thinking of using her mom's credit card earlier that day. Focus on "Writer's World" she thought. She fell asleep reading Tip #5, Listen to Dr. Loering's chanting every morning in a quiet space.

\- - -

Walking in she felt like a stranger in their shiny clean, mid-sized suburban home. She took off her shoes and walked into the kitchen.

"Hailey, you're here," her mom said eyeing her up and down. Her mom was wearing an apron over an emerald-green pant suit. She gave the usual scan of judgement Hailey received upon entering her mom's presence. As an only child, Hailey didn't have the luxury of a sibling to take the attention off her.

"I see you got a new jacket. I hope that wasn't too expensive," she said as she organized vegetables on the counter for a salad.

"You know," she said grabbing an onion, "It's not like dad I won't help you at all if you need a few things. It's such a shame you didn't get that job at the bank. Mr. Drucker really went out of his way to get you an interview. If you show more enthusiasm, you'd have enough money for all the new blouses you want."

"Mom, it wasn't that expensive," Hailey said grabbing a glass of water, thinking of how she switched tags with another cheaper jacket at Marshalls because it was too expensive. It was a trick her friend from high school taught her. She hated asking her parents for anything. It always meant something in return, like these mandatory dinners. As she poured herself a glass of water her mother ran into the garage.

She could hear her mom scuffling around in the garage. It wasn't until middle school that Hailey realized it wasn't normal for mothers to use ovens in the garage. Hailey's mom was so worried about dirtying the newer, super expensive oven in their kitchen. The oven she bragged about every time guests came over. She insisted they keep the old oven and put it in the garage so as not to tarnish the new one. Hailey spent many evenings watching her mom cook a pot roast in the garage. The smells of grass stuck in the blades of their lawnmower, oil, gasoline, and the marinade of the pot roast all mingled together in what Hailey considered the smells of childhood nostalgia.

Hailey's mom ran back into the kitchen. "Your father should be here any second now and I hope he's ok with my dinner choice. Jewels was out of his favorite kind of pork " she said fiercely chopping an onion straight down the middle.

"Why don't you just use the oven in here Mom?"

"Oh, you know your father likes the stovetop clean, I'm just trying to make things easier..."

"Easier by running back and forth to cook dinner?"

"Hailey, why don't you help prepare your father's drink for the evening." Betsy said, motioning toward the liquor rack.

Hailey started to mix together her dad's whiskey with vermouth." Listen, mom I need to leave early tonight. I have a ticket to see Dr. Loering speak. Remember, I told you a few weeks ago..."

"Oh, that writer guru guy that I'm always hearing about on the news? Hailey's mom looked up at her, "You didn't spend a lot of money on those tickets, did you? Oh god I hope not. Don't mention it to your father, he'll be upset that you're wasting your time and money on that man."

"You don't even know Dr. Loering. His writing methods helped me, I've finished three short stories and I think one of them is..."

"Listen Hailey," her mom said interrupting again. "That's another thing I wanted to speak with you about. You're spending all your time alone, writing. She put down her knife and gave Hailey a look of purposeful guilt. "I'm worried about how much you're getting out and meeting new people. Your father is too. We want you to meet a nice man, someone stable, Hailey. Like that guy, what was his name? Thad? No, Chad. Chad, the golf player you dated in high school."

"Chad? He was about as exciting as wallpaper." Hailey hated it when her mom mentioned Chad.

"A nice, quality, wallpaper, one that would have supported you nicely. I worry about you." Hailey's mom walked over to her. She was beginning to show signs of aging, some of the glow of her prior years gone, replaced by worry lines. Her facial expression indicated the start of what was one of her worrying lectures about the state of Hailey's life.

“Do I smell burning?” Hailey asked.

“Shoot,” Betsy said immediately abandoning the conversation, running to the garage.

Hailey’s heard her dad come in the door. "Where's dinner Betsy?" He went straight to the fridge and grabbed a beer. As usual, almost oblivious to Hailey until he opened the beer, happily taking a swig.

"Hailey, hi.", He glanced over at her. "How are you? How's the job going? Is Kevin playing fair?"

"I made you a drink," Hailey said, setting the whiskey in front of him.

"That's my girl, giving me the opportunity to double fist," he said chuckling.

"Now give me the scoop on the company, how is work going? You like it there?"

"It's fine Dad."

Betsy called from the garage, "Frank, I need you to go take out the garbage then dinner is going to be ready.”

"Yes, Ma'am," he said as he started to collect the garbage while chugging down his beer. Hailey heard her mom's shoes as she ran back to the kitchen and suddenly, a loud thump.

"Oh rats."

"Mom, are you ok?"

"I'm fine honey, this happens all the time. There's that darn tiny step there," Hailey was trying to help her when the fire alarm went off.

"Betsy, are you cooking in the damn garage again? Why don't you use the damn stove in the kitchen that we paid a fortune for?" Frank called from the bathroom.

"Hailey, how come we never see you at Church anymore?" Frank said as he helped himself to a heaping pile of potatoes.

"I live in the city Dad. Plus, on the weekends I have writing classes."

Completely ignoring Hailey's comment, Betsy added, "There's that nice neighbor boy David that goes to our church. David Tassel, I play bridge with Mrs. Tassel. She told me that David works at the bank nearby, I hear his job has great benefits, a 401K and lots of perks. She said he's trying to get into the club nearby."

"He lives around here? Where?"

"Oh, I think he lives with his parents. His mother Sally mentioned that he's saving up for a house. What a responsible young man, right?" Betsy said, glancing over at Hailey.

"Time you settle down Hailey, think about a family." Frank stated.

"And what if I don't want a family?" Hailey mumbled, trying to evade eating the pork roast that she didn't care for, but her mom tended to make a lot. It was dry.

"And what else do you possibly think could have meaning in this life?" Frank said angrily.

"Frank," Betsy said trying to intervene.

"She's completely ungrateful, the job, the education, it means nothing to her." Frank got up from the table and threw his napkin down.

"I'm going over to Bill's to play poker, thanks for dinner."

Frank stormed out of the room leaving Hailey and her mother. Moments later they heard a door slam.

They both sat in utter silence for what seemed like an eternity. Hailey stared at her plate, wishing it was anything else, anywhere else.

"Hailey, I don't know why you have to test your father like that, after all he's been through. You know he's worked his entire life to provide for you, provide for us. We bought you that fancy education, helped you with rent the last few months..."

"Sorry Mom." There was no use arguing, she'd gain nothing.

"You could make it up to him by coming to church one of these weekends."

Hailey said nothing, standing to help her mother collect the dirty dishes. Her mom knew she had no desire to do such a thing on her weekend or at any time. She succumbed to the dinners, but church was out of the question.

Later that evening, after tea and cookies, Hailey needed to leave to make her train. As she started to leave her mom stopped her.

"Hailey, wait, I want to give you something." Her mom held a book in her frail looking hands. Hands that never figured out their passion. Hailey noticed her mom's age. Her hair looked thinner. Her back was more stooped. She seemed smaller, feebler every time Hailey saw her.

"Here," she said offering it to Hailey. "I know it's probably outdated." Hailey looked at the cover, Emily Posts' "Etiquette".
"I thought since you *are so* into Dr. Loering's kind of work maybe you'd like this. I read it when I was your age, and it changed the way I think. Rules of a different kind,". She said smiling at Hailey.

Hailey said a quick thank you and left her mom standing alone in her empty suburban home.

_ _ _

The streets were glistening with water, reflecting the bright city lights. When she walked over the grates on the sidewalk, she could smell the burnt rubber from the train tracks drifting up. People walked hurriedly by, unfolding their umbrellas in the increasing drizzle. She'd spent the train ride back trying to distract herself from the unpleasantness at her parents'.

Her pink heels were difficult to walk with on the slippery, cobblestone, cracked pavement. It slowed her pace. As usual her mind wanted to go faster than she could walk, she thought, praying that she wouldn't slip and fall. When she neared the event, her heart began to race. It was a similar feeling to meeting someone for a blind date. A nervous excitedness, a hope for the possibilities. Would she have a chance to impress Dr. Loering tonight?

Of course, she couldn't expect that tonight all this would happen. The possibility of a seed being planted was enough hope for the moment. She thought of all the times she'd been excited about something. The excitement derailed as soon as reality arrived. She found the venue and stopped before the door to search for the ticket. She'd paid special attention and care to the ticket over the last few weeks. It was specifically placed in the smaller side pocket of her purse. An area that only held the most important items.

There was a split second of panic when she reached inside the pocket and didn't feel it. As she searched for it, someone bumped into her. The force almost knocked her over and caused her purse and everything in it to empty onto the sidewalk.

She watched as the man who pushed into her hurriedly walked inside without taking any notice of her. Between the angle and the lighting, she couldn't see who it was.

"Thanks a lot," she said to herself. Her mom's critique of her tone floated through her head as she watched the door shut.

"They don't even see me," she said to herself picking up her items from the wet pavement.

She was almost done picking everything up. A wallet, pens, Chapstick, lipstick, and a handful of change when she heard a voice say, "Are you ok?"

Hailey looked up to see the women who she recognized. The one from the video she was watching earlier.

She stood up and brushed herself off, "I'm fine, thank you."

She nodded and walked inside, flashing what looked like a press pass to the door person.

Hailey thrust her hand in the pocket, feeling the edge of it further down than she would have expected. Sighing with relief she smiled, she found the ticket.

Her nerves wrought; she arrived a few minutes before the start of the event. She entered the door, thankful that there wasn't much of a line to check in. A frumpy, dutiful middle-aged man with an uninterested flair stood waiting. His name tag read "Olin." He took her ticket, scanned it, and asked, "You a writer or writee?"

"Writee," Hailey responded as quietly as she could. There was a level of shame that she hadn't been published yet. "Here you go," he handed her the infamous purple badge that said "Writee" on it. Hailey begrudgingly took it, thinking that she would hide it under her jacket so people couldn't see.

She entered the lobby. From where she stood, she took in a view of the entire auditorium. A sparse few speckled inside. Early arrivers like her, all women. She couldn't tell how many writees versus writers were there. Regardless, Hailey wondered for a moment if they were all hoping for an early glimpse of Dr. Loering before the event, like herself. Maybe they all bore the same hopes as her. That he could save them from their horrible jobs and give them the life of a writer. The hopes that something more would come out of a paid event than being starstruck for an evening.

For a moment she stood, contemplating where the best seat would be. She'd bought a ticket where she could sit anywhere in the front 8 rows. Where would he notice her? Her gut told her directly in front of his lectern. That would be the best choice. She walked up to the front and took her jacket off, draping it on the back of the chair. Settling into her chair with purpose, now was the time to respond. She sat down, got her phone out and pulled up the email. With several glasses of wine, the response seemed straightforward.

Hey Dr. Loering,

Thank you for reaching out. I am excited to meet and have lunch with you. Could you please confirm the place and time that our lunch will be tomorrow?

Kindly,

Hailey

And hit send. A burst of relief hit first immediately followed by doubt. She wondered if she should spell her name the same way (Hali) to avoid questioning. Hailey decided that Dr. Loering would respect her more for being who she was rather than trying to appeal to him. As a salutation hopefully “kindly” sufficed. She loved that it read, “our lunch”. Email sent, seat in place, now it was time for a glass of champagne before the event began.

Droves of women filed in. Dressed in their finest clothing. Sparkly dresses, bright lipstick, curled hair, high heels, ornamental jewelry draped around their elegant necks. For a moment Hailey second guessed her outfit choice. Was it enough? It wasn’t casual but it wasn’t elegant either. It didn’t matter. She knew she possessed something they didn’t, access to Dr. Loering. Hailey booked it as fast as she could in her hot pink heels to the lady’s room and did her business. After washing her hands, she double checked her makeup in the mirror.

With a final look she left and approached the line to buy a glass of champagne.

She heard the final bell warning. Her heart felt like it was racing a million beats a second. Her hands shaky with nervousness. Her voice tight and shrill as she bought her glass of champagne and handed the cashier money.

She went to sit down hoping to overhear peoples’ hushed conversations. Tonight, could be the beginning of a new life for her, she thought.

Shit. Was that Writer Marie? A few seats down Hailey could see Writer Marie's mousy brown hair, always styled the same way. The last thing she needed was for Writer Marie to ask her for a favor right now. Hailey tried to stoop down so Writer Marie wouldn't see her. She hadn't heard from Writer Marie today. A blessing with all that was going on. Especially since the last time Hailey was over Writer Marie mentioned that she needed new bras but didn't have time to go shopping. Hailey thought of her sagging breasts, the nipples that reached out like they were desperately grabbing for territory in a shrinking land.

The black lectern loomed on stage alongside a small black stool. Sitting on top of the stool was a glass of water. Women sat on both sides of Hailey. From her vantage point she could tell there were a few men there. Most likely they were well-wishing husbands accompanying their wives. It was predominantly women, as usual. The sound of heels echoed on the floor as the last few rushed to their seats. Glasses clinked in the now quiet crowd.

The smell of Chanel drifted through the air. The lights dimmed and the anticipation was palpable in the packed auditorium. Hailey loved this moment in any show. The moment in which she was allowed to disappear. Her body gone, melding in a sea of people who were all disappearing, alongside her.

No more of her angst, longing, or suffering. It all dissipated when the lights dimmed, and another show started that wasn't her own life. A well dressed, beautiful woman walked out on stage. She was elegant, tall, lanky, and shone with composure and confidence. She had chestnut brown hair, cut to her shoulders with bangs. She wore thick framed glasses. Hailey wondered if Dr. Loering's glasses were her inspiration. Slowly the lights turned on, revealing Writer Marie looking over at her and frantically waving.

Chapter 4

Becoming a writer isn't easy. If you get published easily, you are doing something wrong.

Now she's going to ask me to buy her bras. There was very little chance of an escape.

"Good evening and welcome to all writers and writees! My name is Annabelle. I'm proud to introduce our guest tonight, Dr. Loering. His fame started when he was the subject of a famous documentary, "What It Looks Like to Write Right in Life." You all know the one."

Hailey was surprised she was mentioning this. She knew that it hadn't shed Dr. Loering in the best light as it showed him before he was famous. Struggling to start his writing workshops earlier in his career.

"We fell in love with him right then and there because he looked like a spectacular failure. But then, he went on to write one book, one magnificent book that has become a bible for all you writees and writers. I know if you are sitting here tonight you understand the importance and weight of his work. Nobody could have done and said the profound things that Dr. Loering has said. He gave up everything in life to do his work. Relationships with his family, money, and at one point, his dignity.

Writer Marie was sneaking glances at Hailey for a while now and it was hard to ignore. The women next to Hailey tapped her, "I think that woman over there is trying to get your attention..."

"Oh, really? I didn't see." Hailey whispered back.

"I think she wants to switch spots with me, I'm totally fine with that," she said shifting upwards.

Writer Marie and the lady next to Hailey continued to motion back and forth to one another. Much to her dismay, Writer Marie was now seated next to her.

"Hi Writer Marie," Hailey whispered.

"Hello Writee Hailey, good to see you," she said placing her cold clammy hands-on Hailey's arm. There was nothing Hailey hated more than the feeling of clammy hands on her skin.

"I'm sure it is," Hailey said under her breath imagining the large, beige, brown bras she'd be sifting through at Macys.

"Never once did he question his path or get a job that paid his bills. Instead, inspired followers supported his art. And thank goodness they did! I know that when "How to Write" came out all our lives changed. We all needed the advice that this sage man had to offer.

I know I speak for most of you out there today that his words changed our lives. Our way of being. We thrive because of his words. So tonight, reading from his New York Herald Bestseller, "How to Write: Doing Is More Important Than What You Think" followed by a brief Q and A from the audience, we have, the one and only, Dr. Loering."

The lights dimmed. I Gotta Feeling by The Black-Eyed Peas started blasting. Hailey felt chills all over her body, the energy was electrifying. Writer Marie was bumping and grinding next to her. Everyone stood, bursting into hysterical screams, flailing their arms, and dancing.

Hailey wasn't a dancer. She didn't like this song either. Writer Marie would give her crap if she didn't follow along. The lights slowly turned on, capturing the outline of Dr. Loering's body. He stood with dozens of red roses. He began to run around the stage, throwing roses to the manic crowd.

High pitch screams echoed in Hailey's ears. Writer Marie started to bump and grind up against Hailey. Hailey half-heartedly returned the dance with the tiniest bump she could muster. Writer Marie made Hailey feel uneasy. She always seemed a second away from an outburst. The audience continued their high-pitched yelling and whistling. Dr. Loering ran close to where Hailey was sitting, and she saw two women a few seats down fighting for a rose. One woman ended up aggressively pushing the other. A security guard promptly arrived escorting the aggressive pusher out the theater. She glanced at the name tag on the one who'd been pushed, Writer Rose. Had a writee pushed her? Hailey looked at Writer Marie who was still dancing her heart out.

She wanted a rose, but not enough to get in a fight, she thought mechanically swaying back and forth to appease Writer Marie.

"Fill up my cup (drink), mazel tov (l'chaim)
Look at her dancing (move it, move it), just take it, off (fee-)..."

Writer Marie nodded approvingly. Hailey noticed wet marks around her armpits. Stains she'd surely have to treat while doing laundry.

The music was dying down, but the crowd was still cheering as he walked to the lectern. He wore his trademark glasses. He looked stunning in a baby blue leisure suit with sequin stitches. His black dress shoes shimmered under the spotlight. Under his baby blue jacket his trademark mahogany brown turtleneck stuck out. His magical blonde hair was combed back in its usual style. Each rose he threw accompanied a charming smile that highlighted his adorable dimple.

Hailey felt a rush of excitement, she couldn't believe she was seeing him for the first time in the flesh. For the first time she realized that Dr. Loering wasn't as tall as she imagined him to be.

A huge, almost maniacal smile was plastered on his face as he scanned the crowd and began to speak.

“Fear?" He yelled out. Immediately the crowd died down. "Fear? What is it? What is it that you fear writees?"

"Resistance" Hailey yelled alongside a chorus of voices. Writer Marie patted Hailey on the shoulder. The energy was as electrifying as she’d imagined it would be.

"Tonight, I’m going to start by reading from my new book. I want to talk about something that is important. Something that is life changing, something that shakes the enemy. Because that’s what we want, right? We want to get in our enemies face and beat them down, beat her down." He said, punching his hand into his fist.

Dr. Loering started pacing, “This substance I own, this power I have, this power you have, it’s a paradox…To write, to create, is work. Creation is work. Creation is also complete luck, complete chance. Two different concepts entirely. But in my workshops, as you all know, especially you Writers out there… I made you a road map to understanding one. And I guarantee you won’t get lost.”

He curled his fists and unleashed them holding them in a V shape. He proclaimed, “What I’m trying to say, is that if you follow the rules, you gain the seeds to write. And the more you work, the more experience you gain, the more chance you have of finding your name in print.

I have the power to inspire others. I have the power to share my magic. You came here from whatever job you have, walking in the freezing rain, commuting to be here. I saw a poor woman picking change off the ground like it was the last of her money on my way into the auditorium today.”

“Even SHE has the substance to become a writer, I thought. This woman, scraping the last she has off the ground. This sad woman if she follows the methods, the rules, she’ll see her name in print. She has the magic life creating substance that lies within me, within all of us. All we need is to follow the cues to unlock it. Its magic isn't it," he said nodding his head and smiling.

Hailey's face felt iron red hot. He was talking about her. She was embarrassed he'd seen her like that. She should have left the change on the ground. Every penny counted right now. As he continued his talk, she an unpleasant realization was born. Dr. Loering pushed her earlier.

Hailey pushed the thought away. Distracted, she shifted in her uncomfortable sea. She was curious about what he would say during lunch. At the same time, she dreaded whatever Writer Marie had in store for her that evening.

Almost as if Writer Marie could sense Hailey's attention spanning, she gently put her clammy hand on her arm.

Hailey did her best to direct her attention back to Dr. Loering. "This book explores how we counter the enemy and origins of the enemy itself. With all that's going on in the world today. All the struggles we have, a lot of you are struggling. It's important to remember that we were all made from the same thing. One unifying thing. That same substance. A substance that had to fight to create. A substance that chose where to grow. This substance is the reason we are sitting here today. It was complete luck, complete chance that this substance chose whoever it did to plant itself in. It was complete luck that the substance created me, and now I can create. I possess the seeds to grow.

I have the power to inspire others with my story. I have the power to share my magic to transform you all from writees to writers. Because that's what you want right?"

Catching the audience off guard, everyone yelled a haphazard "Yes".

"You can do better than that writees, let's hear a yes,"

"Yes," everyone yelled in unison, even Writer Marie.

"You came here from whatever job you have, walking in the cold rain, commuting to be here. Because of the magic life creating substance that lies within me can teach you all to succeed. Its magic isn't it," he said nodding his head and smiling.

Hailey wondered if anyone else was as confused as she was. Was he talking about sperm? Or writing? She'd only seen clips of his entire talk, so this was new.

"And this knowledge we hold in our hearts." He held his hands over his heart. Over his firm pecs, Hailey observed.

"Through the tough times that life throws at us." He paused, satisfied and for a moment it seemed as if he locked eyes with Hailey. She'd imagined this moment forever, but the feeling it produced took her by surprise. Uneasiness, nervousness. Knowing she would be one on one with him the following day cemented that feeling.

He continued talking as a screen dropped below him. Lights dimmed and images of dolphins appeared on the screen.

"From Chapter 3:
Going your own way. The true path. This statement is a statement of self-ownership. Own the strong, masculine side we possess. As a writee, to become a writer you must give a statement of self-preservation. A statement that protects your own kingdom above all else. Saying no is the key to this world. Shutting out others around you to protect your words."

The dolphins disappeared and turned into circling sharks.

"Look to nobody else for social cues, forget all preconceptions of what the world thinks you are. Refuse to bow down to anybody and be treated like a thing that can be thrown out. In other words, living by this is common sense if you want to being a writer."

And then whales burst out the air.

Hailey was moved and inspired. She imagined all the time what life would be like if she had the courage not to listen to anybody. Her parents, Kevin, her inner voice of doubt, and became a powerful, published writer.

He paused again, looking around to acknowledge the great wisdom he bestowed. She could see the glimmer of excitement in his eyes. The crowd was eating it up.

"This next passage is one of the most important things you will hear. Maybe some of you writees here today have changed because of me, how many out there have changed? Let me hear you!"

Dr. Loering stood on stage, his hands on his hips, erect and proud. The crowd erupted. Everyone stood up and cheered. The woman next to Hailey smiled warmly wearing her "Writee" badge with pride out in the open. Two seats down a plump middle-aged woman with short hair, sporting a sparkly red cardigan with black dress pants said loudly, "Isn't he amazing"? She dabbed her eyes with a tissue. Hailey smiled while clapping. Everyone sat down and became quiet, eager for more.

Dr. Loering paused. An image of thousands of men's bodies piled upon one another in what looked like a graveyard flashed on the screen.

"Today's people, and especially men, are encouraged to meet resistance while receiving no help. They are told to man up, buck up, while not being given anything to help. If they request anything, they are told that they are being sexist, misogynists. We as people need to define our own terms. We conquer and provide for ourselves, all the while getting the sustenance we need. As writees, if you ever see a man struggling, you need to give him that extra help. And you know what?"

"What?" The crowd yelled back at him.

"It will get you one step closer to becoming a writer."

Hailey looked around, was anyone else hearing this? Writer Marie looked dazed. This didn't sound good. She was reminded of Kevin or Brock at work, the message was tailored to their type. Hailey felt a hint of dread in the pit of her stomach. Maybe she was overreacting, she thought as Dr. Loering continued.

He started to pace the stage like a cheetah stalking its prey. Pouncing when the crowd was least expecting it, taking in the energy from the crowd and using it to pounce again. She sat in a stupor of sorts as he threw his baby blue dress jacket at the audience sparking another fight in the crowd. Hailey was distracted again. The anxiety about what disgusting task Writer Marie was going to ask her to do ruined her experience, it was all she could think of.

Dr. Loering stopped pacing and was sitting on the stool up front. He took a sip of water. “I will now take questions from the audience. You, over there in the red shirt.”

Hailey tried to see who was talking but it was so far back it was impossible.

A shrill, tiny voice began, “Dr. Loering, I'm a huge fan of yours."

"When you introduce yourself, state whether you are "writer or writee."

"Um, writee and my name is Janice. When you talked about substance to write in the beginning, where can we get that substance? I feel like that’s my biggest challenge.”

“You can always look to a source of inspiration. Sex is a good one,” Dr. Loering said playfully.

“Could you elaborate…” Hailey saw Annabelle handing the woman a rose as the mic got passed to another woman.

“You over there in the black dress?” Dr. Loering pointed to another anxious, eager woman.

The crowd remained silent. Hailey couldn't decide if everyone was collectively shocked. The women next to her looked satiated, like she’d just finished a big meal.

A voice “Dr. Loering, my name is Molly and I'm a writee. I want to say that I speak for like everyone in this room when I say that your writing has like changed my life. Like, your book has changed everything in my life. I quit my job, I started to do what I want. I almost lost everything; I was even homeless for a while. I took your advice, “Give it all up and start over” but nothing came of it. I got a job eventually. I still write, I write about the experience. But after 15 years of being a writee, nothing has come of it. I feel I failed. What do you think?”

“Don’t get hysterical sweetheart. You can do this. You were made to do this. There is no timeline to success. " Annabelle handed her a rose as Dr. Loering continued.

“You can never fail if you are doing what you are charged to do. Don’t make excuses and keep going. Listen folks, if you didn’t already know this, the resistance to write is a battle. But I’m looking out here today and I see nothing but writee warriors. Beautiful, strong, writee warriors, willing to battle with the written word." He said doing multiple karate chops.

He brushed his fingers through his hair, "Beautiful warriors won’t let resistance get in the way of writing that page. Finishing that paragraph. Strong warriors that are willing to do the work. You need to stand up to resistance and tell it what it is…Resistance is a hoax."

Dr. Loering often talked about resistance to create. That it is your own self getting in the way of creating. He urged his followers to move past that, at any cost. Hailey felt skeptical for the first time. Especially at the end of a long day and Writer Marie was going to make her run some sort of bullshit errand. What if she could leave before Writer Marie could ask her?

Say that with me, RESISTANCE IS A HOAX." Everyone, including Hailey timidly said "

"Resistance is a hoax" with a few brave souls speaking louder. Writer Marie looked at Hailey with disgust and said, "Louder writee".

"No, no, louder, the loudest you can, everyone stand up. I want to hear you yell RESISTANCE IS A HOAX like it's the only thing stopping you from achieving all you want."

Hailey arose to yell *Resistance is a HOAX*, remembering momentarily how much Dr. Loering could invigorate her. The energy of the moment overtook her, quieting the sea of doubt stirring inside her.

Dr. Loering continued, "I don't believe in this feeling we get when we sit down to do something that tries to pull us away from what we have been charged to do. I believe in people. I believe in you writees out there. I believe that *you* can overcome whatever it is that holds you back. I believe every single one of you can achieve the wildest dreams you've ever imagined and become a writer."

Hailey heard sniffles; the woman next to her was crying. Writer Marie handed her a tissue.

"Shucks, if I can do it, me, any single one of you is strong, able, capable" he chuckled almost knowingly out at the audience…" I know that you can do it. Look resistance in the face and say to it, "I know who you are and I'm not going to let you win. You take resistance and you give an uppercut, just like Jimmy who broke your heart." He punched an imaginary Jimmy several times. And here's one to Fernando. He kicked the air. The crowd laughed and cheered.

"Next question?" He yelled over the now emotional crowd.

Hailey sat stiff as a board, frozen in anxiety. She wanted to ask why he thought resistance was a hoax. She felt mortified even at the idea of attempting. Anyway, she'd have his undivided attention the following day.

Another woman began to ask a question, Hailey couldn't see very well from her seat, but the voice coming from behind her was familiar. Hailey heard that voice before. She couldn't place it. It was a voice well-seasoned to questions, accustomed to being the center of attention.

With no specification of whether she was writer or writee, "You talk a lot about time Dr. Loering. A quote from your book is, "My advice to people who can't find the time" is you'd better keep it on a leash. I know where mine is always, no time for incompetent nonsense." Could you elaborate on what inspired you to write that?"

"Great question. First, are you a writer or writee?"

"I'm a writer."

"Good for you," Dr. Loering said in a condescending tone. "Some of my thoughts might sound like platitudes, right? Sound a bit harsh? I am serving as a model for you, to see how success works. In my new book, I go a step further, I give writees the exact formula to success. I have spent my whole life doing what it was I was charged to do. Nothing else. That's why you are all here, right? You want the formula of someone who had a dream, a vision, and followed it. Success, money, power. Everything that is part of a writer's life." He started to pace again.

"Big crowds followed. Doing what I want to do, followed. That's because I followed my dream. Those who go out and do anything other than what they were charged to do are wasting their time on Earth. Don't be one of those people. When I was a kid…"

The woman interrupted Dr. Loering's train of thought, "Isn't that judgmental of others? People, women, come from different backgrounds and sometimes they need to do what they need to do to survive? Sometimes that is the art itself, survival. Telling people, they should take control of their time to create, like it's a given, like it's just entitled to everyone seems harsh."

Dr. Loering stood on stage, quiet, his face stoic, body rigid. A sea of expectant women looked back and forth between Dr. Loering and the journalist. Hailey sat on the edge of her seat wondering how he would handle his challenger. Writer Marie shook her head.

With a strained voice Dr. Loering responded, "Well I have missed the mark with you then. Sometimes it's difficult for people to see the truth about art and how it's created. My message doesn't work for everyone. It works for these writee warriors" he yelled to the crowd eliciting another cheer full of high-pitched screams.

Once the cheers started to die down, the woman continued, "Plenty of artists have jobs while they develop their craft. Kafka is a perfect example of that. If he didn't have his job would his writing have been tormented? I think that when you say something like, "Keep your time on a leash" you make assumptions. Your assumptions could harm your audience, especially those who don't come from wealth. Not everyone can live off their "art" and only their "art. As a matter of fact, very few people can live off their art."

"My message is about following your calling and beating resistance, procrastination, your inner demons that fight to destroy the art that resides within you."

"But what do you say to members of your audience who can barely survive? What do you say to the single mom raising several children, working several jobs to make ends meet? How can they keep their time on a leash?"

"Let's talk after. Come get your book signed and we'll chat. Now, there are other ladies desperate for an answer, next question please, final one." Dr. Loering, his face slightly shiny, still not taking away from how handsome he looked that evening, his pecs rippling out from his brown turtleneck.

Hailey blinked her eyes, which were wide open. She wanted to side with Dr. Loering, she felt indebted to him for his advice.

She produced triple the amount of material before she started following his methods. Yet, a feeling of uneasiness stubbornly settled within her.

"You over there in the black turtleneck," he said with notably less enthusiasm.

"I'm a writee, Laura. Chicago is your home base, what do you love most about the city?"

"Where are you from?" He responded in a flirtatious tone. While he answered Hailey started to wonder how she could evade a list of chores. Maybe she could avoid Writer Marie.

"Please, I beg you," he said flashing his irresistible smile, "Writees, don't let resistance get the best of you." With that he ran off stage yelling, "Thank you, thank you all" while blowing kisses out at the audience.

The room erupted into enthusiastic applause. Annabelle came back on stage looking like the perfection she was.

"Wow, Dr. Loering. Let's give him another round of applause."
The crowd grew louder, and people began to rise. Hailey stood up smiling and gave a little scream as she applauded. As the standing ovation formed Annabelle yelled over the crowd,

"I hope you enjoyed his reading as much as I did. For all of you that would like your book to be signed we will set up on stage. Please form a line…" The sound of Annabelle giving instructions was drowned out by a woman behind her who was talking about how much she wanted to jump Dr. Loering's bones. "I'd eat him right up for dessert," she said giggling with her friend.

Hailey, distracted from her uneasiness by renewal of charged energy of the evening, started to think strategically. Was there any way to get away from Writer Marie at this point? Writer Marie was talking to a woman behind her. It was now or never.

She beelined it to the bathroom. A line out the door. Well dressed women, mostly elegant and some in more business casual clothing like herself. All different shapes and sizes, some old and young, everyone with the hideous purple badge "Writee".

Most of the women stood patiently, a few were discussing what they should do after the event. There was one voice louder than the rest. It sounded familiar, the heckler from the Q&A. She was deep in conversation with someone who looked like her companion. Hailey didn't have a choice but to hear what she was saying.

"I think he's full of shit. He brainwashed these vulnerable women into thinking he's a visionary, but he's the market definition of a nutbag who's lucky he isn't in prison. There's still time. These women could wake up. The worst part about him is that he knows what he is doing. He's robbing these women. And they are guzzling up the Kool-Aid."

Hailey stretched to see further. It wasn't only the voice she recognized; the woman looked familiar. She was wearing a black dress; stunningly beautiful. Athletic but slim, poised, and utterly outspoken. Her brunette hair laid on her shoulders with minimal curls. Even a few people away it was obvious she had a beautiful complexion, creamy olive skin, with long lashes and full lips. Hailey couldn't quite place her, but she knew the woman was well-known. An actress? Singer?

The woman standing next to the mystery woman did not show the same enthusiasm on the subject. Plain, anxious, short, a stocky looking woman, she gave brief, almost impatient, formulated responses. Anger began to simmer inside Hailey despite her rendezvous with uneasiness. She felt it her responsibility to stand up for him. To tell this woman how wrong she was.

Dr. Loering's words inspired Hailey. His work wasn't Kool-Aid. If it was, it was the kind that prompted her to write. He gave inspiration that moved people. If some of his message tonight was problematic, maybe this woman misinterpreted it.

The words quietly tumbled out, "What's your problem with him? Why did you even come if you don't like his work?" She'd overcome years of her mom's criticism by speaking up for herself. Yet her soft tone didn't rise above all the commotion in the hall.

The beautiful woman walked into the bathroom. She didn't hear Hailey. All the better. A few other women standing in line looked at Hailey with curiosity but didn't take the bait. It's not like someone like this could be reasoned with anyway, she thought angrily. As Hailey walked out of the bathroom stall, she saw the woman again. She was reapplying her plumb red lipstick and the sink next to her was open. Hailey walked up and started furiously washing her hands.

"So, you didn't like his talk?" She said in the most assertive tone she could muster, looking in the mirror at the woman. Her sentence held bravery Hailey didn't use often.

The woman glanced back at Hailey in the mirror, finalizing touches of her lipstick, "No. I think he tries to brainwash people to believe in his nonsense." She placed her lipstick back in her purse and turned to face Hailey who was still voraciously scrubbing her hands with soap and water. Hailey's body was electric with energy she rarely used. Energy that gave her a voice.

"Why is he a scam?"

As Hailey asked, she pulled out her lipstick, started to apply, her hands a little shaky. Jenna didn't seem to notice. She was intensely looking at Hailey. Or maybe that was a tinge of sympathy.

"You'll know soon enough."

Chapter 5

Taking risks is the only thing as a writee that you can do (besides writing) to become a writer.

The woman turned away from Hailey, taking one final look in the mirror, pleased.

"Have a good evening," she said and walked away.

Hailey watched her for a moment then looked back in the mirror. There was lipstick in her teeth. She washed it out with her finger. Drips of water got on her blouse. A stain. Now there was a water stain on her pink blouse, front, and center. It would be tough to get out.

As she tried to dry her blouse, she wondered what the woman meant? Why did she get under Hailey's skin?

"I hate it when that happens," a woman said, drying her hands next to Hailey. "And I'm a total klutz, so it happens often enough".

Hailey gave the woman a quick, dismissive smile.

"What did you think of Dr. Loering tonight?" The lady asked, ignoring Hailey's indifference to her. "I love Dr. Loering, and this is the 3rd talk of his I've been to, but my favorite part tonight was when Jenna Janders handed it to him. She's such a badass. I watch her on COX news all the time. That woman is one hell of a debater. "

"You mean the woman that heckled Dr. Loering?"

"Yeah, that's Jenna Janders. You've never heard of her? She is a famous journalist."

"I don't watch the news." It was the same Jenna Janders her mom adored.

“You must not. I’m surprised she was here tonight. You should watch her show, she just did a riveting expose on Lonnie Gamble. He was that sleaze who wrote all those inspirational self-help books and turned out to be a pedophile. Good luck with your shirt,” she said as she finished drying her hands. Have a nice night.”

As soon as Hailey walked out Writer Marie stood, scowling.

"Writee Hailey, " she said standing with her arms crossed, "I was wondering where you’d run off to. I wanted to speak with you."

"Yes Writer Marie," Hailey said nodding her head to show the respect a writee was supposed to show a writer.

"I have a few things I'd like you to do tonight now that I ran into you. There's a wrap I've been wanting to get at the Trader Joe's in Streeterville, and a delicious kale salad..."

Hailey nodded. She felt stupid that she hadn't thought of the possibility of running into one of her workshop leaders tonight. Hailey was penalized recently because she told workshop leaders, she couldn't take texts or phone calls during work. The punishment was that anytime Writer Marie ran into Hailey, she could send her on errands.

The auditorium emptied significantly while Writer Marie listed off all the items. English cucumbers, papayas, mangoes, fresh fish, the freshest in the store…An impossibly long list of items from Trader Joe's and Whole Foods. Hailey could see out of the corner of her eye that there were still about 15 women waiting in line on stage. The line was moving quickly. If Writer Marie didn't hurry, she would miss Dr. Loering.

Writer Marie finally finished.
“You got all that?”
Hailey nodded.

"Ok, now off you go, I'd like this before I go to bed tonight."

Hailey looked toward the stage, "I wanted to get an autograph..."

"Very well then, off you go."

Hailey heard the judgement in her voice. That could mean a punishment, but Hailey didn't care. The last woman in line left right as Hailey walked up to Dr. Loering's table.

Hailey handed him her book.

“What's your name, young lady?”

“Hailey”

“Hailey, pretty name, ok, alright, let me sign right here. Last one. Save the best for last right?” He looked up and gave her a wink.

“I absolutely love your work,” Hailey stammered. He was even more handsome up close.

“Thank you, I'm working on a new book that should be out next year. I hope you enjoy this one though. It's one of my favorites. Lots of important work here. Here you go.”

He shoved her book to the end of the table and started to get up. Hailey knew this was her last chance. Time was running out.

“Dr. Loering” she called.

“Yes? I have a date; I need to get going.”

“Oh, well, um, I just wanted to let you know that I'm the one you are having lunch with tomorrow.”

He looked at her in utter surprise. “Lunch? Tomorrow? I know nothing of this. Annabelle? What is this young, um lady talking about?” He was now looking her up and down.

Hailey stood frozen in disbelief. How could this be? How could he not know?

“What Dr. Loering, sorry I didn’t hear you.” Annabelle called.

“This woman here is telling me I am to have lunch with her.”

“Yes, remember, it’s a promotion. The people who paid more for their tickets were put in a lottery and whoever got picked gets lunch with you. And you're the winner?” She looked at Hailey.

“Yes. I’m confused," Hailey said in the emotion in her bubbling up to a point where it made it difficult to talk. "I thought Dr. Loering emailed me about this.”

“Oh, that was me,” Annabelle said. I do all of Dr. Loering’s correspondence.”

“Hailey felt the same amount of disappointment when she realized she’d gotten a job only because her father pulled a few strings for her.

“Annabelle, you’ll sort this out? It was nice meeting you,” he said, giving a half glance in Hailey’s direction, a flash of his extraordinary dimple.

With that he was gone.

“Well.” Annabelle's poised, artistic demeanor sized up Hailey with her eyes. “Would you like to sort lunch out right now or is email fine?”

“Email is fine if you need to go.”

“Great, I’ll be in touch early tomorrow morning. Have a good night and thanks for supporting Dr. Loering,” she said, flashing a forced smile at Hailey. She walked off stage, with a feeling of dread. She’d better hurry if she was going to make it to Trader Joe’s and Whole Foods before they close.

Hailey felt like nothing special, nothing but a writee. It was if her identity never existed before now and nothing mattered any more than running errands for Writer Marie. She was a writee that would need to run to two grocery stores before she went home. She was a writee invested in all of Dr. Loering’s products. At least all the workshops she could afford. She kept reminding herself she was on her way to becoming a writer as she briskly walked to catch a train. The cold November rain pelted her.

She hurried through the grocery store, picking up the items for Writer Marie. As she bartered with employees on prices (Writer Marie insisted she try), she reminded herself all the writees becoming writers. This would be worth it, she thought as she sorted through a mountain of avocados for the “perfect ones”. Writer Marie liked her avocados a little underripe. Just a little. When she finally reached her apartment shortly after one a.m. in the morning the first thing she did before falling into her bed was to throw her writee tag in the garbage.

Diving deep into the sea of regret
nothing will save the lost time the tide carries away
far into the sea
of memories, waves swollen
with the past
waves which erode the present
shore you once stood upon

This is shit, Hailey thought slamming her laptop shut. Another morning where 1000 words seemed impossible. She needed time to write, but she had to get to work.

Brock was standing at Hailey's desk, smiling as she entered the office. He looked like he was dressed for a special occasion, wearing what looked like a new brown suit.

"Good morning! Hailey, you ready to hit the ground running?" He asked like he was her coach, giving her a pep talk.

"Sure Brock," she said, trying to maneuver around him to set her things down. The truth was that she was someone with very little sleep. Between Writer Marie's errands and trying to make her 1000 words this morning, her thoughts were muddled at best.

"Listen, can we take this offline?"

She flopped into her seat, trying to reclaim her space. "Brock, I have a ton of work today. Maybe now isn't the best time? I wouldn't want to disappoint the boss." She pointedly glanced in the direction of Kevin's office.

"Right." His face immediately fell. Hailey knew his special suit meant he was hoping for her response to his invitation of deep-dish pizza.

"Ahem" Brock cleared his throat. "Very well." He straightened his suit jacket. "I'll leave you to it and try to catch you at lunch." He nodded and walked away.

Hailey drew a sigh of relief. It was only a matter of time in which she'd have to reject him. The repercussions would not be good.

She glanced around the office for any signs of Brock or Kevin before she checked her inbox. Dr. Loering's name popped up with the subject "Lunch".

Good morning Hali,

Thank you for coming to the event last evening. Please meet me at the Capital Grille at noon sharp. Do not be late, you will have one hour and one hour only with Dr. Loering. His schedule is slam packed today.

Annabelle

Annabelle was the one spelling Hailey's name wrong. Was it a jealousy thing? Also, it said "meet me". Hailey hoped that was a mistake. How awful would that be to have lunch with Annabelle instead of Dr. Loering? This might be one of the only times Hailey could even begin to imagine someone being jealous of her. And why on earth would she be jealous?

The hours drew on. Between her workload and Brock's looks of longing Hailey felt diminished. She needed to make it to lunch and then she could leave. She took the second part of her day off, not knowing how long lunch would last. Hoping it would last longer.

She got up to go to the breakroom to refresh her coffee. The wrath of Gwyneth awaited but coffee was needed to complete the mountain of work Kevin gave her. Gwyneth was on the phone. Hailey passed by, relieved. The coffee pot had enough coffee for one cup. Hailey emptied it and rinsed the pot out. There was an old, faded sign, ink running down the letters on the fridge saying, "Don't Be Disgusting."

"Hailey! I thought I saw you walk past." Gwyneth's voice rang out behind her." Hailey paused for a moment before turning around, realizing she had nowhere to go.

Gwyneth approached, closing in on her. "I've been dying to ask you about last night. So, how was Dr. Loering?" She said leaning on the door blocking Hailey's way past her. "Was he everything you imagined? I saw Facebook this morning, the show was completely packed. Was he hot in person? Did you get your book signed? "

"Yes, yes, and yes Gwyneth. You know," Hailey said, taking a step towards her. "I'd really love to chat more, but I have so much work today. I'm completely drowning."

"Of course, of course. Hey, how about you fill me in tonight? A play I'm doing makeup on is playing. I can get you a front row seat," Gwyneth's eyes were filled with hope. "We can grab a drink at the bar after and make fun of the acting."

The words "Sure" tumbled out of her mouth before she could think. She couldn't believe her own ears. She caught me at a weak moment, she thought. At the very least she could appreciate Gwyneth's persistence. And one drink wouldn't hurt.

"Here's the address," she said jotting directions on a neon pink post-it note. She handed it to Hailey.

"Sounds good," Hailey heard herself say, wanting the interaction to end. It was one thing to privately go out with Gwyneth. She didn't want to be caught with her in the office looking like best buddies. It was rare that someone reached out to her with an offer of friendship. Who knows, Hailey thought, maybe she'd have some advice on how to deal with Brock's relentless advances.

"Can't wait to hear all the details about Dr. Loering!" She said, finally moving out of the way to let Hailey by.

Hailey gave the most authentic looking smile she could and walked back to her desk. Her coffee was finished before she reached it.

Time slipped by and before she knew it, it was almost time to leave for the Capital Grille. It felt surreal. Now she just needed to get out without Brock popping up. She glanced around trying to spot Brock. Kevin was locked in his office all morning thankfully.

She shut her computer down, grabbed her purse, and hurriedly went to the elevator. As she pressed the down button, she felt a cold finger tap her. It was Laurie from finance, “I think he wants your attention,” she said pointing over to Brock who rapidly approached. The elevator doordinged and was beginning to open. Hailey jumped on without a second thought, Laurie took her time, struggling to move forward with her cane.

"Shit, shit, shit," Hailey said under her breath as she watched Laurie painfully get onto the elevator, one leg after another. Before she was on Hailey pressed the close button.

“What'd you say? I can't hear well, speak up. You’re going to shut the damn door on me girl.” Laurie said, as she finally got into the elevator.

Hailey could hear Brock’s hand hit as the elevator lurched and began its trip downward.

“He really wanted to talk to you,” Laurie said, winking at Hailey. “Romantic interest?’

When outside she walked to the nearest cab stand and jumped in the first cab.

“Capital Grille” she said to the driver. She seemed to be in her late twenties or early thirties. Her head was shaved. She was lean, almost skinny. Cute for a cab driver, Hailey thought. She looked like someone that Hailey would have wanted to approach but was too shy.

“How are you today?” She asked.

“Good. And you?” Hailey wasn’t in the mood to engage in small talk. But she didn’t want to be rude.

She was on her way to a life-changing event. It seemed everything in her life, every decision, every plan, led to this moment of having lunch with Dr. Loering. Her brief interaction with Dr. Loering the previous evening stirred doubt in her. She felt the need to be in silence, creating a stoic shell that would protect her from looking at anything less than someone who showed potential. Dr. Loering had the power to make her writing seen by a wide audience. Dr. Loering had the power to see her as special, worthy, a star, equal to his genius.

“I’m ok." She responded in a friendly tone, "It’s been a busy day. You work around here?” she asked with genuine curiosity.

“Um Yeah, in the Prudential Building.” Hailey tried to answer politely but quick enough to end the conversation.

“And what's your job in the Prudential Building?”

Hailey hated talking about her job. “Um, I work as a project manager for a plastic shipping logistics company." She paused. "But I want to be a writer.” Hailey added, although she said it with the inflection of a question.

“A writer, no kidding. Big dreams. I know what that's like. I want to be a writer too. I got accepted into Northwestern's Medill School of Journalism, but I need to pay for my mom's cancer treatment so I’m working as much as I can right now. What do you write?"

"Sorry about your mom," Hailey responded.

"It's ok, she's a fighter. She’s the strongest woman I know. We'll get through it." She said smiling at her briefly in her mirror.

Warmed by her warmth, Hailey offered, "To answer your question, Fiction, short stories. Literary Fiction that is."

"Can I read your work anywhere?"

"Oh," Hailey said feeling caught off guard. Nobody asked her that question, not even in workshop.

"If that's weird to share that's fine, I just thought maybe you were published or online or something and I could look you up. Or here," she said as she was pulling up in front of Capital Grille. She pulled a small silver box out of her pocket, snapped it open and handed Hailey a card.

Hailey smiled, "Me too," and fished for one of her cards. "Here," she said, handing it to her as they pulled up in front of Capital Grille.

"Plastics Logistics huh?" She asked, holding the card up.

"It pays the bills," She responded as coolly as she could.

"Kind of like my job then," she said laughing. "My name is Bella."

"Hailey".

"Just like on the card, nice to meet you, Hailey." She laughed. They both laughed.

Bella's laughter warmed up Hailey's insides. Underneath all the exhaustion and caffeine, she felt a joyful feeling stirring within her. She was about to get out of the cab. Before she closed the door she took a leap of faith, "I'll send one of my stories. It hasn't been published yet, so you know, it's sacred to me. You won't share it with anyone right?"

"I wouldn't think of sharing your work, without your permission of course. It's not like I'm some stranger you just met."

They both laughed again.

"Listen, I feel honored you're sharing. And I promise, I won't share it. If you want me to read it, send it in the mail, I'm old school."

Hailey never shared her work outside of Dr. Loering's workshops. But her warmth and the fact she'd gotten into Medill made her seem credible. She couldn't deny that she was kind of cute too.

"Enjoy your lunch." Hailey stumbled out the word, Thanks, as she shut the door.

Chapter 6

You can only overcome resistance to completing your project by facing your suffering.

Hailey walked up to the hostess, “Reservation under Hailey or Dr. Loering? For two?”

The hostess, who's name tag said Sandy, looked down at her list for what seemed like an eternity. In reality only a split second. Sandy was beautiful, a dark complexion with beautiful natural curly hair down to her waist. She was wearing a formal black blouse and pencil skirt.

Not unsimilar from what Hailey was wearing the evening before.

“Right this way.” Sandy grabbed two thick, ornate looking menus and began walking.

“We have you in a booth, if that’s ok.”

“Ok,” Hailey responded. She anxiously wondered what Dr. Loering would prefer.

As they walked through the restaurant Hailey's heart was beating out her chest. Even with the lack of sleep she was wide awake now. Sandy led Hailey to a booth in the center of the room.

He wasn't there. Hailey felt both relief and disappointment. Was she really ready for this? She could always leave right now, she thought.

“Enjoy your lunch," Sandy walked away.

Moments later a waiter appeared.

“Hello, my name is Clark. Can I get you anything to drink while you wait for the rest of your party?” He asked with the enthusiasm of a game show host.

He looked about 25, dressed immaculately in a black dress shirt and pants. His blonde medium length hair was slicked back behind the ears of his perfectly chiseled face. No facial hair. His shoes were shiny, black, and pointy.

She liked Clark's energy. His warm vibes were putting her at ease. She tried hiding her shaky hands behind the drink menu. As she anchored her hands to the table, she pondered downing a glass of wine to put her nerves at ease.

“I'll wait until my party arrives, thank you.” Her voice was cracked.

“You're welcome, I'll check back in a moment.” he turned and walked away briskly.

Hailey continued studying the wine menu. She wasn't facing the door, so it wasn't possible to see whether Dr. Loering arrived. She was thankful so she could seem more relaxed when he arrived. Time was moving but it wasn't clear how fast it was moving. It seemed fast and slow at the same time. While her thoughts were racing back and forth about the prospect of wine she was going to get, Clark showed back up with Dr. Loering in tow.

He wore a brown shirt with a black dress jacket over it and faded relaxed fit blue jeans. It was the most relaxed outfit she'd seen him in. He wore black dress shoes on with fake looking shoelaces. He looked serious, stoic, in a neutral mood, yet prepared. A look one might have for a job interview or an update from their financial adviser.

He was a short guy. There wasn't any doubt about seeing him up close. It was alarming. An angle of him most women probably never saw. Hailey knew women imagined him towering over them. I have a leg up, she thought, bursting into a giggle.

"Hailey?"

"Yes, it's me" she said her voice cracking on the word me, still laughing.

"Hailey Hailey quite contrary," he said, a smile breaking, immediately easing the tension. "Nice to meet you", he said sliding into his chair.

"Isn't it Mary…?

"You have a nice laugh. Care to share the joke?" He said gazing into her eyes with an intensity that took her confidence down a notch.

Hailey was not the best at thinking on her feet and this was no exception.

"I was thinking of a joke my mom told me."

"What was that?" Dr. Loering asked as Clark placed a menu in front of him.

Brock told her dumb jokes on a regular basis. His latest one, the only one she could remember would have to do. She usually tried her best to forget his jokes.

"Why do men marry virgins?"

"They want a fresh start?" Dr. Loering asked as he looked over the wine menu.

"Um, sort of, they can't stand criticism," Hailey said as more of a question, hoping that he would drop the subject now that she delivered the pathetic punchline.

"Hmmm," Dr. Loering looked up at Hailey with a perplexed look. "You found that funny, huh?"

“Would you like anything to drink sir?” Clark asked, breaking the moment, giving Hailey hope that they would move past this. She couldn’t believe she used one of Brock’s jokes. What an awful choice. Her face was glowing red.

“Give me a moment.” Dr. Loering responded.

“Ok, I'll be back in a minute to go over the specials,” Clark said as he turned and walked away.

“Thank you, “Hailey said. It was a challenging game, to be able to gaze at Dr. Loering just enough. Not too much that she would make him uncomfortable. Up close, she noticed right away that there were three large moles on his face. Those weren’t visible from stage. Come to think of it she’d never noticed those moles on any of his book covers or posters.

Dr. Loering broke the silence, jerking Hailey out of her head.

“So Hailey, what do you have to say about yourself? What did your parents do?” He asked in a tone that suggested he cared.

The question threw her off. Of all the talking points she envisioned this was not one that she imagined coming up.

“My mother is a stay-at-home mom, my father a Financial Adviser.”

“Uh huh,” he said as if examining her face like a doctor at a physical. Did he ask so he could place her in a category? She couldn’t tell if he liked what she said. She felt every word of hers being weighed on an unknown scale. Was it her imagination or was he looking at the dark circles under her eyes she tried to hide? She uncomfortably shifted in the booth.

“What about your parents?” Hailey asked, trying to reciprocate.

“I don’t talk about my parents.” He said shutting the question down.

“Oh, sorry.” Hailey mumbled.

She looked over her menu quietly, feeling his gaze upon her. Could he hear her heart pounding? Ultimately, she wanted to talk about her writing. About the short story she’d completed and wanted to submit. But how to get from here to there?

"So let me guess, you're a writee," he said casting his gorgeous smile. His smile helped her forget that he’d pegged her a writee instead of a writer.

"I am. How'd you guess?" Hailey had a suspicion it was her clothing. Or her parents' boring career. Or the fact she bought a ticket to have lunch with him.

"I just know. How is your writing coming along? Are you getting in your assigned words every day?"

Before Hailey could answer Clark, the waiter came back to the table. “Have you two decided on drinks? We have mimosas and bloody marys on special.”

Hailey went first knowing. Her mom would be proud of her under the circumstances.

“I’ll have a decaf coffee.”

“Cream or sugar?”

“Sugar please.”

“And you sir?”

“Glass of Sancerre. And a Perrier.”

As Dr. Loering ordered the wine she regretted not getting a glass.

“One glass of wine and one decaf.” Clark said with a hint of judgment in the word “decaf.” " I can go over today's specials.”

“Proceed.” Dr. Loering said with ease of authority.

Clark listed off the specials in a well-rehearsed manner.

"I think I will have the steak and salmon special.” Dr. Loering interrupted Clark.

After writing his order Clark paused and looked at Dr. Loering.

“You look familiar. Are you by any chance that famous author, Dr. Loering?”

In a response that couldn't be deciphered as if he were irritated or flattered by being noticed, "My name is Dr. Loering, yes."

"My younger sister loves your work."

"Is she cute?" he asked chuckling.

A feeling of unease hit Hailey's gut. She may as well be out to lunch with Brock or Kevin she thought as she tried to keep a neutral facial expression.

"I haven't read anything of yours," Clark continued. "Not my type of material. But she adores your past work, especially the book, "How to Figure Out Your Writing Livelihood without Dying".

"Excuse me," Dr. Loering abruptly got up.

"I need to use the restroom. Is it this way?"

"Yes sir, right over there around the corner, down the hall to the right.

With that Dr. Loering got up quickly and left.

Clark the waiter looked surprised.

Was it the book Hailey wondered? She'd never heard of it before, and she was required to know all his works as part of the workshop agreement.

"Yikes, I hope I didn't offend him, "Clark said quietly.

"I know what I would like." Hailey interrupted him, hoping to change the subject.

"I'll have the lunch special as well."

“And the temperature on your salmon and steak?”

“Rare on both, please. Also, could I have a glass of Cab?”

“House, ok?”

“Sure.”

“Alright, we have two specials and the two glasses of wine.” Clark said as he wrote down the rest of the order on his notepad.

“And do you still want decaf coffee?”

“No, I’ll just have the wine. Maybe coffee after.”

“Alright then.” He said and was gone.

Wine didn't seem as bad of an idea. Hailey started to wonder if all men were different versions of Brock. She didn't like Dr. Loering's judgmental demeanor. She wondered if everything was a test with him. A test she would fail no matter what. She still hoped to mention her writing and the workshop she was going to. Maybe if she showcased her dedication he would soften.

Finally, he arrived back acting as if nothing happened. “Decaf coffee?” he asked with a condescending tone.

“I changed my mind. I went with a glass of Cab.”

“Why'd you change your mind?”

“Well, I suppose because you were having a glass.”

“Oh, I see," he said tapping his hand on the table. "That's part of what you need to change to evolve. It's part of your journey in transforming from a writee to a writer.”

"What do you mean?" Hailey asked with genuine curiosity.

"Make the choice, own it. Understand your path and don't question it."

Hailey nodded, feeling color rise to her cheeks.

Dr. Loering leaned in, "Don't be shy, don't let it embarrass you. Own it, own your life."

Clark returned with their glasses of wine.

Hailey took a generous gulp from her glass. The wine seemed like it would give her power that she currently did not have.

"I bought a ticket to the final workshop."

"Oh yeah?" He said swirling his wine and smelling it.

Hailey tried to copy the swirling with her wine. It was a departure from the usual boxed wine she consumed.

"I think those workshops are the number one most important thing writees can do to progress. I also think it can make or break a writee. Some writees quit after them. It's too much to be faced with adversity for those people. Then, a few of the bravest go forward with their transformation. Defying all odds, finishing the page they worked on, the book they slaved over, getting it in front of their audience..."

"What do you think makes this workshop so important?" Hailey asked.

"A number of things. These workshops work from multiple paradigms. We aren't just teaching writing; we are teaching living. We teach death. We teach love. To love life, to love your work. To marry the darkness with the light."

Dr. Loering continued talking about how he developed the workshops while Hailey sipped on her wine. Maybe she was on the right track with this conversation. She was enjoying seeing him up close in his element. She was starting to feel like this was worth it.

Clark came back with their food and they both ordered another round of drinks.

"I usually only drink one glass at lunch," Dr. Loering said, smiling as he rubbed his stomach. "But hell, today my schedule is somewhat clear, why not have the second. You see Hailey, I decided to have a glass of wine and I'm happy about it. It's that easy."

Hailey smiled. Feeling good about their rapport, she asked, "So what do you think I need to do? To progress?" This was the question she'd been dying to ask and now she'd asked it.

There was a pause that Hailey took for Dr. Loering finishing chewing.

His phone buzzed, "Oh sorry, I need to check this" he said fishing his phone out of his pocket. He proceeded to type away.

She pondered if she should get her phone out and do the same. Hailey always felt like the phone was a disease. Looking at your phone was contagious, and it gave people an excuse to not engage. Instead, she sat in awkward silence as Dr. Loering did whatever he was doing on his phone.

After what seemed like an eternity, he looked up, "Sorry, I was texting my girlfriend. She's mad at me again." Dr. Loering said as he started to cut into his steak.

“This looks delicious,” Hailey offered. Hoping to redirect the energy into some sort of positivity. The air weighed heavily there; she didn't know how to restart the conversation.

“I’m writing a story”. Hailey offered.

“About what?” Dr. Loering asked.

“It’s a story about a visit to a relative's house that goes horrifically wrong.”

“Interesting, good for you Hailey.” He seemed genuine when he said it.

“Yeah, it’s hard for me to get as much time as I would like writing. I need to survive, you know, pay the bills, so I have a day job.”

“There’s really no excuse to not do your life’s work.” Dr. Loering said this, smiling. When he said this, Hailey noticed for the first time that his teeth were less than perfect. She wondered about what all the women who idolized him would think of his imperfect teeth.

Knowing there was no way to respond without sounding defensive Hailey responded,

“I’d love for you to look at my work sometime.”

“I’d be honored, Hailey.” He entirely surprised her with this unexpected generosity. Her hopes lifted.

Clark then approached,

“How is everything then?”

“Absolutely delicious. These potato puffs are to die for.” Hailey said genuinely.

She looked over at Dr. Loering who was eating methodically. He didn’t pause and look up at her, the focus was on his plate.

“How do you like your food?”

“Good”, it’s fine.” There was a long pause while he ate another bite of his steak, a bit of grease lingering around the side of his mouth, shimmered in the midday light. The silverware sounded like its own orchestra in the heavy silence.

“I wonder what people think when they look at us” Dr. Loering asked when Clark walked away. The question completely caught Hailey off guard, again. She was weirded out that Dr. Loering was asking this. She didn’t peg him to be someone that cared what anybody would think.

“Do they think we are a couple having a silent lunch together, perhaps we are in a fight?” He asked further exploring.

“Hmmmm, I am not sure. Maybe we’re on a business dinner?” Hailey knew the second it came out her mouth that her comment was flat and uninteresting. Dr. Loering didn’t look up from his food, clearly not impressed. Was he hitting on her, she wondered? This was supposed to be her dream scenario, but it was feeling more and more like the bad lunch date she envisioned going on with Brock.

Just as she was working up the courage to ask about his personal writing habits, Clark whisked by the table again.

“Is there anything else I can get you?”

“Just the check.” Dr. Loering responded.

Clark nodded and removed her plate and walked away.

Dr. Loering patted his stomach, “Well, that was good. What do you have going on for the rest of the day?”

As she started to answer Clark returned with the bill and set it on the table in front of her.

Hailey was not planning on paying for lunch. With her small salary she hardly had money for lunch at a place like this.

“I have the rest of the day off. I was thinking of getting some writing done.” She said hoping that he was going to take the bill from her side of the table.

“Writing, yes, that sounds good,” he absently replied as he began to look at his cell phone again, making no movement to help pay.

There was a pause. She decided to look at the bill. It seemed as if Dr. Loering had zero intention to look at it.

Immediately her eyes fell to the total. Over two hundred dollars. That money was her groceries for a week. She looked at the items on there. A feeling of dread overtook her. There was no mention of having to pay for lunch when Hailey bought the tickets. And Hailey had just bought the ticket to the last workshop making her extremely broke in a high interest kind of way.

Dr. Loering was still making no move to pay. He laughed quietly as he looked at his phone. Hailey gingerly pulled out her credit card and left it on the table. Almost as soon as she set it on the table Clark appeared out of thin air and grabbed the bill. Her stomach sank further and further into a pit. Clark returned with the bill.

“Thank you. I hope you enjoyed everything.” Clark said with satisfaction.

Hailey was struck with so much anxiety over how she would eat for the next week, it was difficult to get words out.

"What are your plans for this afternoon?" she heard herself ask. She felt herself outside of herself, detached, almost not wanting to know the answer but having no choice.

"I'll walk over to the bookstore after this and browse. Hailey, thank you for meeting me. It was a pleasure."

Hailey was distracted trying to figure out the tip as Dr. Loering got up to begin his departure out of the restaurant. She quickly signed and got up.

"Yes, of course Dr. Loering. It was my absolute pleasure," she said awkwardly reaching out her hand, which Dr. Loering didn't notice as he turned away already to walk out the door.

Hailey, in an act of desperation shouted, "Dr. Loering".

He stopped, looking a bit startled and turned around, "Yes, Hailey," he said returning.

"My writing, do you want me to email it?"

"I don't read emails, so no, ask Annabelle for an address to send a hard copy to. Thanks again for lunch Hailey."

And with that he walked off quickly. Hailey was shocked. He made people pay for having lunch with him in addition to paying for his lunch? Was it just a way to get free lunch?

She needed to get out of here. It was over, the damage done. She felt a sense of devastation at how much money she spent on this man, his books, his workshops, his talks, and now his lunch.

A small glimmer of hope arose in her. He'd offered to look at her work. As awkward as the lunch was, that olive branch alone was enough to endure the pain of having had to use her credit card until her next paycheck to feed a man who made enough money to pay off the entirety of her student loans in a split second.

She was deep in thought walking. It didn't matter. To her, Dr. Loering's feedback and potential endorsement of her writing was a chance out of the mundane reality that currently existed for her. She thought of all the rejection notices in her inbox, there were a hundred of them. She felt so invisible to the world, especially the writing world. There was nothing special in her radar without him.

She stopped at an area by the lake to sit on a bench. She sat down on a bench and took a moment to collect herself. She stared out at the water. It looked fake in the middle of the city. On one side it was surrounded with big shiny buildings and fancy condominiums. It was a perfect rectangle of water. On the other side there was a small path leading to four benches spaced about ten feet apart. Hailey loved sitting on these benches. She'd pretend that she was just looking out at water, not all the madness of the city surrounding it. Until she looked inevitably noticed the ugly new condos with their sterile soon to be out of style restaurants. Places that were filled with television screens, red leather booths and waitresses that looked like future MBA students. The only thing that made the water seem real was the fact that it led to the Lake. The lake was about two blocks from this inland channel. This was the only place in Streeterville Hailey felt like she could get away from everything. She was on the bench closest to the road that day looking out at the water. Aside from how horribly awkward lunch was, this was a chance. It was a chance out of the shackles she felt every day when she went to her office job. It was a chance to see the world how she truly felt she was supposed to. It was a chance for someone to recognize that she was more than just a cog in a machine.

She needed reality to be something other than what it was.

Hailey reached into her purse to find the receipt from lunch. There it was, crumpled next to her billfold. Sadly, the $260 lunch was a reality. He had taken money she didn't have. He even pushed her down when she was trying to pick up the last of her money, Hailey thought. A cold breeze shifted the environment and gave her the chills. It was time to head back home. She unlocked her phone and opened her email. She typed in the name Annabelle to a new email.

Dear Dr. Loering,

Thank you for having lunch with me. It was a pleasure getting to know you. Anyway, you mentioned you'd be willing to read my writing. Let me know the best address to send it to.

Sincerely,

Hailey
333-222-1111

Hailey felt a huge sigh of relief but instantly wondered when Annabelle would respond. This could be the break she needed. She yearned to have her voice heard.

Annabelle's response buzzed on Hailey's phone.

Send it to this address, paper copy only:

PO Box 381
Chicago, IL 60622

With that, Hailey ordered an Uber and rose off the bench in which she experienced hopeless despair. Her newfound excitement energized her to get home and send her story both to Bella and Dr. Loering.

Chapter 7

When in doubt, reach to your fellow writee community for help and communion to reach your creative universe.

Hailey stopped to drop off her writing at a post office on the way to Gwyneth's show. She slipped her stories in two manilla envelopes. Each with a carefully handwritten note on her finest stationery (her only stationery).

Dear Dr. Loering,

Thank you for having lunch with me. It was a pleasure getting to know you. Anyway, you mentioned you'd be willing to read my writing. This is my story about a girl who visits her aunt in Maine. Things turn sinister when she finds out a secret from her aunt's past. I hope you enjoy it.

Sincerely,

Hailey
333-222-1111

Bella,

I look forward to your feedback.

- Hailey

She took a deep breath and handed it to the unenthused post office worker. This could change her life. Things could be different. Maybe she could quit her job. She dreamt of a job where all she did was travel and write. Perhaps this manuscript could be the ticket out.

Hailey arrived at the James M. Nederlander theater. Hailey searched for her ticket. She liked CATS but couldn't imagine what a play based entirely about cats would be. She settled into her seat. Gwyneth had gotten her 3-4 rows from the front. The lights flickered on and off. Music started, and as humans dressed up as CATS began to jump out of into the audience. Hailey was so startled, she screamed.

As the play wore on Hailey realized that the best part of this was the beginning when she'd been startled. It'd be one thing to watch actual cats singing and dancing. But the premise of humans dressed up as cats singing and dancing seemed entirely ridiculous. Especially two and a half hours of it. The encore finished; Hailey breathed a sigh of relief. She'd spent the entire time wondering who could possibly enjoy this. As the crowd slowly moved out of the theater, Gwyneth appeared, looking stunning as usual. She wore a red vintage skirt with leopard trim, a tight black top and matching red lipstick. Her long curly hair was pulled up on one side, the other side down with loose curls.

Hailey felt unsettled as she walked towards her. Gwyneth was the opposite of someone Hailey would typically be friends with. Her two friends (still approved by Hailey's mother) in college would never wear such provocative clothing. But what did clothing matter, she thought, the two friends weren't even super close to Hailey, especially after graduation. Having a wardrobe from Sara Jane didn't equal lifelong friendship. Both her friends moved back to the suburbs, shot out children and Hailey's mom continuously mentioned how she saw them in church. Gwyneth turned, saw Hailey, and waved her over.

"Hailey, I wasn't sure if you were going to show up," she said waving at one of the cat actors "Hi Frisco," she called.

“That’s a man?” Hailey asked watching calico painted Frisco as he made the rounds to fans and other people milling around, hoping to catch a picture with the cast.

“Doesn’t he look great? That’s all me. I know, I’m talented.” Gwyneth said, waving at another cat walking by.

“Wow, that’s amazing Gwyneth, I guess I can appreciate the work that must have gone into doing all the makeup for this…”

Gwyneth cut Hailey off before she could finish her thought, “I know it’s an awful play, but it’s one of the bigger productions I’ve done. I’m hoping it will open doors.”

“Should we get a drink?”

"I'd have one," Hailey said as they walked to the small theater bar.

“Nice outfit, Gwyneth, only you could pull it off,” Hailey said, sincerely trying to give her a compliment.

"Thanks darling, do you like my earrings?" She asked, twirling what looked like a tiny black cat dangling from her ear.

"Um, yeah those are nice."

"She loves those pussies," the bartender said as they walked up to the bar.

"Stop it George," she said flirtatiously. "I want to hear all about your lunch with Dr. Loering. You have to tell me everything! But first, I wanted to say sorry about Kevin the other day."

"You don't need to apologize." Hailey said, secretly appreciating the apology. "Kevin is an asshole. He really really likes you though."

"What do you mean by that?" Gwyneth asked in a slightly defensive tone.

"Well, you're going for that promotion," Hailey said immediately after, sensing the misstep.

"Yes, I'm going for the promotion, yes, what's your point? I need the money."

"I don't have a point, I think Kevin likes you more than me, that's all." Hailey responded.

"Like? What does like have to do with it sweetie? Guts are the reason I get into Kevin's inner circle. I asked Kevin what I need to do to get it and he told me. And I did it. And then I have to put up with all the office gossip that I'm a slut."

"I'm sorry, I shouldn't have said anything about the promotion."

"Listen, I'm not special. I'm hungry, that's all. I was hungry enough to grab the meat for the taking." She paused looking over at Hailey, "That didn't sound right, did it?"

They both let out a laugh of relief.

Gwyneth turned to Hailey, "Let's hear about you, I haven't heard a word about your date with Dr. Loering."

"Date, no, no, it wasn't a date, just a lunch."

"Tell me about him, Dr. Loering," Gwyneth said propping her head onto her hand. "What is he like in person? Is he as captivating one on one as he is on television? I've seen some of his shows, but I'm always wary of those self-help guru types."

"No, he isn't like that, I really think his methods work and help people to become better writers. There are success stories. Like the one woman who got on the New York Herald Bestseller List."

A strange voice said, "By people you mean vulnerable women."

Gwyneth and Hailey looked over to see Jenna Janders standing in between them.

"Well, if it isn't the one and only Jenna Janders," Gwyneth swooned and gasped. "Oh my, you have to forgive me, I'm a little star struck. Jenna, I am a huge fan of yours. I watch your show every week. Please please let me buy you a drink, George get over here," Gwyneth frantically waved. "Get Jenna another one of what she has, oh let's see, looks like a vodka drink?" Gwyneth continued gushing, hurrying George to bring a drink.

"Dirty Martini", Jenna said, holding up what was almost an empty glass. "I'm sorry for interrupting but I overheard you two talking about Dr. Loering. Do you mind if I join you two?" Jenna asked as she grabbed a stool, putting it in between Hailey and Gwyneth.

"Hi, my name is Jenna," she said looking at Hailey. "What's your name," she said, extending her hand.

"Don't you recognize me?"

"Should I recognize you?" Jenna asked, scanning Hailey's face.

"Here we go," Gwyneth said, handing Jenna her martini. "George makes the best martinis but I must warn you, they hurt."

Jenna responded laughing, "I'm no stranger to George's martinis. I live right around the corner, and I pop in here for a drink from time to time. I like seeing the actors, it's something I've been doing ever since I moved into this neighborhood. Plus, it's never crowded in here. "

"Did you see the play tonight! Gwyneth asked, and before Jenna could answer she nervously held out her hand, "I'm Gwyneth and this is my friend from work, Hailey." Hailey noted how Gwyneth called her a friend.

"Hailey, Hailey who I am supposed to recognize. I don't recognize you, Hailey. How do I know you?"

"The event last night, Dr. Loering's talk, in the bathroom, remember?" Hailey realized that Jenna was the one that passed by her when she was picking her change off the ground. Thank goodness she didn't recognize her from that moment, Hailey thought.

Jenna paused and took a sip from her drink. "Oh, you were the girl who was offended by me telling the truth. Yes, I remember now."

"I wasn't offended," Hailey lied with color rising to her cheeks.

Gwyneth interjected, "Ladies, ladies, ladies, let's drink to liars. We've all known a liar or two, or three, haven't we? Hell, I just kicked one out of my apartment the other week, lying three times cheating son of a bitch. That's why I prefer dating women. Men are more trouble than they are worth."

Hailey was surprised to hear this side of Gwyneth as they all held their drinks up, clinking glasses.

"I would agree about men being more trouble than they are worth." Jenna said as she sat her drink down on the bar.

"Jenna, I want to hear all about your latest investigation. You are beyond talented, I watch your show every week, " Gwyneth gushed.

"I like your enthusiasm," She smiled at Gwyneth. "I came over here because I heard you two talking about Dr. Loering. Gwyneth, as you probably know, I've been following him for a while now."

She paused and looked at Hailey, "I believe he's brainwashing women into quitting their jobs, families, lives, with false hope that they can become famous. I also think he uses his methods to sleep with women. And if that doesn't alarm you, what about the fact he uses new attendees to run personal errands for "leaders" who have been published? It's a way to keep control over people. A pyramid scheme."

"I need to stop you right there," Hailey said. "How do you know this? What's your proof? And if you have proof, why hasn't it been shared?"

"You should really watch her show Hailey," Gwyneth said looking slightly bored with the conversation. "I don't want to hear about boring Dr. Loering, I want to hear about some of the stars you have interviewed. Like Dale Hickner, the famous Scientologist? He's such a hunk."

"And such a nut," Jenna said laughing at Gwyneth.

"If you don't want to talk about Dr. Loering, that's fine. I thought you should know he's a scam. Women have been shelling out money to destroy their lives. I think he is hiding a deeper secret, but I haven't been able to get any evidence. My editor pulled me from the story."

"I saw your interview with him on television. Honestly I might have been sold on him entirely if I hadn't seen that." Gwyneth offered.

Hailey slowly steamed. Dr. Loering might occasionally say problematic things but so did every big figure. "His method has done the opposite for me. He was kind enough to read one of my stories."

Hailey said a little too defensively. She had no idea if he would really read her story.

"He doesn't care about success for anybody but himself." Jenna said, looking at Hailey. "I'm only trying to help you."

"Thank you, the only help I've needed has been with my writing. Dr. Loering's methods have helped me, they work." Hailey said with less confidence than she wanted.

"Listen, this conversation is boring ladies," Gwyneth said, smiling and winking at Hailey, softening up the mood. "How about we finish our drinks and go back to my place for an afterparty smoke party."

"I'm on a big assignment, but you know, maybe it's George's martini speaking, I'm in." Jenna said.

Gwyneth and Jenna started to discuss where they lived in comparison to one another while Hailey sat ruminating. If there was any truth to what Jenna said she sent her writing to the lion's den. What would he do with it? Burn it? Defecate on it? Laugh hysterically then send it to all his literary connections and warn them of her? She hoped with all her heart he would see potential in her. What if it was the opposite, she thought, trying to pull herself out of the darkness. All the positive possibilities that might come out of Dr. Loering looking at her writing would be worth it.

They paid their tab. Then, the trio stumbled over to Gwyneth's.

Gwyneth's apartment was only two blocks from the bar. A high rise, complete with a doorman, they entered from an elevator into what was a spacious one-bedroom apartment loft. Gwyneth mentioned how spacious it was several times. It was nice, obviously newer and with a modern look.

"Go ahead and make yourself comfortable," I'll get us some drinks, she said with a slight slur to her words, walking into the kitchen. Hailey plopped onto a red loveseat while Jenna sat in an armchair. There was a glass table in the middle of the living room assorted with various nail polishes and lipsticks.

"I can't believe Jenna Janders is sitting in my apartment right now!" Gwyneth called from the kitchen.

Hailey and Jenna gave each other a knowing look. Hailey rolled her eyes and Jenna started laughing with Hailey following suit.

"It must be interesting working with her," Jenna said plopping down on the couch.

"I can hear you two, " Gwyneth called.

"Did you really pay to have lunch with Dr. Loering?" Jenna asked.

Hailey, her tongue loose from the alcohol, responded, " I did." Her drunkenness made the fact she was broke seem like it was no big deal. She paid to pay. It was possible nothing would come out of it except an awkward conversation with her parents to borrow money.

"How was it? I've only interviewed him one time. After that one he wouldn't agree to doing another, I'd love to get one on one time with him like you did. Away from a larger audience. I think he feeds off larger groups."

Gwyneth entered the room holding a silver tray with three glasses of champagne and two joints. She set the tray on the table and handed Hailey and Jenna the drinks. She grabbed one herself and settled on the couch next to Jenna. Jenna eagerly grabbed one of the joints and lit it up, taking a big inhale.

"Sure," Hailey said as Jenna passed her the joint. She awkwardly took an inhale, one too large for someone who only smoked twice in her life. A huge cough erupted.

"Careful now," Gwyneth said laughing. "We have a rookie on our hands."

Hailey took a moment from her coughing to wet her throat with the champagne. A rush went to her head. She took a deep breath, trying to gain composure. "We went out to lunch, and I didn't get a great impression of Dr. Loering, but I was so nervous. I admire and fear him at the same time." She paused, taking a sip of her champagne. Her phone started buzzing. She had a feeling who it was. Then it buzzed again and again. Annoyed at the interruption she fished for her phone.

WRITER MARIE: I need you tonight

WRITER MARIE: KIDS acting up

WRITER MARIE: Also, I'D LIKE 5000 words tonite so I know you are keeping your daily counts up

WRITER MARIE: BE HERE IN 10

WRITER MARIE: ?????????

Hailey turned her phone off. She'd deal with Writer Marie later. Plus, she was in no condition to be around her slimy hands or her spoiled children.

"Regardless of what you think Jenna," she said while Jenna took another large hit, Dr. Loering was a light in my life when I had nothing else. His writing classes and methods gave me direction." Hailey started to feel a disconnect between the words that were coming out her mouth and the sound. Was there an echo in Gwyneth's apartment? She was high as a kite.

"Anyway," she said as the joint came back around to her, "Maybe he had things on his mind, who knows, but he was kind of an asshole." She didn't dare mention that she'd paid for lunch.

"That he's an asshole is a well-known fact for anybody who knows the truth about Dr. Loering." Jenna said as Hailey passed her the joint.

Hailey took a giant puff while wondering why it seemed there were so many asshole men in the world? And so many wonderful women? She pictured her mom slaving over the perfect dinner for her ungrateful father. Then she thought of Bella. She was genuinely kind. Why couldn't she think of even one kind man?

"Jenna, tell us about the investigation you've did on him. I think Hailey should know," Gwyneth said looking at Hailey and gently nodding her head.

"I did an investigation on him awhile back. I was immediately suspicious when I heard only women were joining his groups. People passed it off like women need more empowerment than men when it comes to writing. So, I joined one of his groups, to test it out. I'll admit, at first, the language was empowering. Then, after a while it started to seem sprinkled with sexism. Things like, "Women are weak and need help and direction to follow their dreams...". I got kicked out of workshop and told I couldn't come back for questioning the language. Then I got a big break. Dr. Loering accepted an interview with me. Maybe you two saw the interview. Every time I mentioned his past, he was especially evasive about his time in college. He repeatedly asked to not speak about his past work, including one of his most famous books."

"Why do you think that is?" Gwyneth asked.

"I don't know. Maybe he didn't develop his program, maybe he's stealing his ideas. That's not enough to nail him. Lots of programs are built on stolen ideas. This one over here doesn't want to believe it," Jenna said, glancing at Hailey who was sat in disbelief.

"Believe what?" She managed to utter. She was extremely high now and everything was amplified. Gwyneth's voice, Jenna's hands. She couldn't stop staring at her hands, they were beautiful. The long, graceful fingers neatly trimmed. The hands of a writer, she thought. Writer, writer is why I wanted to meet Dr. Loering in the first place, the thought snapping her back into the present.

"Believe that he's into some deep shit and has brainwashed all of these women into believing him."

"Believe that he isn't who he says he is. "Gwyneth added.

"I understand if his methods aren't for everyone. They aren't meant for everyone. I've gained so much from them, so much." Hailey loved to talk about writing so she carried on," The fourth method he taught got me out of a huge rut. It's about setting aside time to do what's important and carrying through with it even when you don't feel like it. I know it sounds obvious, but at the time, hearing it pushed me to finish my work. It also put me with others that have the same goals. His videos are motivational for me, whenever I'm stuck, I've watched him. Even just to get through my workday. Everything seems so hard, but he makes it seem easy. Maybe it's the way he simplifies things... I..." The strong weed overtook her, or maybe it wasn't even strong. How would she know? She never smoked.

"I have a feeling he's a phony. I hate his overconfidence. I'd love to take him down and see him burn." Gwyneth chimed in, relieving Hailey who was inwardly thankful for having the spotlight off her.

Jenna looked over laughing, "I didn't realize you had a mean bone in your body Gwyneth."

"I'm not all sugar all the time, she said, flashing a mischievous smile at Jenna. "But I have sugar all the time, and I think this group could use some, " she said as she got up and went into the kitchen.

"If there's any truth, what you said," Hailey said almost quietly enough that Jenna couldn't hear, "Then what?"

"Then we need solid proof."

Gwyneth approached with a tray of assorted cookies.

"I still think it's crazy, " Hailey said, stuffing a chocolate chip cookie into her mouth.

"Let's play a game," Gwyneth suggested.

"Oh, I'm really good at Farkle," Hailey shouted out excitedly.

"The champagne is working on someone," Jenna laughed, and then all three erupted into giggles.

"No, let's play a game with real stakes, Truth or Dare." Gwyneth suggested.

"Ladies, I am out for the evening," Jenna said finishing her champagne. "I'm on deadline"

"No!" Both Hailey and Gwyneth screamed. They looked at one another and started laughing again.

Jenna gathered her things while laughing. "Listen, if you two ever need anything," Jenna said, digging in her purse, "Here's my card," she said, handing it to Gwyneth.

"We might need some pizza," Hailey said as she reached for another cookie

Gwyneth rolled in laughter on the couch. "I can't stop laughing."

"Have a good night," Jenna said and left.

"Well, I guess it's just us, the cookies, and champagne," was the last thing Hailey remembered Gwyneth saying that evening.

\- - -

Hailey woke up in a strange bed. A new gaggle of text messages from Writer Marie polluted her phone. Text messages that she was feeling less and less inclined to read, much less respond to.

WRITER MARIE: Where are you? You MISSED LAST NIGHT...

It smelled like stale roses in the room she was in. The second sensation was a horrible headache. Her mouth was completely dry. Her memory fuzzy on what happened after Jenna left. As she slowly awoke, she took in her surroundings. She was enveloped in a huge down comforter. As she arose, she realized she was wearing someone else's pajamas. As she looked over, getting her bearings she realized that she was in Gwyneth's room. She realized that because Gwyneth was asleep beside her.

Gwyneth was peacefully asleep, looking meticulous given the night before, although her makeup was washed off. It was the first time Hailey saw her being natural. Gwyneth was beautiful, Hailey thought. The questions were beginning to form in her aching head. Why hadn't she left the night before? She saw her clothing on a chair near the bed. Gwyneth's room was cluttered with photos, clothes, and knickknacks from her life.

It was messy but comfortable. Hailey realized that the smell of roses was perfume Gwyneth wore. Hailey tiptoed to her clothing and left Gwyneth's room. She closed the door quietly and made her way to the bathroom to change. Not remembering where the bathroom was, she opened the first door in the hallway. It was a spacious room with a giant vanity, a mountain of makeup lying on and around it, wigs, what looked like a closet full of costumes. Not the bathroom, she thought.

She opened the second door in the hallway and sighed with relief when it was the bathroom. She pulled on her pants and shirt after checking her phone to see what time it was. 10 am on Saturday morning. She'd slept late. She hadn't finished her words for the morning and didn't have any motivation to write. Writer Marie would be a horror show when she went to the next workshop. In Hailey's hangover haze she couldn't care enough to deal with her.

Glancing in the mirror it seemed that she washed her face at some point. Luckily her makeup from the night before wasn't all smeared across her face. She imagined Gwyneth helping her. assuming that she hadn't been able to do it herself if she wasn't able to remember what happened.

What Hailey needed more than anything was coffee and a glass of water. She walked out to Gwyneth's kitchen to fumble around for coffee. After fumbling around she found a pot, coffee and was looking for mugs when she heard…

"Second cupboard to the right of the sink, second shelf."

"I can't remember the last time someone made me coffee," Gwyneth said as she plopped onto a dining room chair.

"Well don't get your expectations up, I typically get my coffee on the way to work." Luckily the coffee pot was fast. Hailey poured cups for both her and Gwyneth and came to sit down at the circular, glass, dining room table.

"You know what I hate?"

"What could you possibly hate Gwyneth? Besides Kevin's invoices?"

They both laughed.

“I hate how they put liquid sugar in the coffee at McDonalds,” Gwyneth said, taking a sip of what was decent coffee.

“Me too,” Hailey said. “Thankfully, this coffee is strong, I’m completely out of sorts after last night. What happened last night?”

Gwyneth laughed, “You don’t remember?”

“I don’t remember anything after Jenna left.”

“Well, after we talked about playing truth or dare you told me all about your writing. You talked about your parents. Told me about your suburban childhood. You were a chatterbox. Until you weren’t. I was worried you were going to be sick. But I got you to bed alright. I hope it’s ok that you slept in my bed.”

“Thanks,” Hailey said softly. “That was one of my first times smoking.” She felt a little embarrassed at her overindulgence.

“I could tell,” Gwyneth said laughing again. “You’re a lightweight.”

“This morning, I was wandering around to find that bathroom and I walked into your other room. I would love to see all your costumes sometime.”

"You really were out of it if you don’t remember where the bathroom was, you were in there a few times last night," Gwyneth said as she got up and started to rummage around in her cupboards.

Hailey felt the same twinge of shame. She was a lightweight. The one that always stayed behind to study or read books versus going out.

“I’m looking for some breakfast, are you hungry?” Gwyneth asked.

“Starving,” Hailey said, aware that even though she ate at least seven cookies and loads of chips last night, she felt hunger pains.

"I always wanted to be a makeup artist.” Gwyneth said as she pulled out eggs and a loaf of white bread. “That's what I went to school for. Since I was a little girl, I loved playing dress up. I would make myself and my friends into different characters. I have some pictures here," she said, grabbing an album from under her table.

The first photo was a horrific mask. An old man with no teeth. There was blood in the corner of his bulged-out eyes and drool coming out from the corners of his open mouth. "This is horrifying Gwyneth."

"Isn't it?" She responded with pride. "Keep going."

Hailey flipped to the next photo, it was labeled "Before" and was a picture of a guy who looked to be in his twenties. He was good looking, handsome even. A nice smile, striking facial features, beautiful head of brown curly hair, he was a man who looked like he would turn heads. She flipped to the next page. There was a picture of an old man. His teeth were yellow, hair thinning, there was a sad look in his eyes even. It took a moment for Hailey to realize that the old man and the younger man were the same.

"You did this? This looks amazing."

"Isn't it? I am most proud of that one. The transformation was exquisite," she said, walking over to Hailey and looking, admiring her own work. "What was this for?"

"It was for a play titled “Life Progression.”

"It truly doesn't look like the same person," Hailey said as she flipped through the pages of the album." Gwyneth went back to making breakfast.

"You're so talented. Why aren't you doing this full-time?"

"That's the plan, my dream is to do makeup on movies. I've been trying to get experience over the past few years. I'm really hoping to get my foot in the door on a set. Or maybe move out to LA in the next few years."

"You should Gwyneth. Quit, go tomorrow. I have no idea what's holding you back. If I had that kind of talent I wouldn't hesitate."

"I can't leave my dad. He kind of needs me. He's been lonely ever since my mom died."

"Can't you get work around here?"

"I have, in theater mostly, but I need to get to New York or LA to find more projects."

Gwyneth's hair was shining a golden hue from the sunshine. She looked angelic, her frame fragile as she cleaned up the morning's breakfast of eggs and toast. Every movement, full of life, energy, despite their late night. But mostly she observed her grace. Grace and style that were foreign to Hailey. She felt lucky to know her.

Hailey felt privileged in her intimacy with Gwyneth. Perhaps she contained multitudes that spanned beyond her office persona. Yet a feeling of dread crossed her mind as she left to catch the train. If Hailey was wrong about Gwyneth, it was very possible she could be wrong about Dr. Loering. Hailey's phone dinged with more messages:

Writer Marie: Writee? Where are you? ANSWER ME.

Writer Marie: When will you be here? YOU ARE NOT FULFILLING YOUR WRITEE DUTIES.

Writer Marie: I am very disappointed that you are ignoring your duties as Writee...we will talk tomorrow. THERE WILL BE CONSEQUENCES.

Chapter 8

A poised response to anger is finding the root cause of your anger and expressing it with creativity.

The Interview Part I

Jenna: "Sitting here with me is Dr. Loering, a multiple New York Herald best-selling, elusive author, teacher, and entrepreneur finally giving us what I know a lot of us want. Insight into the man behind the success.

Millions of women subscribe to his channels on YouTube. Buy his self-help books. And attend his revolutionary workshops that promise ambitious writers a publication upon completion. His last book was adapted into blockbuster hit starring a star-studded cast. Let's get started. "

Jenna turns to Dr. Loering: "How are you Dr. Loering?"

Dr. Loering: "I'm good, wait no, I'm fantastic."

He was beaming, lounging on the couch, looking comfortable. He wore a brown turtleneck with a plaid leisure suit. His brown shoes matched his brown turtleneck.

Jenna: "Fantastic. So, let's get right into it."

Dr. Loering: “You mean, let’s get right into it.” He said crossing and uncrossing his legs.

Jenna: “That’s what I said.”

Dr. Loering: “No, you said, “So let’s get right into it”. That’s not a real sentence.”

An awkward pause while they stare at each other.

He starts laughing.

Dr. Loering: “I'm kidding, you can take a joke, right?" He adjusted the thick black framed glasses on his nose.

Jenna pauses before saying: “And that's why your audience is so fascinated with you Dr. Loering, you seem to always get it right. Let's talk about that a little bit. How did you form your writing methods?”

Dr. Loering: If I tell you about the secret behind how the methods were formed, I give away the only secret I have.

Jenna: (persistent) I bet the audience would love to know your secret of success at the very least. Let me ask another question. Did you follow your own methods to obtain your current success?

Dr. Loering: I did. I followed my methods to get to the next level of success. And I stress to follow the methods to every writer that takes my workshops, for that reason. It’s a formula. When writees start complaining writing is hard, or they don’t like the place they are at in the process, I point them back to the methods. It’s the path to success. My workshops improve their writing process, storytelling skills, and allow them valuable feedback. The methods give them insight and grit. If you follow the methods, writees have a high percentage of getting published. They become writers. It's simple.

Jenna: You began your workshops in college, correct? Didn't you form them with Katya Jones? She played a huge role in your earlier work, didn't she?

Dr. Loering (Folds and unfolds his arms twice): I started the workshops in college. It was an experiment at first. A way to work through homework I didn't like or writing for projects that I procrastinated on. I wasn't a natural academic, so I needed to learn how to stay afloat. I decided to form a series of methods that would help me do the work and do it well. I also wanted the methods to be testable and transcendent. I wanted writers to apply them to any project so they would finish and succeed. In other words, I learned how to knock success out of the ballpark.

He gets up and fake bats at a ball.

Jenna: (not impressed) Tell us about Katya's role, does she still work with you?

Dr. Loering: Katya? No. She helped me a little but decided to take a different path. I don't talk about her or any of that past stuff. Out of respect for her privacy, you know.

Jenna: I don't know, that's why she's intriguing. Her name came up a lot when I've talked to people who knew you in college. Speaking of which, it was hard to find people who knew you intimately. It's tough to find people who know you now. Dr. Loering, who are you close to? Friends, family, romantic relationships? I'm sure your audience is dying to know.

Dr. Loering: I don't mix personal issues with business issues. That's referring to several of my methods. And still to this day, I stick to those methods. They're my bible. Besides, I don't think it's fair to put the spotlight on those I'm close to. I chose the spotlight, people I'm close with didn't.

Jenna: (Jenna nods). Millions and millions of women look to you as a guide, almost a spiritual master in the guise of a writing coach. Why do you think your message resonates with women? Especially young women?

Dr Loering: I've wondered the same question. My workshops are open to anyone and everyone. I don't pay attention much to who reads my books. I don't see a woman, I see a writee. I don't see a man; I see a writer. It's more about where someone is at in their journey to become a writer.

I am much more interested in helping people reach inside themselves to find the most captivating material. To stay inspired. I think that's my life's work, and I can't help if that resonates more with someone like you rather than a man.

Jenna: Someone like me, you mean a woman? (She asks in slight jest). Some might see that as sexist, or that your methods are geared towards women.

Dr. Loering: I certainly didn't have that in mind when I made them, and men do take the class.

Jenna: They do. I tried to obtain attendance records from your workshop, but your team wouldn't give that to me. All I have to go off are your public talks.

Dr. Loering: We don't give away people's information.

Jenna: But this is general information we are looking at, males to females.

Dr. Loering: I don't see how that's relevant; the workshop is for anyone as I said.

Jenna: Do you think your past relationships have anything to do with how you see males or females in your work?

Dr. Loering (caught off guard): You're asking again about my personal life; I don't mix my personal life with business.

Jenna: Well then, that brings me to my next question. I think a lot of people will be wanting to know this, what are you currently working on? We haven't seen much work from you for the last few years.

Dr. Loering: I am working on another novel, but it's a secret as to the subject. My agent demands I don't give any hints. I assure you; it will knock the other novels out of the park.

Jenna: That's exciting. Truly. There were so many insightful thoughts in "What I Need to Tell You About Writing" And before that "Thinking the Write Way". If you don't mind, I am going to read a passage from "Thinking the Write Way"

Dr. Loering: Smiles smugly. "Ok.

Jenna: "A persistent problem is judging others. We look at someone, either their appearance or behavior, and develop snap judgments—often negative—from years of doing so out of habit. We think we know better than others. At the same time, shouldn't we judge others around us to understand what is going on in the world to keep ourselves sane? How can we discern between bad judgment and righteous judgment?"

There's a pause.

Dr. Loering is smiling.

Jenna: "You talk a lot about judgement. Let's explore this passage because your quote is so... so, fascinating. What's your own experience being judged?

Dr. Loering: You know, I'm judged all the time. Some people don't like my work. My work isn't for everyone, it's for people who want to battle fear and live their life to the fullest.

Jenna: "When is the first time you remember being judged? The very first time?"

– – –

He never felt so empty, like that trash can on the front lawn, being kicked around. He, the lonely kid who is waiting for a bus that seems like it will never come, full of friends he will never make, because he is different. He's different and they know it. They know that he knows it.

He is different because he has laser beams for eyes.

No, she thought, not laser beams.

He is different because he has a cat named Pickles that can talk.

Hailey's phone buzzed. She grasped around for it, feeling the stages of a hangover creeping into her.

Hey, it's the cab driver (Bella) from the other day. I'm reading you right now. I thought I'd give you one of mine.

She'd sent a link to what looked like an article from "The Insider."

Another buzz followed, from her mother:

Hailey, your dad and I would like you to come to dinner again this week. How is work going?

Then, yet another text from a number that wasn't in her phone:

"Call me right away. Dr. L."

Dr. Loering wanted her to call him. The persistent feeling of loneliness she felt in her apartment when she was alone snapped into anxiety, loneliness gone. Like it had never been there in the first place. Before she spoke with Dr. Loering she needed to wake up and gather her scattered thoughts. She was starving. She searched for her favorite pizza place and ordered delivery. Deciding to shower, even though she only wrote 200 words, she walked through her mostly empty apartment, her steps echoing through the empty hallway. She could always finish writing later.

She noticed the wood creaking below her and a draft of cold air blew through the hallway, pushing her to rush even more to a hot shower. As she felt the hot water pour over her, she imagined what Dr. Loering would say. He'd gotten back quickly, that was good. Massaging her rosemary soap and shampoo on her body she pondered the different ways she could respond. What if he offered her a job with him? Or what if he would set up a meeting with his agent? Her life could change today.

She put the pesky flashbacks of the warnings she received the night out of her mind. The night with Gwyneth had been fun. More fun than she'd had in a while, she thought stepping out of the shower grabbing a towel she'd bought at GoodWill recently. She felt a feeling of exhaustion and relief. And Bella had gotten back to her. Bella who wanted to read her.

It felt good to be clean. A fresh start, a new chance, maybe even a new life. She put a towel around her wet hair and ran to her bedroom. Time to put on clothing other than sweats.

As she was picking and pulling a sweater and jeans out of her closet, she heard the buzz of her door. Grabbing money from her purse for a tip, she ran downstairs to see a delivery girl standing with her pizza. She had long hair dyed pitch black with a lip ring and looked like she was barely 16.

"How are you doing today?" with a genuine tone. This surprised Hailey who assumed by her appearance she would be too angsty to ask such a question.

"Better now that food is here," offering more information than she typically would be due to her unabated excitement.

As Hailey signed the slip on the pizza box and handed her the tip the angsty looking delivery girl offered, "My boyfriend says, "I have to keep my girl fed because otherwise she gets "hangry". "Hangry, you know angry because you're hungry..."

"Yeah, I know," Hailey looked up and smiled at her. It was the hope of the moment that led her to doing what she did next.

"Hold tight, I have something for you," she said, running back up the stairs. "I'll be right back, one minute." She ran into her apartment and grabbed one of Dr. Loering's older books, one that opened her eyes to a whole different world, one in which she felt spoke directly to her, "Thinking the Write Way."

She ran back down the stairs to what now looked like an impatient angsty pizza delivery girl.

"Here," she said, handing the book to the girl. "This changed my life. I hope it does the same for you."

The girl looked at it, perplexed, “Oh yeah, I've heard of this guy, Dr. Loering. Um, cool, thanks. Well, I gotta go but I hope you enjoy your pizza."

"Thank you," Hailey called with pride as the girl walked out the door. Hailey watched as she climbed into what looked like an old junker of a car feeling pleased. She walked back up to her apartment and scarfed down a few slices of pizza, not even bothering to get a plate. As she swallowed the greasy lukewarm slices, letting her hangover absorb the grease she started to become nervous of the impending call. She texted Bella:

Hi Bella, thanks for sending me your work. I look forward to reading it!

She stopped typing. Did she want to see Bella? She closed her eyes and pictured her, a smile forming on her face. She was super cute. Those kind eyes and that dimpled smile. A woman cab driver though, her parents would love that. Maybe she was misreading the situation. Hailey wasn’t even sure what her own sexuality was. She was attracted to men she thought. But she also liked women. Since being gay was a taboo in her small world she kept her feelings to herself. At the very least Bella’s going to be a journalist though, and maybe she could help her she thought.

She erased her text and tried again:

Hi Bella, thanks for sending me your work. I'll take a look. It was nice meeting you, maybe we could meet up to discuss our work sometime soon.

She hit the send button. No going back now, but at the very least maybe she'd get to see her again.

She stuffed the remainder of her pizza into her overcrowded fridge, turned the television off and went to sit in her bedroom. The quietest room from all the noises of the streets and neighbors. It felt like she was about to give a speech in front of an audience of 300 but it was one person she was calling. Taking a deep breath, she pulled up his number and hit the call button. It seemed like the phone rang forever. waited for the phone to ring. Suddenly, she heard Dr. Loering's voice.

"Hello Hailey"

"Hi Dr. Loering, thank you for getting back to me so quickly."

"I read your essay. "

There was a pause as Hailey waited for him to continue. She nervously said, "Wow thank you, that was quick."

"The first thing I wanted to say is congratulations for finishing it."

There was another pause. Hailey wasn't certain what to say or if she should respond. As soon as she began to say, "Thank you..."

"The best part about this essay is that you did it. And good job on that. It takes a lot of guts to get out there and do something and you did it."

Hailey, feeling encouraged, responded, "Well, thank you. I had a lot of questions while I was writing, like if this was good enough? Am I describing this moment in the best way? I appreciate that, because it was challenging to do..."

He quickly cut her off, not acknowledging anything she said, "As far as the piece is concerned, what are you trying to write here? Because it is unclear. It starts off "I was headed east on the highway past all kinds of signs... "You aren't giving your reader any information. What does the character look like? And then a few paragraphs later, "Uncle Pat was an intelligent man" what does that even mean? Everyone is intelligent. You aren't telling me anything interesting here."

Hailey started to feel sickness in her stomach as he went on.

"He had the appearance of a meathead. What does that mean? Romance? Freedom? This story has no style, or arc, it's simplistic."

His voice was thick with condescension and each thing he said was a little worse than the last.

"I struggled finishing it, what is the order of things? What really happened? I'm not sure who your aunt is."

"Well, I appreciate your feedback." She squeaked out. All she felt was panic, she was frozen in horror. Her worst nightmare was unfolding in real time, the money she spent, the hope she put into things all gone. Her mother being right about her inability to be a writer.

"I mean, this is definitely not something I would send out. If I were you, I would rewrite the entire thing from scratch. This sentence, as he said in a mocking voice, "I went into the bar and looked around seeing nothing but leather" that's not a real sentence. Anybody could see that. It's not interesting at all. I really don't know what to say other than that this needs to be rewritten, it's not good."

Hailey felt like a dagger had been shoved into her stomach and twisted around. She'd written several drafts of this piece. She'd workshopped it. This was her best piece of writing. It was the most interesting one. And now it seemed her work was reduced to something a two-year-old could have written better. It was difficult to respond without choking up. But she managed to get out,

"Thank you for reading it. Is there anything that did work for you?"

“You’re welcome, Hailey. There wasn't much that worked for me in this besides the fact that you tried. If you decide to rewrite it, I’d look at it again. A lot of people are cowards when it comes to doing something. A lot of people don't have what it takes to do something until it's right. So, I understand if you don’t."

There was silence for a moment as Hailey once again tried to get a response out with choking up. “You know what, I'll take you up on that Dr. Loering. I’ll rewrite and I"ll send it to you. I'm going to do it."

"Great, good for you (in a tone that indicated he didn't believe her). Right now, it’s bad though, it was difficult to get through. Don’t give that to anyone else. Ok?”

“Ok Dr. Loering. Thank you so much for taking the time to read me and give me feedback.”

“Yeah, ok. Bye.”

And with that he hung up. It was over. Her life, it felt like, was over. There was no hope left in the world, nothing to look forward to. The person she admired the most ripped apart the piece of writing she admired the most. And he made her pay for lunch.

Hailey laid down on her bed and cried. Every part of her felt defeated. And she knew deep down in her heart she would never rewrite the story. She could never see or talk to Dr. Loering again. Because the person she respected so much, had taken so much advice from over the years, turned out to be an awful person. He believed that what she knew was a good piece of writing, was the worst thing he’d ever read. Why would he do that other than to make himself feel better? And why did he need to feel better? He had everything.

Her phone buzzed:

I'd love to get together to discuss our work. Next week? Monday? You name a place.

A new feeling of horror overcame her when she realized that she sent what was supposedly her worst piece of writing to Bella.

Chapter 9

A writee's ego is a trap and is only released when you pursue the path to becoming a writer.

Hailey walked into the office determined to work. Work was a place she knew she could at least get things done. Even if she was berated, her job held the tangible reward of a paycheck that her passion had yet to yield. She felt productive that morning, and slightly rebellious as she skipped her writing duties. She made her way to her desk, starting her computer. Ready to throw her energy into something that didn't end in a catastrophe.

Even Brock's glance of longing didn't get under her skin as much that morning. At least he didn't have the power to kill her passion to write, she thought as he awkwardly stood over her desk telling her about his mundane weekend at an arcade out in the suburbs.

Around mid-morning she wanted coffee. She slowly made her way to the break room. She was dreading seeing Gwyneth. She didn't want Gwyneth asking about Dr. Loering. Or to ask about anything for that matter. Yet, as she wandered towards the break room, there was Gwyneth.

“Hailey!" Gwyneth blurted out loud enough for the whole office to hear. I've been waiting to see you all day. How are you? How was your day off yesterday?” Hailey felt her face starting to color.

“Fine. Not as expected but it was fine.” Hailey revealed more details than she wanted to despite her best efforts.

“What do you mean? Did something unexpected happen?" Gwyneth asked taking a sip from her Diet Coke. "I have some chocolate, chocolate fixes everything," she said as she sifted through her desk taking out a bar.

Hailey felt the thing inside of her that she forced to push down all day coming to the surface. "Gwyneth, I need to go to the bathroom," her voice choking more than she wanted. It was the act of kindness that put her over the edge. Kindness felt strange in Hailey's world. The world she was used to was full of condescension and never being enough. She ran to the bathroom hoping that nobody would see the tears sliding down her cheeks. Once inside she went into a stall, locked the door, sat down, weeping. Shortly after she heard the door open.

"Hailey, it's Gwyneth. Are you ok?"

Hailey was quiet for a moment hoping she'd go away. Hoping that the entire situation would go away. That Dr. Loering never existed in the first place and that she'd never found him.

"Sugar," Gwyneth called gently knocking on the bathroom stall. "Listen, I know we haven't known each other for long. But I want you to know I genuinely care about you. You can tell me whatever it is. I'll listen."

Maybe it was that there was nowhere to go. Maybe it was Gwyneth's voice, it was sweet. Maybe it was that she said she cared. After a moment, Hailey opened the door.

Gwyneth stood, looking beautiful as always in a vintage black dress with puffed sleeves, white collar, and lapel.

Hailey didn't have strength to hold back anymore as she blurted out, "Dr. Loering gave feedback on my writing and he said it's shit," Hailey said as Gwyneth handed her tissue.

"It was my best essay, one that I stupidly thought would get me out of this job. I hate this job, I hate Kevin. I hate coming here every day to do work for an asshole who doesn't give a shit about anything else but his fragile dickhead ego. I hate that the only reason I got this job is because my dad is friends with the giant douchebag that is Kevin. And to top it all off I gave the same essay that Dr. Loering thought was shit to another woman and I might have a crush on her..."

"Whoa whoa whoa, slow down." Gwyneth touched her hand and Hailey noted how soft it was.

"First, Dr. Loering is a scam. His opinion is worth just about as much as two cents." Gwyneth's attempt at a joke made Hailey smile.

"Listen, I've never read your writing. I would love to, and I am sure it is great. Even though the reports we write are boring, yours always sticks out to me because it's beautifully written, in prose. You don't need Dr. Loering to get published. What you do need is to keep on trying. Don't worry about him and fuck Kevin. Kevin is a sad boy trapped in a man's body, just ignore him. You're better than this office, than Dr. Loering, you'll find your way."

Between her soothing voice and soft touch, Hailey's crying subsided. "You're just saying that." Hailey said.

"Why would I lie to you? You know I say what's on my mind. That's what gets me into trouble all the time." She said laughing.

"Say," she said grabbing Kleenex and handing it to Hailey, "Why don't we blow out of here? Let's go down to the place around the corner. Get some drinks and blow some steam off and you can tell me all about this girl you have the hots for?"

"I don't know if I have the hots for her, we just met."

"You've got a thing for her. Behind those tears I see some budding love."

Hailey couldn't help smiling a little as she said, "But what about Kevin, you know he hates it when we ask off, and at the same time? And Brock, he'll gossip about us. "

"That's why we don't ask, we tell him. I'm not scared of him. He's thinking the sun comes up to hear him crow. Let me deal with Kevin. And Brock needs attention, just treat him like a kid. Give him some but be clear about your boundaries, then he'll back off. We've got this. Go grab your things and meet me by the elevator."

What they didn't see was Brock up against the wall in the men's bathroom, listening to every word they said and jotting down the conversation.

Hailey nodded to her own disbelief and immediately Gwyneth left the bathroom. Hailey splashed icy water on her face, taking a deep breath, leaving moments after Gwyneth. She walked quickly past Kevin's office. She could make out Gwyneth's muffled voice behind his closed door. She quickly shut down her computer, grabbed her belongings and left for the elevator before her common sense kicked in.

She heard her phone buzzing and checked it:

Writer Marie: Hailey, I'll need you to come by tonight for a few hours. We can talk about the workshop this weekend too...

The blessing in finding out that Dr. Loering's true colors was that she wouldn't have to deal with Writer Marie anymore.

After waiting for a minute in front of the elevator Gwyneth appeared with a smile on her face.

"I took care of it," she said pressing the down button. "Let's blow this backwards joint." Laughing and holding arms they both left the office together while Hailey wondered if she was going to have a job to come back to and promptly after wondered whether she cared. Having a friend seemed more important than anything else.

"Two whiskeys neat with beer backs, whatever cheap ale you have on tap," Gwyneth barked at a bartender who she also seemed to know. "You got it lady," he said in what sounded like a thick Italian accent. Thick clouds of smoke swirled around them. There were jars of boiled eggs sitting on the shelf and a sign that said, "Eggs for $1".

"This place is sketchy; I can barely breathe through all the smoke. I didn't know you could legally smoke inside." Hailey fanned her face with her hand, like it would make a difference.

"And Whiskey? That's a strong choice?" Hailey said settling into her bar stool, wondering if this was going to be a huge mistake. The place was dimly lit in addition to the smoke which Hailey was thankful for.

She didn't want to be seen. She felt like she was going to get in trouble despite knowing that none of her co-workers would be here this time of day. There looked like a regular or two sitting at the bar and what looked like a business meeting with a few men, all smoking cigarettes. Hailey was thankful for the lack of interest from them in herself and Gwyneth. She wanted to feel invisible.

The bartender, who was beginning to look increasingly like Ray Liota from Goodfellas, quickly deposited their drinks as quickly as Gwyneth got a bill out to pay. "Keep the change." She picked up a glass of whiskey and handed it to Hailey.

"To us," she said raising her glass. "Overcoming a monstrosity of a day with the best medicine." Hailey clinked her glass and shot down the whiskey backing it with beer.

"Is that a payphone over there?" Hailey asked, she was starting to feel like she was in a different era.

"There's rumors this place is run by the mafia. People come here to get messed up and hide. For that reason, I thought it'd be a viable choice," Gwyneth said taking a drag from a clove cigarette, looking pleased with herself. She handed it to Hailey.

"Thanks for doing this," Hailey said taking a hit. "Out of curiosity, how in the hell did you talk Kevin into letting us leave?"

"Simple," I told him we are both taking a personal day because you found out some horrific news and if he has a problem with it, he can take it up with HR."

"Are we going to get in trouble?"

"No," Gwyneth said, placing her hand on Hailey's for the second time that day. "We're good," she said taking a swig of her beer with her other hand. "The words "sexual harassment may have slipped out of my mouth."

"Are you serious? What happened?" Hailey asked, turning towards Gwyneth, wondering if the office rumors were in fact true.

"Not me, Sugar, but the last girl, the one before me. She told me to watch out for him, that he was a creep and that she was quitting because of it."

"Damn," Hailey said, the hit of the clove starting to make everything feel heavy and light at the same time, like her body and emotions were being stretched in two different directions. "I'm so angry right now. Kevin, Dr. Loering, Brock, they're all scum bags. I never really thought about it before, maybe because I'm so used to it, but men are assholes."

Gwyneth burst out laughing, "You've never thought about it before? Have you dated in this city?"

"No, I haven't been on many dates. One or two. I've been here less than a year. And I don't know, I haven't found anyone that interested me."

"Fair enough, as someone who is well seasoned in the dating world, I can say you aren't missing much." Gwyneth said flashing Hailey a smile.

"So, tell me about this taxicab girl. You know," Gwyneth said taking another hit off her clove cigarette, "You're full of surprises. I didn't peg you for someone who would go below their class, if you know what I mean."

"I don't know what you mean," Hailey responded, self-consciously looking down at the outfit her mom bought her from Macy's.

"You know, you're like an upper middle-class gal from the burbs. Let me guess, your parents paid for your degree in finance. The conditions were that you marry a nice young man. They helped you get set up in the city. Help pay your bills, but they are already planning for your return to Highland Park where you'll buy a house with a two-car garage and give them several grandchildren. But what does Hailey want?" Gwyneth asked, turning toward Hailey.

"And what do you want? A cab driver." Gwyneth said laughing, "Her parents' worst nightmare."

"First of all, she's more than a cab driver, she's a writer. Also. I don't know if I like her like that, it's just a feeling." Hailey responded, annoyed that she was so easy to read but impressed by Gwyneth's accuracy. "Second of all, what about you, what do you want?" Hailey said trying to shift the subject.

"I'm tri-sexual," she said laughing, "I'll try anything!"

They both laughed, and for a moment Hailey was forgetting all her troubles in the world.

The drinks and weed were also helping calm Hailey. Feelings of despair still lingered over her like the thick blanket of smoke currently surrounding them. "Seriously though, what am I going to do?" Hailey asked staring at the mafia bartender who was chatting up the men at the bar like they were old buddies. He looked over at Hailey and winked, running his fingers through his slicked back, greased hair. Hailey quickly averted her eyes. Gwyneth motioned for another round.

"What do you mean what are you going to do Sugar?" Gwyneth asked, turning towards her. What do you want to do? What would you do in your wildest dreams if you could do anything? No consequence, no restraints, anything you want. What, your parents don't like your passion to write? Can't you convince them? Does it even matter what they think?" Gwyneth asked as the bartender set their drinks down.

"I doubt I could convince my parents of anything. But," Hailey said, looking up in thought, "If I could do anything, right now, I'd make sure that men like Dr. Loering and Kevin got what they deserve."

"Oh yeah, and please do tell me, what do they deserve?"

Hailey smiled, because inside her was the perfect mix of booze and weed to let her revenge fantasies rip. "Sometimes I fantasize that I get to beat the shit out of Kevin." She said palming her fist into her hand.

"Just beat the pulp out of him. A fight that would go down in the books as the most infamous fight of all time. Of course, I'm the underdog in this scenario but I'm a trained MFA fighter."

"You mean MMA?" Gwyneth asked laughing.

"Yeah, MMA, but I've always wanted an MFA." Hailey continued, her imagination now in fighting gear. "And we'd be fighting at Madison Square Garden, tickets sold out. The press is all over the fight, lauding it as one of the most anticipated fights of the year. Kevin would be 100% certain he'd win it, giving hundreds of interviews gloating about what he would do with his trophy, money, and all the hot women he'd get when he won this fight. He'd talk about all the fancy cars he'd buy and how he'd be sad to quit his job as the big, important job as Manager of Revenue at Quicksand Industries..."

"Ah, it makes me cringe how he brags with customers about being the Director of Revenue, what a boring title!" Gwyneth interrupted. "And is Kevin still the same physique in this scenario, because in real life he's a Napoleon."

"Shhhh," Hailey said laughing, "Let me finish. Meanwhile, while he's spending all of his time bragging about how big his muscles are and how he's going to win the fight, I'm training. And I'm good already, but the extra training, and the media focus on him gets me to train harder than I've ever trained. I spend day and night laser focused on the fight. In my interviews, which are few, I focus on what I know to be true, how hard I've trained, and that no matter what, I'll be ready for the fight.

I talk about how I know that no matter what the outcome is I put the most effort in I ever have." As Hailey continued Gwyneth ordered them another round and motioned for her to continue.

"It's the night of the fight. The stadium is packed. Girls Girls Girls by Motley Crue comes on. Kevin makes his grand entrance. His robe is over the top, ornate with a big middle finger on back. I come out to the Hammer Smashed Face. I'm wearing a plain black robe. Kevin is dancing around on stage like an idiot. Already celebrating, thinking the joke's on me. He's convinced that all he really has to do is show up. Effort doesn't apply to him. He's ready to win, I'm ready to fight.

The fight begins. He tries a right hook, a left hook and misses completely, falls. I stand there, I could gloat, or make fun of him, because his shots are weak, but I don't. I simply prepare my next move. He gets back up, I jab at him a few times, playing with my prey, confident I can take him out. He's slow, weak, and he doesn't have the concentration to win.

The stadium is going wild because they start to realize that me, the woman, might kick the man's ass when they thought it'd be the other way around. A man beating a woman's ass. Kevin bought out the first few rows of seats for the office employees so he could directly see the looks on their faces when he won. And now, I can see the surprise on their faces as they see their beloved boss going down.

Now, as he struggles to get up after being punched out, he wishes he wouldn't have. Blood is coming down his face, his nose busted, one of his teeth are loose. I'm just waiting for the final blow, dragging it out. He yells to the crowd, his voice barely audible, "I will always be better than her," and right as he says the word "her", I give him the final blow and knock him out. The crowd goes wild. It's the first fight in history where a woman beats a man and beats him to this level. Kevin lifts his head enough to see all the people in the office giving one another high fives and hugging in the front row. They were never cheering for him. Kevin is wheeled out on a stretcher. After the fight Kevin sustains serious injuries. He suffers from the aftereffects of concussions. Headaches, memory loss, confusion, soon he is demoted to a position in the mail room. Everyone forgets about him except for when the fight is mentioned."

"Why, I had no idea there was a fighter in my presence," Gwyneth said laughing, raising her glass again.

"I want to hear your version," Hailey said laughing.

"My version needs some food, I'm famished. Let's go to my place, it's not too far."

"My clothes reek of smoke." Hailey said as she took her jacket off and plopped down on Gwyneth's couch. "I've got you covered," Gwyneth said as she disappeared into her bedroom. She came back out and tossed Hailey a pair of pink silk pajamas. "Gwyneth," this isn't necessary. "But it is," she said as she moved around in the kitchen. "Can I help with anything?"

"Play some music?"

Hailey found a speaker and put on The xx.

"Silk pajamas," Hailey said to nobody as she went into the bathroom. Discarding her clothes she put on the pajamas, feeling silk against her skin. She still smelled of smoke. "Gwyneth," she called out the door, is it ok if I rinse off, this smell is too much."

"Absolutely, towels are on the rack. Help yourself to anything you need."

Hailey took off the pajamas and showered, taking extra care to double wash her hair twice with Gwyneth's designer shampoo.

Gwyneth entered carrying a silver platter. There was wine and a tray of joints neatly rolled.

"Gwyneth you know how to put together a spread," she said in genuine awe.

"Anything for my girl," Gwyneth said jokingly.

As Hailey popped what looked like chocolate toffee into her mouth she called out, "I could get used to eating like this."

Gwyneth appeared, also changed into a silky crop pajama top and shorts.

"Thank you for all this," Hailey said.

"Wine?"

"Definitely," Hailey said as she lit up a joint, taking a bigger hit than she could handle which ended in a coughing fit. Gwyneth was gathering a plate of pizza and chocolate. She sat down across from Hailey and smiled.

"I'm so glad you're here."

"Me too," Hailey said coughing and laughing at the same time."

"What if Kevin could see us now?" Hailey asked passing the joint over to Gwyneth.

"He'd definitely be trying to manage us," Gwyneth said with a mouthful of check mix.

"Or Dr. Loering, do you think he ever has fun? I've always wondered if he has friends. He seems so serious. Someone famous like him, it must be hard to get close to people."

"Hailey, there is no sense in trying to make sense of that man. He's only interested in himself and a man like that who feels like he has nothing to lose, who feels on top of his power, is only interested in sucking the life out of the people around him."

"You make him sound like a vampire," Hailey said taking a big sloppy bite of pizza.

"Maybe I'm the vampire, and he's my prey," Gwyneth said. But I'm a vampire that's under a curse, and the curse can only be broken by taking out misogyny. Once that happens, my curse breaks, I live forever, but as a human, not a vampire. And Dr. Loering is the ultimate prize for me, a self-proclaimed healer, writer, know it all that destroys people one by one with his charisma, his charm, his ignorance on how he scams women into thinking they are less."

"Oooh, I like this..." Hailey said as Gwyneth passed a joint over to Hailey and moved closer to her on the couch, grabbing her phone to create a chiaroscuro effect.

"I'd stalk him slowly. For years he'd feel my presence, but he wouldn't know exactly what I was. He would constantly feel fear and be looking over his back every day. I would have been turned in my prime, so I would be irresistible to any creature on this cursed planet. But I'd develop a taste for misogynists.

I take pride in finding the most misogynistic blood and I'd take even more pride in my hunt. Anyway, as I said, Dr. Loering would come onto my radar as he becomes famous, and I put him on my list of prey. Others that make the list are Mel Gibson, Charlie Sheen, Tom Cruise, Woody Allen, Roman Polanski, and finally, Johnny Depp, because the reality is he isn't that good of an actor. I cannot stand those Pirate movies.

"Same," Hailey said, "Absolutely overrated."

"Now, Dr. Loering is going to be my most prized hunt, because his fame comes from convincing women to do things that ultimately harm themselves. He's also the most untouchable because he knows of my kind, knows I'm out to hunt him. So, I do my research and since at this point, I've been alive 100 years, I know how to find every detail in his life. Things nobody knows. Parts of his history that humiliate him. Like the fact that in first grade a girl used to beat him up occasionally. Not too bad, just enough to let him know that she was in power. He has an aversion to cold and snow because as a kid she would hold his face down in the snow while he screamed, only letting up when his mom could hear his puny little screams."

Hailey didn't know if it was the day of drinking, smoking, or a combo, but the story had her entirely enthralled. Gwyneth continued.

"I read all his stories, all his past, that leads him to being such a phony and fake. Someone who clearly feeds off women. I want to get him at the right place and the right time and that takes time, many years. One dark stormy night, when he is leaving one of his events, I follow him. I am more hungry than usual; I've killed enough people that the world is starting to change. People are accepting one another for who they are, women are rising in the world, taking power in places they never have before. He's one of the last big ones, but he is the big one, the one that is changing what I've done so far. Undoing my hard work. And as I said, I'm hungry, I haven't fed a lot in a while. I'm also sick of being a vampire, sick of the hunt, and I think that he might be one of the last ones I need to take out before I can start eating real food again.

I follow him to a bar nearby his place. I watch from afar as he orders a drink and ends up hitting on a woman. She's beautiful. There is an innocence about her, the perfect victim for him. I see him making her feel special, like the sphinx he's made her out to be. I can tell that she knows who he is, she understands his power.

I can tell she is young, vulnerable, and inexperienced. She's looking for validation.

I decide to interrupt them, I buy them both drinks and begin to charm them. I can't let him take her back home alone. I get them drunker. I can tell Dr. Loering wants me to leave but likes the show I am giving, flirting with this beautiful girl in front of him. She likes the attention. I throw it out to them that we should have a threesome. Dr. Loering immediately agrees, pays for our tab and we leave the bar. We get back to his place and I'm invited inside.

His place is huge, and he has giant metal, phallic statues everywhere. While Dr. Loering goes to get us drinks, I put the beautiful woman in a trance. I start kissing her. I don't want her to be harmed, I don't want her to think this is anything but realizing something about her sexuality. She confessed earlier that she had never been with a woman before. Dr. Loering comes back, and we are both naked now. I am starving, I see the thick, pure misogynistic blood pumping in Dr. Loering's veins, and I want it, I want it bad. He takes off his clothing, and we see his chiseled body, another tool he's used to enrapture innocent minds.

The beautiful girl doesn't notice it because she is exploring my body. He hungrily comes toward me, and I receive him, and gently bring his neck towards my mouth. As he grabs my breast, I bite into his neck. He moans softly and I begin to drink like I have never drunk before. I drain him entirely clean while the beautiful girl is exploring my body. I finish him, push him off us, and finish with her, as his drained body lies next to us. My curse begins to break, and the hunger that once held me prisoner now frees me to be human again and frees all women to be equal in their power.

"I have two questions," Hailey said, now finished eating, sitting close to Gwyneth, feeling a warmth she hadn't felt in a long time. Could this be real friendship? She thought as she watched Gwyneth take a sip of wine. "Anything for you sugar."

"My first question is, what did you do with his body?"

"Simple, I have one of my familiars take care of it. They are prior Evangelical Pastors or Spiritual Leaders who were bad people. Think Jim Jones reincarnated as a slave. When I turned, I started to employ them to do all my dirty work."

"But doesn't the beautiful girl see you doing all this?"

"Remember, I put her in a trance."

"Isn't that kind of rapey?"

"No," Gwyneth said, stretching out. "She wanted me before the trance. I only give her a trance when I need to hide Dr. Loering, I want to make it, so he doesn't exist anymore to her. He never did. Wouldn't you enjoy that?"

"Why does it matter what I would enjoy?"

"What's your second question?"

“Are we really friends?”

“Of course, we are dummy. We are stuck together whether you like it or not.”

Hailey smiled. As Gwyneth went to put in what they collectively decided was their favorite movie, *9-5,* Hailey’s phone buzzed. The sound of her phone immediately broke her out of the warm moment.

She picked it up seeing the reminder of the writing workshop she was starting the following day, the special workshop she signed up for with her mother’s credit card that was supposed to be one of the best of all of Dr. Loering's.

And then another text from Writer Marie:

If YOU DON'T SHOW TONIGHT, YOU'LL BE BANNED FROM WORKSHOPS FOREVER (no refunds either)

Chapter 10

<u>*Writer*</u>

"Who is going to clean all of these dishes?" Writer Marie yelled at nobody. Stacks were piled up since the morning. It had been a long day, turning into a long evening. Full of commitments that Writer Marie never felt there was enough time to complete. She texted her Writee several times and was becoming increasingly frustrated. No time to shower in the past 48 hours.

From the children's bedroom she could hear Greg trying to console her son Albert. Albert was screaming and crying all night about his sister, who consistently bullied him.

She told Greg, her twerp of a husband, that she needed time to organize her women's group. Really, she was tying up loose ends for Dr. Loering's workshop the next day. She also needed to send out an email for her church group about their bible group meeting. Greg gingerly offered to cook for her daughter's bake sale tomorrow at school. Writer Marie could smell something burning in the oven despite her best efforts to give him direction.

"Ugh," she gasped, making her way out into the oven, with one clean dish in hand.

"Greg, these are burning!" As she opened the oven to a cloud of smoke the doorbell rang.

"Greg, I need you to answer that," Writer Marie screamed. She was losing her voice from the constant yelling, the constant screaming, there was never enough time, enough help.

Why did I have children? She thought as she sat down at the kitchen table, hearing Greg quietly talking to whoever was at the door.

"Who's there?" She yelled, trying to hide the tone in her voice.

"Greg," she yelled loud enough that she knew old Ms. Crown would bang on her ceiling shortly.

"Yes, honey, "Greg said walking into the kitchen with her Writee, who appeared dissolved.

"You showed up finally." Writer Marie said angrily.

"Greetings Writer Marie" Writee Hailey said, trying to act as sober as she could. This was the last place she felt like she should be now.

"Greg, get her a glass of water, she looks like she needs it," Writer Marie said as she combed her fingers through her thick black hair that she knew looked knotted and windblown.

She watched as Greg stood on his tip toes, stretching as far as he could get a glass, his fingers barely able to touch the edges of one to move it closer. Sighing in exasperation, "I have to do everything around here." She pushed past him to grab a glass on the upper shelf, the glass slipped out of her cold clammy hands, and fell to the floor, in a crash that startled all three in the kitchen.

"Shit," Writer Marie screamed.

Greg and Writee Hailey scrambled to pick up the glass shards.

"Ouch," Writee Hailey said as blood started to flow, dripping onto the yellow Formica kitchen floor.

The pounding from Ms. Crown started again, followed by what sounded like her cane bumping up against her ceiling.

Writer Marie went to get a band aid for her writee, scorning under her breath her less than average height husband. Maybe her mother was right, she thought angrily, grabbing the Band-Aids out of the disorganized medicine cabinet. People didn't describe him as handsome either. But she knew that he would always listen to her and that was what made her stick with him after two bratty children, a foreclosure on their house, and his lack of being able to figure out even the simplest task.

Writer Marie threw the band aid at Hailey, "Something smells like it's burning," Writee Hailey said with a slight slur in her speech.

"Shit, can you get those out of the oven writee," Writer Marie asked, hearing a yell from her son in the other room.

"Greg, go talk to your son, now. And I asked you to bake not burn. It's not that hard to make cookies..."

Greg rushed off to the bedroom with what looked like a sense of duty.

"Darn," Writee Hailey said beginning to pull out the tray, "OUCH", she screeched as the tray of cookies fell to the floor. Writee Hailey ran over to the sink.

Exhausted Writer Marie pushed a large pile of unpaid bills she'd been ignoring out of the way so she could sit down.

"The oven mitts might have a hole in them." Writer Marie said quietly. She felt like she might lose her mind.

"Why didn't you tell me?" Writee Hailey squealed as she stood holding what was now a burnt and bloody hand under cold water.

Ignoring her as she sifted through the bills, Writer Marie said, "The children are horrible tonight. We need to have a conference with their teachers, I don't know what they are being taught in school," Writer Marie said to nobody, again.

She turned to Writee Hailey, "Their behavior is getting worse and worse. Especially since you haven't been showing up. We need you to show up when you are called," she said in what came out as a low growl.

Writee Hailey glanced up at her with a look of defiance that Writer Marie hadn't seen on her before. Was this girl losing her marbles?

Greg reentered the kitchen and softly said, "We used to be able to have a hand until you lost your job, we've all had to get creative..."

"Lose my job? Writer Marie snapped, "I got fired because I had to cover for you with the kids a number of times..."

"You don't trust me to do anything," Greg quietly said.

"What did you say?" Writer Marie scowled as her writee stood in dismay, sipping on her water.

"You need everything to be perfect..." Greg started and stopped as suddenly mid-sentence as Writer Marie slammed her hand on the table.

"I don't know how long I can go on like this, I'm working 7 days a week at jobs I hate and taking care of the children in almost every spare moment I have. Nobody helps or keeps their word around here." Writer Marie said glancing over at her writee who still awkwardly stood.

She then directed her gaze at her husband with disgust," Greg, plenty of parents can handle two children in addition to the other duties they have in life. You are an exception." She pushed away from the table, getting up and motioning for Writee Hailey to follow her. "And, when you bake cookies set a timer on your phone, so you don't burn them. And clean the dishes, it smells in here." She said leaving the kitchen.

"You should shower too, you stink" she called after him, leaving Greg standing in the kitchen in dismay.

As she headed back to her crafting room, with Writee Hailey in tow, Writer Marie grumbled under her breath, " My life wasn't supposed to turn out like this..."

She always imagined being big in the church community, but after the first scandal with Greg and some of the younger parishioners in their congregation those hopes were scrapped. She would never forget Pastor Todd calling her into his office. The humiliation she felt when he told her that Greg was no longer allowed to be a youth leader due to complaints of his flirtatious behavior. She felt betrayed. Greg knew how important her church life was. They never went back to that church again and moved to the city. They joined a church where she knew nobody. But it wasn't the same, and word reached eventually, casting a negative light on Writer Marie before she could redeem herself. She silently went to service and sporadically went to women's groups. Greg was no longer invited to church with her.

She found Dr. Loering's workshop through a friend from her old neighborhood who invited her to go to one of the introductory workshops. She quickly found that Dr. Loering's workshops were a place where the rules mattered, and nobody knew of Greg's interest in younger girls. Learning the vernacular came easy to Writer Marie. Religion was full of parables, poetry, labels, and narratives that contested the present reality. Dr. Loering's workshops were a place where she could flourish and regain control, she felt was absent in her life.

Writer Marie settled into her chair, glancing at the brochures and workbooks she would assemble for the weekend retreat. She motioned for her writee to sit down while letting out a big sigh.

"Now to deal with this," she said. motioning again to Writee Hailey. "At first you seemed more than eager to rise up in the ranks, just like me. "But," she said tapping her fingers lightly on the coffee table, "As of late, you are full of excuses. What do you have to say for yourself?"

There was a long pause as Writer Marie sat, looking at her writee directly in the eyes, knowing that she would have to punish her eventually or risk being called out as lenient with the other Writers in her group. Punishment was an incentive to gain more writees. The more she showed that she could discipline her writee the more power she would have. Writers were promised a total of three Writees as they continued publishing pieces for the journal.

She would punish Writee Hailey fairly and to the rules.

"Quiet aren't you, you know, despite having very little writing experience I found myself published after following the rules. In case you forgot, those rules include being a writee for 2 years. I suppose I can relate to how you feel." Writer Marie didn't mention the fact that being friends with Writer Samantha hadn't hurt her prospects of getting published and moving up in the ranks.

Of course, getting published for her only meant in Dr. Loering's journal. But that was the bulk of the Writers. Most Writees didn't know this information, some did. But the ones that did get published outside of the journal were the ones showcased, not Writers like Marie who quietly moved up in the ranks.

"Did you come here drunk?" Writer Marie asked, astonished that a Writee would even consider doing such a thing. She'd heard of writees gone bad but assumed her writee wouldn't do such a thing.

Greg appeared in the doorway, his mouth gaping open in awe at the unfolding situation.

"Greg, go to the kids."

"Yes, Ma'am," he said walking away slowly.

"Read a story to them, I want them asleep," She yelled irately.

"What's the point of being a writee if you're going to show up drunk on the job?" Writer Marie asked.

"You know, I'm going to have to punish you for this by writing you up. It will mean a two-year delay in getting published, but I suppose you already know that. Unless you're too drunk to remember." Writer Marie went on while Writee Hailey stood there, looking oddly composed despite reeking of booze. There was a moment of silence.

"Are you too drunk..." Writer Marie started to ask before Hailey interrupted.

Writee

"Punish me?" Hailey asked, standing up and trying to lean on the doorway but instead stumbled until she fell into it. This was it for her, she couldn't take anymore.

The whole evening she'd been wanting to point out that she was supposed to be running errands for Writer Marie. Not Greg and her bratty children, but she knew what Writer Marie would say.

"Punish me? That's interesting because I thought this was the punishment. Isn't burning and cutting myself enough? Isn't it punishment enough to have to do four loads of soiled laundry every time I come here? With urine-soaked underwear from your daughter who still pees her pants? She's 9! And how both of you leave your dirty dishes until I'm around to clean them? Isn't it punishment enough that I have to deal with your spoiled, entitled children at bedtime and listen to your troll like husband complain about how powerless he feels?"

Hailey was wringing with anger. It seemed as if years and years of repression were rising to the top of her and she couldn't stop it from coming out.

Writer Marie calmly turned and looked at Hailey, "Listen, there are rules and I need to follow them. But from all my experience running women's groups at my church, I've been around the block a time or two." Writer Marie knew her life was anything but interesting or like the women who came to her groups. She'd heard enough to guess the kind of issues that her writee might be having and felt a spec of sympathy at what those issues might be.

"What is it? Work issues? Domestic issues? If you need to step back from your duties, you need to let me know so I can go through the proper channels to reinstate you when you are ready again. But whatever it is, I cannot have you showing up late and... drunk, " Writer Marie said firmly.

Writee Hailey sat silently after her outburst. Too quiet. In the background Greg briefly yelled, "Lights out, no further discussion."

Hailey was tired. She was already beginning to feel hungover. Finally, after what seemed like an eternity Hailey said, "What I want isn't possible at the moment and might never be. I don't see how what I want is relevant in this discussion. Dr. Loering's workshops were supposed to be a route to publication. I'm having trouble seeing that possibility anymore. And mostly, I'm tired. Tired of being everything for everyone else, tired of taking care of people's dirty work, and tired of doing things I don't want to do."

"Doing what you don't want to do is part of life," Writer Marie said. The calm she established was wavering.

"Doing what you don't want to do is part of your life," Hailey said back. "That's your choice. It doesn't mean it has to be mine."

"Are you saying you're quitting?"

"No, not yet. But I'm done working for free for you, or at all for that matter."

As she left the room she heard Writer Marie call, "So you aren't going to the workshop this weekend then?"

Ignoring her Hailey made her way to the door, pushing past Greg, who obviously been listening on to their conversation. She briefly paused before she left, feeling that he was looking at her, she turned around.

"You don't have to stay with her," she said, then left, making sure to quietly shut the door behind her, a learned response from years of living under the same roof as her mom more than anything.

Chapter 11

Releasing your ego requires enduring the ultimate pain and it is the true path of the writer.

Hailey was late to the workshop. Both her head and hand throbbed as she pulled up to what looked like a cabin. The setting surrounding the cabin looked like Northern Wisconsin. Not Palatine, the suburb it was in. Hailey pulled into the circular drive behind a blue BMW. The driveway was full of cars. She grabbed her sleeping bag, water bottle, and a backpack full of other items she'd been instructed to bring.

The whole drive out to the suburbs she second guessed going. Initially she'd imagined the class being an exciting experience, a joyful one. A writee had to attend a certain amount of feedback groups before they were invited to attend a workshop. It was supposed to be a milestone. Hailey didn't care anymore about pleasing writers, she didn't want to waste any more money and the class was non-refundable. She hoped she be able to get something out of the weekend.

Yet, she played the game and act like she cared. Chills went up and down her spine when she thought of seeing Writer Marie. The consequences could be dire for her behavior the following evening. She'd regretted her behavior. Mostly because she was a lightweight and knew she shouldn't have went over to Marie's drunk. Even if the Writer/Writee relationship was bogus and abusive she could have handled the situation better. Her first thought waking that morning was that she could have prolonged her outburst until after this weekend. She hoped Writer Marie would go easy on her.

The cabin wasn't what she expected, it looked large enough to be a family's vacation home, not a retreat for a large group of people. She entered the cabin into a large room cleared out room, except for giant portraits of Dr. Loering on every wall. Each one was a little different, one of him speaking at an event, one of him signing a book, another of him with a group of smiling women.

Hailey stood taking them all in, "What a narcissist," she said aloud, just as a woman dressed all in white robe approached, with such grace that she had the appearance of floating.

"Hi, are you here for the workshop?"

"Um, yeah, my name is Hailey, this is the workshop about writing methods, right?" Hailey glanced around, almost wondering if she was in the right place.

People were setting up their sleeping bags around the room, some standing and talking, a few sitting by themselves, looking deep in concentration. A bald man, with a black beard was sitting at a desk, a line of people behind him.

"Yes, you're in the right place. My name is Ginger. Dallas over there will check you in and help you get settled. Welcome." She said as she ethereally walked away, floating to what looked like another newcomer.

Hailey walked over to the line, she felt uneasy. This wasn't what she pictured, a big room with everyone sleeping on the floor? I paid a lot of money for this, she thought. With that price I thought I'd at least get my own room.

As she approached the front of the line, she looked up front and noticed what looked like an alter with a bunch of ornate pillows, sages, speakers, and a few drums. She was starting to realize the mistake she made by not thoroughly reading the instructions. With everything that happened in the past few days she'd only skimmed them.

"Hello, your name is?" Dallas looked up at her quizzically.

"Hailey, my name is Hailey," she said awkwardly.

"Hailey Hailey had a little lamb," he said breaking out in laughter while Hailey wondered if it was a requisite for men to make childish rhymes out her name.
"Isn't it Mary?"

"Mary what? You're Hailey, right? Doing the one night?" Dallas wore a tie dyed T-shirt with an eagle and khaki pants.

"Yes, the one night."

"You could have done two."

"Oh, well I can only afford the one."

"For the future, there's scholarships, you can apply and get 5% off."

"I'll keep that in mind for the future," Hailey said knowing that she would never attend one of these workshops again. At least it was highly unlikely.

"You a writer or a writee?"

"A writee, but does that matter?"

"No, I like to guess, and I bet that you were a writee."

Hailey now annoyed, "Am I checked in? Is there a program of events? I didn't print out the instructions."

"Oh, that's not a problem, you can find a spot to spread out on the floor and the workshop will begin promptly at 9. Bathroom is over there," he pointed to the corner. "We ask that when the workshop starts you don't go outside and follow the instructions from Ginger. Here's a copy of Dr. Loering's methods to review before we start," he said handing Hailey a copy of the acclaimed methods. "And we will need you to sign this disclaimer," he said as he handed her a form on a clipboard. "Sign and date."

"The workshop begins at 9 but is there a program with what the schedule is? “Hailey asked, signing, and agreeing once again to something she didn't read.

"At 9 Ginger will go over the schedule, you can relax. Get settled and mingle until then."

"If this is a writing retreat, don't I need something to write with..."

"Next," Dallas called motioning the next person in line. Hailey stood for a moment, irritated that he wasn't answering her questions. Why was the agenda secret?

Hailey looked around for a spot, grabbing one where she felt she'd have enough room. As she settled in the room began to fill, more and more people arriving, mostly women. Every time someone entered Hailey wondered if it would be Writer Marie, but no signs of her yet. Hailey unrolled her sleeping bag and got settled. One woman after another arrived.

Hailey smirked and wondered how Dr. Loering was so good at getting into women's heads. Then she remembered how she fell for the same spell. She sat, feeling nervous, hungover from the day before. She wished she’d decided to eat the cost of the workshop. She wished she was hanging out with Gwyneth. This seemed ridiculous, why did they need to spend the night? As she was ruminating, the spaces around her were filling up. Soon she was smack dab in the middle of two people. The lights began to dim, and Ginger started to give an announcement to what Hailey guessed was at least 50 people. She hadn't seen Writer Marie, but she knew that didn't mean she wasn't lurking around somewhere. Writer Marie was a staple at these events, she always talked about them.

"Welcome everyone to the ultimate workshop. One that addresses all 10 of Dr. Loering's writing methods in one weekend. We are proud to be the hosts of what we consider one of the most effective writing workshops of all time. Dr. Loering's methods are standalone advice to all you writees aspiring to be writers. These workshops are the added benefit to get you to that next step of your process. We ask that anything that happens within these walls remain confidential as you have all signed your NDA. Anyone who breaches that will be subject to legal action, so I hope you all read it carefully. Moving on, " she said smiling. "Some of you may only be here for one night, we always suggest you do two nights, but you can still get something out of the experience."

A giggle burst out of Hailey as she thought to raise her hand and ask if Dr. Loering would be willing to pay her costs for the second night in exchange for the lunch she bought him. The woman next to her nervously looked over at her and Hailey whispered, "Sorry."

Ginger continued, "For those of you who haven't yet experienced a workshop like this I'll briefly go over the instructions. We will promptly begin the workshop at 9. Beforehand I'd like you to review the writing methods beforehand and set an intention of which one, or two you'd like to focus on this evening. Then we will administer the medicine."

Hailey hadn't heard anything but the medicine part which she was unaware of. In her feedback groups she'd heard from some of Dr. Loering's writees that the weekend workshops were the most fulfilling and worth it. But there never was any mention of medicine.

"Some of you may get sick, that's ok. We expect that, and for that reason paper bags are being passed around so you can eject your impurities into that." The girl next to Hailey passed her a flimsy paper bag, like one she'd find on a plane when she'd go visit her grandma in Florida. We recommend that over the toilets and we prefer you don't use those if you are going to be sick, we've had some plumbing issues in the past,".

As Ginger described the procedure for getting sick in more detail, fear was beginning to creep in, medicine that would make her sick? What the hell was this? She looked around to see if anyone was startled, but most people looked ready, quietly staring straight ahead absorbing every word.

Ginger listed all the information Hailey failed to read. "I hope you all read about the dieta and general contraindications. As the night progresses, I ask that nobody talks to one another. Everyone has a right to their own experience. I will be sharing some of Dr. Loering's newest work and asking everyone else to share something they are working on around midnight. I ask that everyone participates in this even if they don't feel like it. It's part of the process and we want you to get the most out of this workshop. We also ask again that you don't go outside until instructed, which will be after around the time we share. If you do go outside, please be mindful of the neighbors, we are in a neighborhood. After we pass around the vomit bags we will pass around sage. Then you can expect to take turns coming up to get your medicine at the altar. If anyone has any questions now is the time. "

Hailey raised her hand immediately, noticing that nobody else was.

"Yes, you, please remind me of your name," Ginger acknowledged her.

"Hailey. I'm sure I'm not alone here, but what is the medicine? I don't remember reading anything about that in the instructions. I thought this was a writing workshop, where we would be, you know, writing." Even though nobody else raised their hands Hailey felt confident she was addressing something that others had to be concerned about.

"Did you read the instructions? We mention the medicine..."

As Ginger went on about the importance of the instructions and reminding people about reporting what medications they were currently on the girl next to her whispered, "It's ayahuasca, you didn't know that?"

Hailey didn't really know what ayahuasca was or why it was relevant to Dr. Loering's writing methods.

"Does that answer your question?" Ginger asked her.

"Yes, um yes, I think so." Hailey said now realizing she may be the only person who wasn't privy to what was going on by the looks of some of the people around her.

"What's ayahuasca?" she asked the girl next to her.

"It's the drug of choice for Dr. Loering's classes, the one he thinks can help us all. It shows you your ego and darkness. It's super intense."

"Oh, ok, thanks, have you done it before?"

"Yes," The girl whispered back, "It changed my..."

"Please no talking and pay attention, you will have a chance to socialize tomorrow after ceremony," Ginger scolded them.

Changed her what? Hailey wondered. Her face? Her writing? Her life? A part of her felt like running out the door, calling Gwyneth to laugh about the entire experience. Another part of her was curious. She could also hear her mom's voice in her head lecturing her about wasting money. How bad could it be if the girl next to her did it? She looked kind of frail and like she could use a cheeseburger or two. Ginger was still talking about a few other details including further reminders on where they should purge their impurities.

"We now will begin. Dallas, please proceed with the drumming. Dallas went up to the alter and began to drum while Ginger began to chant Dr. Loering's methods and started to pour liquid into what looked like a shot glass. Hailey and the girl next to her exchanged a glance.

"My name is Bethany," she whispered to Hailey.

"Nice to meet you, I'm Hailey," she whispered back. Hailey could feel Ginger's eyes boring into them.

"Don't worry, just let the medicine help you, you can always tell it to back off," Bethany whispered.

"Thank you," Hailey said as she watched people, one by one downing the shot glass and lighting what looked like some sort of incense, letting the smoke spread around their bodies. Hailey caught a waft of it, it smelled sweet. Better than the nagchampa she often smelled in the college dorm rooms.

Before she knew it, it was her turn to take the shot glass.

"Just take it, you won't regret it, " Bethany whispered.

Hailey downed it before she could second guess.

LES RITA MITSOUKO, MARCIA BAILA PLAYING SOFTLY

INT. WRITING WORKSHOP at UCLA

HAILEY-

Late 30s, still kind of looks young, short hair like a boy, confident, independent, works in some capacity as a writer

STUDENTS-

All the writer's faces are blurry; voices are garbled and hard to understand, their bodies look like their melting…

HAILEY-

Alright class, today we are going outside of the box. We aren't just going to talk about writing. We are going to talk about life, the story of your life. Let's show a raise of hands, how many of you would die in 10 years if it meant you could be famous?

Everyone in the class raised their hands.

HAILEY-

Ok, how many of you are inspired by what you write?

Nobody raises their hand.

HAILEY-

Why, why can't you find inspiration? That's what we need to work on. Last week I assigned you to go out and kill something with your bare hands. I told you to save the bodies. Raise of hands, how many of you completed the assignment?

Students raise their hands.

HAILEY-

How many of you felt challenged by that?

Everyone raises their hands.

HAILEY-

Most of my classes have the same reaction.

The students laugh.

HAILEY-

Our next assignment will be butchering your dead creature. Then, I want you to write your next assignment in their blood. Please don't dispose of the remains yet. We'll work with those next week.

A student raises their hand.

NICKELBACK PLAYING SOFTLY

STUDENT-

Whaaaaa do need to know...if mine is.... Still alive....

HAILEY-

Sorry I can't understand you; can you repeat that?

STUDENT-

Student: Whaaaa do need to know....to save.... Who I love....

HAILEY-

I still can't hear you; can you speak up? And will someone turn that music down? Is that Nickelback? If it is I truly may be in hell. Turn that down! I can barely hear everyone as it is....

Hailey snapped back into what was her current reality. She felt sick for a moment, and scared. Music was playing from stereo speakers. Banana Pancakes by Jack Johnson. Why this? Why right now? Hailey thought. She hated Jack Johnson. She smacked her lips. She was thirsty but decided she would follow the instructions of not drinking any water while under the influence of the medicine. It was too difficult to focus her eyesight, so she laid back down and closed her eyes.

Chapter 12

CANDYMAN REVISTED PLAYING SOFTLY... CLATTER OF SILVERWARE...A BURP

INT. MANSION-NIGHT LARGE WOODEN TABLE WITH MEN

MAYBE HITLER

"Pass the salt please," a voice said to her right.

She mechanically grabbed the salt and passed it, thinking vaguely that her mother *and* Emily Post would be proud. As she passed the salt, she got a closer look at the man on her right side. Was she sitting next to Hitler? This man looked exactly like Hitler, the mustache, the beady eyes, pointy nose, wearing some sort of military uniform...

MAYBE HITLER

"Thank you," he said pouring salt onto what was an empty plate.

HAILEY'S VISION

"Are you Hitler?" Hailey asked.

KEVIN

"Hailey," a voice she recognized as Kevin's, "It's rude to ask people if they are Hitler."

MAYBE HITLER

"No, no, it's fine, I get this all the time," Maybe Hitler said holding his hand up, smiling at Hailey. "Despite what it looks like, I'm not Hitler, my name is Richard. You can call me Dick if you like."

HAILEY'S VISION

Hailey looked in horror around the table, she was at dinner with Kevin, Brock, her father, Dick who looks like Hitler, and Dr. Loering.

BROCK

"You know Hailey, if you aren't good, we aren't going to allow your special guest to come in. She's been waiting for you to stop messing up." Brock said, smiling at her, displaying a mouth full of yellow, rotted teeth.

FUCKED UP HAILEY

"Where am I? Dad, where am I?"

HAILEY'S DAD

"You're at dinner honey, eat up, we have a special guest for you." Her father looked like he had aged 20 years and his skin was falling off every time he went to take a bite or a drink. Exposed muscle was beginning to show.

FUCKED UP HAILEY

Hailey got up from the table, "I'm getting out of here, let me out of here, now," she said to a table full of men who were eating dinner off empty plates, smacking their gums, and grunting as they took imaginary bites from their forks.

DICK THAT LOOKS LIKE HITLER

"You just got here," Dick who looked like Hitler said.

DR. LOERING

"Sit down Hailey, you need to wait for your special guest, she'll be here any minute," Dr. Loering said. He looked the same, except he had short stubby horns growing slowly out of his head.

FUCKED UP HAILEY

"I don't know what this is, but I want to get the fuck out of her, right now," Hailey said, "NOW," she screamed.

Everyone stopped eating.

DICK WHO LOOKS LIKE HITLER

"Perhaps we should invite her special guest in, so she calms down," Dick who looked like Hitler said.

KEVIN

"Alright then, since Hailey can't handle anything on her own..." Kevin said getting up from the table, exposing his belly which looked to be slowly growing.

Kevin got up on the table, took his pants off and crouched over a giant, empty, silver platter. Hailey was horrified, was he going to take a shit on the platter? She watched as what looked like a body part started to exit out of his backside, a leg, another leg, a torso, wait, that dress looks familiar she thought as Kevin continued to give birth or whatever it was, although it was looking more and more like...

FUCKED UP HAILEY

"Is that Gwyneth?" a full body plops onto the silver platter. Hailey gets up on the table pushing Kevin's deflated body out of the way.

DICK WHO LOOKS LIKE HITLER

"Careful," Dick who looks like Hitler said, as he began to suck on his spoon.

FUCKED UP HAILEY

"Gwyneth," Hailey said, shaking her, she was limp, and covered in some sort of clear slime." Gwyneth, wake up, wake up, please," she begged, trying to wipe off some of the slime from her beautiful porcelain skin.

The men around the table started laughing.

BROCK

"Even though she kind of looks like a guy she can't save her."

Kevin's deflated body, that looks like a flattened tire of skin in an ugly suit started laughing, soon every man at the table was laughing hysterically while saying "Hailey looks like a man." Hailey continued to try and revive Gwyneth.

FUCKED UP HAILEY

"I love you," Hailey said, tears pouring down her face, "I can't do this without you, I can't, I need you..." Hailey started to sob, feeling for the first time how much she cared about Gwyneth, how much she had grown to need her, to want to be her friend.

GWYNETH'S VOICE

"Wake the fuck up Hailey,", and all the sudden Hailey felt a warm substance on her face that smelled like the dumpster outside her house, or the faint smell of sewage from the river.

Hailey opened her eyes to Bethany sitting over her, "I'm so sorry," she mouthed.

"Did you vomit on my face?" Hailey started to say but was interrupted by her own vomit exiting in a fashion that would have inspired scenes for The Exorcist. Writer Marie appeared, grabbing her fiercely by the arm and pulling her into the bathroom.

"You shouldn't be here, and you will pay the price," Writer Marie whispered as she threw a roll of paper towels at Hailey and left her in the bathroom.

When had Writer Marie arrived and how hadn't she seen her? She thought as she started to wipe the vomit from her face, feeling the chunks rising in her again.

Hailey had no idea what time it was. It was dark. Some people around her were making noises like they were in pain. Others were sick. Puking out there demons. After she'd been sick, she laid in her sleeping bag. She felt the warmth with the feelings of love that filled her up. Her feelings of love for Gwyneth, for her friend, her loyal, beautiful, funny, friend. Bethany was curled up in her sleeping bag and seemed lost in her own world. Hailey was lost in her own universe of love when she felt the cold, clammy, fingers of Writer Marie grasping her hand...

"What the fuck?" she said out loud accidentally.

"No talking please," Ginger said sternly from her alter. She looked like she was floating with light all around her, coming from every corner of her body. Writer Marie was nowhere to be found. Hailey wanted to tell her what she saw, but instead, again, she felt chunks of vomit rising into her throat. She got up to gather herself, can I use my legs? She thought, or maybe she said it again, she couldn't tell if it was the drug or not, but Ginger was always glaring at her.

She ran into the bathroom on autopilot where she retched into the toilet. When she got out Dallas was standing there shaking his head.

"Please use your vomit bag next time," he said walking back into the large area.

Hailey felt like she was drunk, high, and on some sort of cocktail of drugs she'd never experienced before. There was no room to respond.

She stumbled back to her sleeping bag and curled up into it, feeling like it was the only protection she had. Closing her eyes, she saw Gwyneth's soft hand appeared, helping to lift her out. Before Hailey could see anything, else Ginger began to speak.

"Now I will read you a passage from Dr. Loering's most recent story. this was published and given high reviews in the New York Herald, so we are so excited to be able to share it with the group. Once I finish reading, we will take turns going around the room to share our work."

Hailey could barely sit up straight and felt like it would be impossible to talk. Thankfully she was one of the last in the room, so she had time to collect herself, she thought. It felt weird to be listening to a story by Dr. Loering when she was in the middle of such a beautiful personal journey, she thought. Maybe it wouldn't be so bad.

"I'll start with the review of his story, then I'll get right into it:

Dr. Loering jerks at our heartstrings with a brand-new short story. His first of its kind, it has been well received. The self-help guru stirs his pot and comes out with a coming-of-age story about a girl who risks everything to visit her relative out west who is dying of cancer. There are surprises waiting in every paragraph..."

Hailey was intrigued for several reasons, maybe it was the ayahuasca, or that Dr. Loering didn't write short stories. She started to feel dread as Ginger read on, the premise of the story sounded uncannily like her own.

"I headed out west on 90. It was the first time I ever felt the feeling of a wide-open road. It was the first time I was away from my family. The first time I knew what being alone truly meant."

These are my words, she thought, this is my story. Is this a sick joke, she thought looking around? Bethany was still wrapped in her sleeping bag; it was hard to see other people's expressions, but nobody was looking at her.

"How could he get away with this?" She said out loud to herself.

Ginger stopped reading, "Please save your comments until the end of the reading, you'll have a chance to respond when it's your turn to speak."

Hailey felt the medicine unlocking a part of her that would usually shut up or take whatever it was completely out of control.

"No, that is my story. I'm not going to be quiet. He's a liar, a thief, and he stole my work."

Hailey realized she probably sounded crazy, none of the people in this room knew she had lunch with him or that she shared her work with him. She couldn't even prove it through email entirely as she mailed a paper copy to him.

"I'm going to ask you one more time to please be quiet and respectful of the people around you. The medicine is trying to tell you something but if you keep speaking you will not be able to hear it."

Hailey retorted back," What I hear is a carbon copy of the story I sent Dr. Loering after having lunch with him. And speaking of lunch, he made me pay for his lunch. Can you believe that? On top of all the other money I've spent to hear his worthless methods, methods that I could have come up with on my own, I bought him a $200 dollar lunch. And then he steals the short story he told me was a piece of shit..."

Writer Marie approached the alter and was whispering to Ginger, then she said loudly, "This writee is a fake, phony, and is going to be permanently removed from all of Dr. Loering's programs. She's also the reason I was late tonight. Once again failing to show up for her duties. I've seen her work. There's no way she'd get in the Herald."

While Hailey was ranting there was noticeable movement in the cabin, and she could see Ginger making motions with her hands. Bethany was fully awake and sitting up, staring at Hailey in horror. She couldn't tell how much of this experience was real or in her head though. What was becoming exceedingly real was Writer Marie and Dallas approaching her.

"Are you two, here, wait, is that really you or is just another vision?" Everything was swirling with black and grey clouds.

"You're coming with me," Writer Marie scowled. She didn't seem to be on the same medicine as everyone else. Hailey couldn't tell in the state she was in. She felt outside of her body, outside of the walls, looking in, from above, and could see a girl she didn't recognize getting kicked out of Dr. Loering's Ayahuasca Retreat.

"Gather your belongings and let's go."

"I don't even know if I can walk, where are we going?" Hailey said, looking frantically at Bethany for help. Everyone was sitting up, watching the spectacle.

"Do the best you can, but let's go, now." Writer Marie said firmly.

Hailey stood up slowly, falling back to the floor instantly, the sickness she felt before coming back with a vengeance and with no time to stop herself she vomited all over the floor in front of her sleeping bag. While she was leaning over Dallas picked up all her things, shoving what he could into her backpack with what seemed like anger.

"I'm sorry." Hailey said, feeling scared, weak, and like all she wanted was her bed.

"We know," Dallas said pulling her up. "You can come with me, and everything will be better.

"He's a liar," Hailey said one last time.

"Enough," Writer Marie said sternly enough to scare Hailey.

"You're ruining everyone else's time here. Is that what you want?"

Hailey glanced around, she realized then she didn't know any of these people, there was no reason to trust them, and was still extremely high.

As they walked through the room, stepping past people. They were headed to the front door.

"Where are you taking her?" She could hear Bethany call.

It comforted Hailey for a split second that somebody might care what happened to her. Dallas and Writer Marie opened the front door and they all stepped out into what was an overcast, cold, pitch-black night.

"Listen, I hate to do this, but I'm going to have to ask you to go to your car and sit there until you are well enough to drive. Preferably until it gets light out. That's about when the medicine should wear off."

"Are you serious? You want me to sit in my car the whole night? Isn't there another room or area that I can go?"

"That's the problem, there isn't besides the kitchen, and we don't think you'll be safe there."

"But I'll be safe by myself out here?"

"It's the best we can do. Try to get some rest and you'll feel better in the morning."

As Dallas was talking there was a red glowing aura around him, something that if didn't calm her, made her realize how cold it was and that she needed her jacket.

"Why am I being kicked out? I'm telling the truth."

"I believe you," he said unconvincingly.

"I don't, neither does anyone else." Writer Marie offered. She was silently standing with her arms crossed, a look of disgust so intense that she almost seemed like a vengeful apparition.

"But you read my story, you helped me draft it, how could you not remember... "

"She's lying, I did no such thing, Writers don't help writees with their projects until after this workshop, everyone knows that."

"What? Writer Marie, please, I promise I'll do anything to be able to lay in the kitchen. I'll sleep it off and leave quietly tomorrow morning. I won't bother anyone and I'll puke in my brown bag..."

"It's very much too late for apologies, you dug your grave little girl, now go ahead and get in it," She pointed to the parking lot.

In a more agreeable tone, Dallas said, "We need to think about the other participants. One of the rules in the instructions was to listen to abide by the rules and if you didn't you'd be asked to leave."

"This is bizarre, why am I being punished because of him?" She said knowing that Dallas would understand the who she was talking about.

"It seems like you might be the one punishing yourself, the medicine shows your ego."

It was the last thing Hailey wanted to hear, another person, another man, telling her how to feel or what she should feel. She started to walk off into the night, trying to remember where her car was parked and whether she could even figure out how to open it.

"I'll check on you in a few hours," Dallas called after her softly.

"Don't ever come back. To this place or the workshops. This serves as a permanent suspension," Writer Marie sneered loud enough for Hailey to hear but obviously quiet enough that she wouldn't bother anyone in the ceremony.

" If it's permanent it's not a suspension," Hailey tried to argue back but Writer Marie walked away. Hailey watched as she struggled to get the door open with her cold clammy hands.

"Don't bother coming to check on me," Hailey yelled at Dallas as he helped Writer Marie inside. She could hear the door open and shut again as she struggled to find her way to her car. At least she'd be safe in there, she thought. After opening the door of a car that looked identical to hers and realizing it wasn't hers after seeing piles of cigarette butts in the middle console, she made her way to what was her actual car, unlocking the door. She fell into the backseat. She ripped the sleeping bag out, it was cold. Then, she thought, she'd call Gwyneth, she could pick her up and could worry about getting her car another time. The parking lot was a circular drive, people would be able to get around her car if they wanted to leave.

"Ha," she said out loud, even in the middle of what was the most intense high she'd ever had she was still thinking of being considerate to other people. A flash of her mom appeared holding a burning copy of the Emily Post book. Instead of going down the rabbit hole further she fumbled to turn on her phone, which looked like a tool meant for extraterrestrials. The numbers were blurry and difficult to look at, but she managed to find and call Gwyneth, who sleepily picked up the phone after several rings.

Chapter 13

"What the hell?" Gwyneth exclaimed loudly, somehow looking beautiful even though it was the middle of the night.

"Did you go to sleep with your makeup and hair done?" Hailey asked, sliding into the seat and immediately hugging Gwyneth.

"You know I never leave my place unfinished. Hailey, jeez, you're going to squeeze me to death," pulling away, "You owe me an explanation for driving all the way out here in the middle of the night."

"I'll give it to you but let's get the hell out of here." Hailey looked back at the cabin. By now Ginger would have finished reading her piece to all the workshop attendees. She did a double take. She swore she saw Writer Marie standing outside, watching her leave, arms crossed, her body floating slightly above ground.

"I always knew she was a witch," Hailey said under her breath.

"What? You sound weird." Gwyneth said as Hailey fumbled around to turn up the heat.

"I'm on a drug right now, everything is weird, and it's freezing in here, I'm so cold, so cold and so grateful for you being here, being here in general." Hailey took in the comfort of feeling safe. She looked over at Gwyneth, with her coat over her silk pajamas. She felt herself falling into a feeling of safety feel deeper than anything she had experienced before. Like she was falling into a deep, dark well, but it was warm, comfortable, and would save her. The darkness would save her.

It took almost an excruciating hour for Gwyneth to get there but thankfully she'd found the cabin. As soon as Hailey saw headlights she ran into the road, frantically waving her hands, desperate to get out of there, desperate not to see Writer Marie again.

At that point, the medicine was beginning to wear, coming, and going in lesser waves of intensity. The hour she'd spent waiting for Gwyneth in her car, vision after vision entered and exited her. It was like the entire universe had been welcomed into her. Her mom was handling her as a baby, the lack of joy on her face. Her dad in and out of the house, constantly finding a way to get away, her mom going through all the motions, politely, stoically, never missing a beat, everything in perfect unison.

But then Hailey lay in the backseat of her car, with nothing but the tune of the heat blasting. Hailey saw something she'd never seen before. She saw her mom in a vision, shutting a door, and reaching into a closet with her hand, she drew her hand out, in a fist. As she stepped away and closed the closet door, she unfurled her fist, and a butterfly was unleashed, and flew away. Hailey's mom stood there, a single tear drop, falling down her face.

As soon as the butterfly left, she saw her parents trapped in their bedroom, with no way out.

For the first time in her adult life, she understood that her parents felt as trapped as she did. They told themselves that there was no way out. It made her feel a warmth she never felt before for her family, that they needed her help, not the other way around.

There was a longer vision of Dr. Loering chasing her by foot through Lower Wacker Drive. They both were running as fast as cars could drive, knocking each other over, smashing one another into the sides of the tunnel, which would crumble into pieces, collapsing the entire tunnel. Now it was a race to see who could get out before the entire structure collapsed. Realizing there was no time to escape through the tunnel they both jumped into the Chicago River, just as the entire tunnel collapsed and exploded. They wrestled one another in the water, Dr. Loering dunking her down until she could barely escape or breathe. She always had enough strength to rise above the water, enough time to breathe and finally, knowing that his energy was waning, she was able to push him off her, and swim to the shore, pushing away floating dead rats as she found her way.

The vision gave her new insight. That, oddly, even though Dr. Loering took her most prized possession, she was herself, she could prevail. Her demons weren't as scary as she imagined them to be. The last vision she'd had before opening her eyes to search for Gwyneth was of Bella. Bella stood with a single red rose, trying to say something Hailey couldn't understand as one rose petal after another fell onto the ground, until she was in a circle of rose petals.

There was a release in her. She felt that I was the right thing to leave the cabin. It was meant to happen, maybe the first time she hadn't soured at the thought of serendipity, rather invited the feeling in. Rather than be brainwashed by Ginger all night, she'd found her own way.

Gwyneth broke the silence as she pulled onto the Kennedy, "What happened in there Hailey? You sounded weird on the phone, and you look messed up. Did they hurt you?"

"Yes and no. I can't believe it, I really cannot believe it," Hailey said feeling another rush of the medicine. "Or maybe I can."

"Believe what? You better tell me or I'm going to drive you straight back to that weird ass cabin in the woods. I felt like I was up north in Wisconsin and what, are we in Skokie?"

"He stole my work. He took it and published it under his own name." Hailey said.

"What? What are you talking about? Who stole your work? You never mentioned giving your work to anyone, wait, except, oh no..."

"He stole my story, Dr. Loering, the one that I've been working on. The one I gave to him for feedback, the one that he said sucked and that I shouldn't submit, that one, he stole that story."

"No way, how could he have done that? How do you know?"

Hailey began to explain the past two nights best she could, starting with Writer Marie and ending with Dallas escorting her out to her car.

"Let me get this straight," Gwyneth said, lighting up a joint, "Dr. Loering does workshops where he drugs people out and tries to push his work on them and make them feel like shit. On top of that he stole your work and submitted it to the New York Herald."

"You got it," Hailey said, waving away Gwyneth's offer of a joint. She didn't feel the need to mix anything with the ayahuasca. Everything was bright, Gwyneth was glowing. It was still hard to talk, like maybe the language she chose as a human wasn't right, maybe there was another way to communicate with her body. She felt in her heart, a glowing warm energy of safety, and she knew that it was partly because Gwyneth was there, beside her.

"I hate to ask you this, but you are on drugs. Are you sure it was your story? What is your story about and what is the story that this shaman woman Ginger was reading? Are you sure she wasn't just chanting some sort of misappropriated Native American song?"

"I can prove it," she said digging out her phone which still looked really weird to her. She pulled up The NY Herald and fished out the review of the story, then finding a link to it. There it was in, in print, her story.

Gwyneth was pulling into a White Castle. "I'm hungry for sliders. Wow, he stole your work and published it. What an ass. What was your story about?"

"Here," Hailey handed her phone to Gwyneth. It was about a trip I took to see my aunt out west. I have no idea how he could even get away with it. It clearly wasn't written in his godamn voice. That's the crazy part, who would believe that he wrote that story?"

"Nobody knows anything about the man so I guess that nobody could assume that he didn't take a trip out west to visit his aunt." Gwyneth pulled up to the window, ordering sliders, fries, and a bunch of other items.

"Is there anything I can do? I'm so sorry." She looked over at Hailey, grabbing her hand. "At least your work was good enough to get published. I know it's not the same, but now you know."

"He can't get away with this." Hailey said with confidence that she didn't recognize.

"Listen, I need food to absorb all this, let's go back to my place since you aren't in any condition to do anything other than lay down. Eat some food and we will figure this out, " Gwyneth said as the clerk handed her a giant bag of food.

"Figure it out, yeah, if figuring it out means I won't have a story anymore. He just tried to take the last little bit of hope of me ever getting out of my stupid job, my stupid apartment, the stupid little world I have to breathe and eat in, shit in, die."

"Tried to is the key phrase. Listen, there's a solution to this, but I need some sliders and sleep before I can think, " she said pulling back onto the Kennedy.

Hailey felt chunks rising in her, it was the food, the smell of food revolted her right now.

"Gwyneth," and before she could tell Gwyneth to pull over or do anything she threw up all over Gwyneth's lap.

After pulling over and dumping a jug of water Hailey had to clean up Gwyneth, they commenced to Gwyneth's apartment. Gwyneth remained calmer than Hailey imagined. Hailey felt horrible.

Hailey profusely apologized all the way to her apartment where Gwyneth deposited her in her spare makeup room on her chaise lounge to sleep. Hailey didn't feel tired. She tossed and turned, looking around at all the wigs and costumes in the room. Finally, she got up and walked over to one of her vanities, picking a platinum blonde wig, the kind of hairstyle she saw on the likes of Gwen Stefani. She turned on the lights over the vanity, startled at her appearance when it came into view. She looked amazing, like the knockout she never thought she could be. She started to call Gwyneth's name but stopped, realizing that she Gwyneth had done enough already that evening. She turned off the light, keeping the wig on and made her way to the chaise, sprawling out. She felt a strong energy of love, and for once, it seemed to be for herself.

_ _ _

"Yeah, what kind of solution could there possibly be? Because he is the most powerful man of his kind, you know it. And he doesn't give a shit about anything but being famous and powerful."

Gwyneth and Hailey started their Sunday morning late, deciding to head to brunch.

"Finally!" Gwyneth yelled loud enough that several people turned to look at her.

"Finally, what?"

"Finally, you understand what a scum bag he is."

"That's not the point Gwyneth."

"Oh yes, it is," she said taking a sip of mimosa. "Now that you don't care about him, you won't care about taking him down."

"Take him down? Me? What am I going to do? Make an excel spreadsheet with all the reasons he's an asshole? Write a shitty story and give it to him to steal?"

"The second idea isn't half bad. But that's not what I was thinking."

"And what were you thinking? Killing him? Kidnapping him?" Hailey asked right as the server placed two plates of eggs Florentine down on their table, glancing with concern at Hailey and quickly walking away. The post ayahuasca glow of Hailey gave her an electric charge, she didn't care as much what people thought.

"Ha, not quite. I was thinking we will just steal his hard drive and give it to Jenna Janders. She'll help us."

"How are we going to get his hard drive? Ask him, " Oh hey would you mind if we just borrowed your hard drive for a few hours? Our isn't working and we need to transfer some pdfs off our laptop because we are out of space on our mutual laptop? And what will we find on his hard drive?"

"No silly. Let's finish breakfast and talk to Jenna. I have a plan we can run by her. He has shit on his hard drive that will incriminate him. Plans from the workshops, evidence of drugging people, evidence he stole work from people. I think it will work. Stop worrying. We are going to figure this out."

Hailey was staring at her glass. Gwyneth's promises of a plan weren't reassuring her. All she could think of was the time she spent on her story. She knew it was good even though it was a simple premise. She'd known that when she gave it to Dr. Loering it was good. That was why him saying it was so bad punctured her. It was the one good thing in her life, the one thing she was proud of and the moment she gave it to someone who she respected they tore it away from her, and now took it from her. That story was her ace, her golden ticket, the way out of Brock and Kevin's world.

Hailey felt a tear falling down her face.

"That story meant a lot to you, didn't it?"

Tears falling freely now as she picked at the food, she knew she couldn't eat, "It was the only thing I had going for me."

"The only thing, huh? There are no other stories? No other people? No hope in your life for happiness? Sweetie, life is more than one story. Now listen here, we're going to finish our breakfast, or rather, I am, then we can call Jenna and make a plan. We'll get that story of yours back, you have my word."

"Gwyneth, you've done enough, really."

"Aren't that what friends for?" she handed Hailey a Kleenex from her purse. "Why don't you try and finish up your Benedict. It's divine."

"I can't eat."

Gwyneth looked at Hailey, studying her face, pausing as if to search for something, “Listen, you are beautiful, intelligent, kind of shy and stuck up, but I like you. I really do." Hailey never noticed how beautiful her hazel eyes were. They reminded her of stones reflecting sunlight, glistening in the spray of a waterfall. Even in her turmoil, she felt grateful for her first friend in the city. She felt grateful she had Gwyneth.

"Let's call Jenna. Right now. We’ll tell her what happened, and she can help us make a plan."

"Don't you think she has more important things to do than help us? Plus, I have to get my car from that cabin."

"It's worth a shot to take Dr. Loering down, it's not just about you Hailey, it's about all the other women who have fallen for his shit. Think of what you went through with Writer Marie. There are other women out there right now performing acts of invisible labor in hopes that they'll get published Yet to me it sounds like getting published means little for the few that do. Do you want women to suffer like you did just to find out that Dr. Loering will steal their work if its's good?"

Hailey imagined Writer Marie with her rotting teeth, her cold clammy hands, the smell of her dirty apartment...

"Ok, fine, get a hold of her. But I don't think she will be able to do anything, she already tried to interview Dr. Loering, and it doesn't seem like that did anything to stop him."

"We can't know until we try, plus I have an idea," Gwyneth took out her phone, "I put Jenna's number in the night after we all hung out. We can get your car later. By the way, you look hot in that wig, nice choice."

"Thanks," Hailey said smiling, feeling the warmth of the late fall sunshine on her face, as she bit into her Benedict.

Chapter 14

The Interview Part II

Dr. Loering: "The first time I was judged?" He said as he looked like he was searching around. "Interesting question," he said as he took a sip of water, dribbling a few drops onto his shirt. He glanced down at what now was a small wet spot on his chest. There was a moment of dismay that quickly turned to anger as he abruptly stood up.

Jenna: "Are you alright?"

Dr. Loering: "Can we pause this? I have this fucking water stain on my shirt. It looks ridiculous. Annabelle? Where's Annabelle?" he demanded, leaving the set, and walking toward his dressing room.

"This is bullshit," he said under his breath.
"More of a fucking therapy session than a fucking interview," He snapped at a younger no name employee, some intern girl, he thought as he flung open the door to his dressing room.

"Annabelle," He yelled as she ran into his room, looking poised as usual.

"Here's your shirt," she said moving toward him. "Take off the one you have on and let's put this new one and finish this."

As he took his shirt off, he locked eyes with her, he loved to toy with her. He could easily have her, but he kept her around, on the low pay she accepted by giving her just enough hope to be his. It was less complicated that way. He liked fucking when it was no strings.

"Button me up," he commanded, and she dutifully came over to button his shirt. "Hurry then I need you out of here."

After she dutifully left, he sat down in his dressing room mirror with the full intention of making Jenna Janders wait.

"Fucking cunt," he said, realizing over the years the disgust he held for women who tried to shake him. For almost 50 he looked good still. He knew it. Muscular, not a ton of wrinkles, but enough wear and tear to push a rugged look.

"They love a wise man." He combed his hair, running his fingers through it in the way that he knew drove most women crazy.

"That fucking bitch though, prying for personal information," he said to his reflection.

"You ok in there?" Annabelle called.

"I am fucking sick of women, sick of them asking, asking, asking." He felt his blood starting to boil up. They were so fucking useless; how could they be so desperate when it was so easy out there to do anything you wanted...

Enjoying the feeling of his undoing Dr. Loering continued to his reflection, "And you, here now, no way we continue with your questions Jenna Janders, before you tell me why you are such a sad, spinster bitch, yeah you..." He threw a jab, intending a mock punch, for a moment fantasizing that he was hitting her face.

– – –

Jenna was waiting for fifteen minutes before she called asking one of the production assistants to check in on him.

He came back out with the production assistant who looked rolled her eyes when he sat down and settled into his position. He cast a smile at Jenna that was meant to charm her. The smile that intended to charm millions of his women followers.

Jenna: "I barely noticed the stain on, your, um, shirt it and I'm sitting right across from you, I doubt the viewers would have seen it, but that's part of your perfectionism, isn't it? I get it, I seek the same kind of perfectionism in my own work."

Dr. Loering: "If you don't seek perfectionism in your work, why even bother, that's what I tell my writees all the time. They don't get to jump from Method 1 all the way to publication in one swift move, but I give them the tools to be able to become a writer."

Dr. Loering: "So where were we?"

Jenna: "I was asking you about the first time you ever felt judged?"

Dr Loering:" We're still on that question?" He said laughing. "Judgement isn't something I really think about other than when I'm trying to help other people. It's not something that has prevented me from moving forward if that's the kind of answer you are looking for.

Jenna: "I'm not looking for an answer, I'm looking for your truth. I want to know some of your, how should I say it, elusive history. I want to know what makes you tick and understand your influence over your predominately female audience."

Dr. Loering shifts in his seat, looking uncomfortable.

Dr. Loering: "I can't help my audience is mostly female, I put out what I put out, it's up to people who find worth in my message to decide whether it works for them or not."

Jenna: "Ok then, let’s talk about that for a moment. If you aren't targeting women, why do you think your message resonates with them?"

Dr. Loering: "Honestly, I'm not sure. I didn't set out to target women, I wanted to create content and methods that would appeal to writers. It's my good looks," he said laughing. "No, honestly I'm kidding, I know that I am good looking by societies standards, but I think people, and by people, I mean both men and women, because I do have men that attend my workshops, I look at the numbers, because they see what can come out of having confidence in understanding the nature of the beast. And in my case, I understand the beast I'm trying to tame is the beast of writing."

Jenna: "That's fascinating, let's talk more about your methods and how they were developed."

Dr. Loering: "I'd love to, I really would, but the way I produced my methods are secret and are intended to be kept a secret. I think of it more as a spiritual process than, let us say scientific. That's what you're looking for right, what scientific method I used to develop them?"

Jenna: Smiling, uncrossing, and recrossing her legs, “Once again Dr. Loering, I'm not looking for an answer, I'm looking for the truth. And I ask the question about the development of your methods because you don't talk about it in any of your work. Are you telling me they appeared to you one day, kind of like Joseph Smith? Is your audience aware of that?"

Dr. Loering: Becoming agitated, "I'm not sure where this questioning is headed, but I'm done," he said standing up and ripping the mic off him. "Annabelle," he called, "Let's get out of here, this interview is over."

"Done," Jenna said. "We caught him."

"We should celebrate," Larry said, slowly walking across the room. Larry was a huge man, towering above Jenna at 6 ft 3 ft. He was just as wide as he was tall, and he was out of breath by the time he got back to his desk with two glasses.

She put her phone down just in time to see the secret hiding spot where he kept his whiskey under his desk. It was the first time she had seen Larry, her editor, in months.

"So," he said as he poured a generous amount of whiskey into the glasses, "Tell me how you're doing, I know this one was tough for you."

They clinked glasses, "What do you mean Larry? I got the guy, isn't that all that matters? He can't hurt women anymore."

They both knew that Jenna's last assignment almost put her over the edge.

"Do you think he'll give you an interview?"

"I don't know yet, the cops just booked him today. He loved the publicity; I doubt that will change. I don't know if I want to give him a platform, but yes, most likely I will interview him. I just need to nail down my angle."

Larry took a sizable gulp and lit up a cigar as he leaned back into his chair, his shirt showed a grease stain, "Listen, nobody is happier than me that you got the guy. I think out of all the cases you've had; this one was the most gruesome."

"This was the most gruesome. He beat women up to the point of death for a sport and filmed it. He wanted to show his work to the entire world, and he would have if we hadn't caught him. This case was more than catching the guy and getting my big interview, this was my chance to make a difference on a larger scale, it's what I've been working towards my entire career."

"Yeah," Larry said taking several puffs of his cigar. He stood up and looked out his window, not bothering to open it in what was now a cloud of smoke.

"Remember that guy you took down, the one who was drugging and raping his wife? It was a high-profile case; he was a big figure in the oil business. Had his hands on a lot of money, but his wife, he just beat the shit out of her, it was impossible for people to ignore. But they did...until you got involved."

"I remember the case, yes, initially I interviewed him about being an entrepreneur, but that was what made me suspect him..."

"And your divorce was going on at that time..." Larry was looking Jenna square in the face.

"Listen Larry, I thought this meeting was about a new assignment, what's going on? I appreciate this," she said swirling her glass around, "but usually I'm rewarded with pitching my next assignment."

Larry ignored her, as he sat, rather plopped into his chair, "Good job in catching him. Them all. Jenna, you've made an impact. And I'd like to hear your next pitch if you have one, but that's not why you're here. I wanted to meet with you today for a different reason."

"You want me to do a few more high-profile interviews to switch it up? Right," Jenna said interrupting him," I have an idea..."

"Hold on," Larry said, placing his hand on his pristinely clean desk, which looked out of place next to him. "You haven't taken a break in over 3 years J," Larry said, straightening his tie. Even though Jenna worked for him for almost 10 years he still scared her a little. His smile was a frown, all business was his demeanor, dressed in a suit, a deep demanding voice with a temper that was easily ignited.

"And the last break you took, you ended up finding a story," He said nodding to the wall where a headline "Jenna Janders Tracks Down Serial Rapist".

"I have a pitch..."

"Stop there," Larry said in a tone that was one decibel above losing it, "I don't care if it's the break of the year if it's important we'll get someone else on it while you are out and you can pick back up in a week."

"A week? I can see a day or two, but Larry, you know my work is my life, if I needed a break, I'd let you know," Jenna knew that was a lie when it came out of her mouth. She felt too tired to argue. She was so used to being on the run all the time she didn't know what the breaking point was. If there was a breaking point, she'd recently felt like she might be close to breaking it. The nightmares she was having were consistent, every night she woke up drenched in sweat. She knew her job was the love of her life, yet she always felt like she was chasing something that wasn't there

Getting up and motioning her to the door, Larry insisted, "Go home, go visit family, friends, whatever it is you haven't done the past 20 years of your life, and come back in a week."

"How about we compromise with 3 days? A week isn't necessary, I promise, " she said, mostly to the door that was shut in her face. She smoothed her shirt, realizing that since she'd on this assignment she hadn't showered in a day or two. Or was it 3?

An intern popped his head up and smiled at her, "Do you need help Jenna?"

"Unless you can talk him into letting me take another story, no." Jenna said pointing to Larry's office as she turned around.

"Maybe I can help, what's the story?"

"Find your own story intern," Jenna said walking off. Harsh, yes, but these interns were too hungry to be trusted. All waiting around in the office with their MacBook's. NYU and Northwestern degrees, funded by their parents to sit and wait until their big chance came. Hell, if Jenna was going to let one of them take her idea. They do grunt work. She rarely trusted any of them for anything more.

"He wants me to take a week off," she said to herself chuckling as she went to her office to grab a few belongings. She had never taken a week off. Holidays, birthdays, milestones, all passed by her while she was living in a story. A feeling of loneliness washed over her. Friends, family, they were very rare these days. Most of her friends were from college and moved on to families and the people that filled in the gaps with that lifestyle. It was true that Jenna was tired to the bones.

She'd been so addicted to bringing down powerful men that she lost everyone in the process.

Bad men got under her skin in a way that no matter how many of them she brought down, she never felt her job was done. After she caught the serial rapist, the nightmares started. Anxiety started creeping in, waking her up at night. Seeing so many victims, and so many crime scenes she started to wonder if it would be her turn next.

It was the first time she felt her time was coming, yet she didn't know why. When she started her career, she was just a newscaster, but she realized she was good at interviewing. Then she realized she was even better at investigating.

She sat down at the desk she rarely used. The spa was what she needed. She couldn't remember the last time she had been to a spa. Jim, her ex, had bought her a massage, that would have been six years ago now. Six years since the divorce.

For now, going home would do, she thought as she put on her jacket and took a moment to look out the office window towards the Chicago skyline, dark and spectacular at the same time. Her view faced west, and she could see Milwaukee Ave. stretching out for miles, cars reaching into an expanse, inching further and further away. She realized as she left that she never truly took the time to look outside.

She unlocked the door to her apartment and stepped inside. Throwing her jacket onto a couch she rarely sat on she went into the kitchen. She opened the fridge. Only a few leftover containers and a bottle of half-finished white wine. She poured herself a glass and went to turn on the water to take a bath.

She caught a glimpse of herself in the mirror and stopped to look. She couldn't stop thinking about the woman she interviewed in her last story; the woman looked identical to Jenna's best friend from high school. She studied her face in the mirror. She tried to take care of herself the best she could, but lines were starting to spread across her forehead. For as many men she took down, she hadn't figured out how to beat age and its cruelty to women. As she continued to look in the mirror, she could see herself ten years ago, twenty years ago, the plans and hopes she had to be a journalist were already there. Yet, it was early enough where anything could have happened. But it didn’t. What happened was exactly what she thought would happen. Life. And it was messy. Especially when she cared about making a difference, she cared about the truth, she cared about taking down men like Dr. Loering. Men who pretended they saved people, women especially, while secretly they were one's women should fear, the predators. The fog from her bath crept in, Jenna wiped the mirror again. Her present self-looked sad, determined, tired, and resolved. She knew that her primary purpose in this life wasn't the prescribed one of society. She was a truth making machine, not a baby making machine. A man she dated once told her she was beautiful without makeup. And she was wearing makeup that day. As much as she wanted to believe that she knew that makeup enhanced her beauty, at least according to society's standards. She grabbed her brush and started combing her hair. Her phone vibrated.

She ran a brush through her hair, still the same thick brown hair she'd always had. No grey hairs yet, she plucked them from her scalp as soon as she saw them.

As the tub filled up, she searched for the remote and turned on her television more for background than anything. Noise to get away from her thoughts. Maybe it was the fact she was almost 50, it started to bother her that she didn't have anyone in her life. It was something she hadn't even considered she was so busy over the last decade.

She turned off the water in her bath, it was scalding hot, so she decided to wait a few minutes before getting in.

Over the last year, she started to notice that despite all the trauma the survivors she interviewed endured that they all seemed to move forward, find love, and build families. The first channel that popped up on her television was the news. She half-heartedly turned up the volume grabbing for a throw blanket her mom had sent her as a gift in college. Kicking the papers off her couch she lied down. Surprisingly this felt good.

She looked on her phone for the nearest spa and scheduled a massage there for the following day. It felt good to take at least one step towards taking care of herself. Maybe next she could cook something in her kitchen...she thought as the news played in the background.

A weather report. Nothing gruesome, just the temperatures. Jenna drifted asleep. She jerked awake, managing to hear the last of a newscaster talking about Dr. Loering's and he became a powerful new voice in fiction. Jenna turned up the volume but not in time to hear anything else about his story. She searched around for her phone, lost in the couch, finding it with the intent of ordering food when she noticed a text.

"Jenna this is the cute woman with the strawberry blonde hair you met the other night, Gwyneth.

We need your help. We have a story for you (Dr. Loering), when can you meet up?? We promise it will be worth your while. :-)"

A flash of Larry yelling at her earlier went through her mind, dissipating as quickly as it came. Dr. Loering was the case she'd never been able to crack, even though Jenna knew he was scum there wasn't anything on him. Jenna immediately texted back, planning to meet them later. She took a quick bath, throwing on the most comfortable jeans and shirt she could find, glancing around her apartment one last time as she left, wondering when she would be back.

Chapter 15

Hailey immediately answered the door. Jenna walked in briskly, looking Hailey up and down. Hailey spent the last few hours pacing around, trying to brainstorm ideas while Gwyneth had been getting ready in her bedroom. Walking helped Hailey think.

"Please sit" she said motioning her to sit. Jenna sat across from Hailey and they both nodded at one another.

Gwyneth came out of her room, her hair curled, wearing a red dress with pink lipstick. She looked even more fabulous than usual.

"Jenna, we are so glad you could make it. Hailey's been freaking out..."

"What's going on?" Jenna asked

Gwyneth and Hailey looked at each other. Gwyneth began, "He stole her story. He took it and now he is being claimed as the next best fiction writer."

"He took your story?" Jenna said now noticing the anger radiating off Hailey.

Hailey couldn't help it, she started to break down, "Yes. The no-good piece of shit bastard took my best story. A piece of writing that I worked on for the last two years."

Gwyneth handed her a tissue, "I can't believe I was stupid enough to give it to him. I can't believe I was stupid enough to follow him. I also cannot believe I found out after being drugged at one of his workshops. Did you know that he's doing that? People that go to his workshops work up to one last final workshop where you take drugs. Apparently, drugs are the final barrier to getting published. In reality it's another scheme to get money..."

"Whoa whoa whoa, that's a lot to take in, let's start at the beginning and hear the whole story." Jenna said as Gwyneth placed a few cold beers out in front of them.

They were onto their second beer when Hailey finished explaining everything, from the lunch she paid for, to sending him her story through the mail, the horrible feedback, to the invisible labor she was forced to do as a writee, then finding out that he stole her work while on drugs at the writing workshop.

"Those drugs are definitely illegal." Jenna said. "Is there anyone you can think of in the workshop that would be willing to talk? What about Writer Marie? Do you have any evidence from her?"

Hailey thought of sweet Bethany from the workshop. She'd hate to ask her. She already seemed so fragile.

"I can't think of anyone from the workshop," Hailey lied. "I have all my text messages from Writer Marie. I don't know, as horrible as she is I'm not sure I want to get her in trouble. Her life is so miserable. Dr. Loering is who I want."

"The writee errand running is a scam. Writer Marie used you for free labor. There must be others who thought it was a scam. Do you know anyone else in the workshop? Anyone who quit? Do you have a registration list or a list of people that were coming?"

"Can we stop calling her "Writer Marie"? Gwyneth asked.

"Certainly," Hailey said smiling. Turning to Jenna she said, "They keep attendee information confidential. Everything was hush hush in workshops. In the beginning I liked that workshops were mysterious. I liked feeling like I was part of something special. I liked that we were writers out to change the world. I was sold by the idea that only the most committed would advance. But the drugs aren't what I want to get him on anyway, honestly the drugs helped me in a weird way. And the writee errands were awful, but that's not what I want either. I want my story back. And I want the world to know he stole my story."

Gwyneth silently listened to Hailey and Jenna talk, occasionally rubbing Hailey on the back. "I'm going to make us tea," Gwyneth said disappearing into the kitchen and returning with one of her ornate trays complete with tea.

As the three sat drinking their tea Hailey continued. "Lots of women have made that same mistake, giving him something. Whether it be money, ideas, time, lots of women believe in him. Men want that, for us to fail, for us to be less than we are. We need to fight back; we need to take this asshole down as an example." Hailey stared straight ahead, the tears subsided, a numb feeling overtaking her, "He took the best thing I had. The only thing I had."

"The best thing?" Gwyneth said winking at Hailey. In return Hailey gave her best attempt at a smile.

Jenna stood up and smiled. "Ladies, I've been hunting this man for years. Waiting for this moment. And now it is here. I think we might have enough evidence between the requirements to join the workshops, the language of what it means to be a writee and the drugs. I need to confirm a few details, but don't you see, this is our chance to bring him down."

"That doesn't answer how we can get my work back" Hailey said giving Gwyneth a look as she took another sip from the tea. "I essentially gave him my work; how can we prove that it's mine?" Hailey said as she grabbed the bottle from Gwyneth and took a swig. "I'm ruined, I'm stuck being Kevin's little bitch for the rest of my life. I will live in my shitty little apartment and hell, why don't I marry Brock while I'm at it?"

"I don't think you and Brock make a good couple; I think you'd look better with Kevin."

Jenna and Hailey glanced at Gwyneth, trying to decide if she was serious.

"I'm kidding!" She said laughing. "Listen, I told you, I have a plan. Jenna, that's why I wanted you to come here," Gwyneth said looking up at Jenna.

"Let's hear it Gwyneth," she said glancing at Hailey, glad that her tears subsided. Jenna had never been a crier and crying made her uncomfortable. Both were now looking at Gwyneth, Hailey was not optimistic of Gwyneth's plan. Regardless she wanted to hear it.

"Now ladies, I've thought this through. And I really think, no matter how crazy you might think this sounds it could work. So, let's give this an open mind, how about?"

"Our minds are open and ready to receive," Jenna said, motioning for her to continue.

"Alright, this is the plan. First, we set up an interview with Dr. Loering that he cannot refuse. "From what I know of him, the New York Herald would be the perfect way to get him out." Jenna nodded from the couch. "I don't think he's ever refused an article with the Herald; he loves them because they love him."

"They do kiss his ass," Jenna added in.

"Either Hailey or I will act as the reporter and meet him out."

"Wouldn't that obviously, be you? He knows what I look and sound like," Hailey said.

"True," Gwyneth said. "It just so happens you know a talented makeup artist." She said pointing both hands at herself. "And hear me out, you know him, Hailey. You might know him better than any of us. I think you would be the best person for this part of the plan. Plus, you have a coach. Jenna can help prepare you."

"I don't know about that. I might just drop kick him and spit on his face, but continue," Hailey said looking at Jenna for validation.

"Yes, let's hear her out," Jenna said.

"Hailey will act as a reporter for the New York Herald and set up an interview with Dr. Loering. Jenna, do you think he would interview with the Herald, even if it is a male reporter?"

"As long as the interview is with the Herald, he'd probably do it, yes. He does have a reputation for wanting female journalists to interview him. His go-toes are usually Sharon Hinderskinny or or Patti Topland."

Gwyneth set her tea down loudly. “Ugh, I cannot stand Sharon Hinderskinny. She is so fake!”

"Why would a male or female matter?" Hailey asked, ignoring Gwyneth’s comment. This wasn’t about Sharon Hinderskinny being fake. She was concerned that she might be part of a plan that wasn't only crazy, but dangerous.

"Gwyneth has a point," Jenna said, "We know Dr. Loering has an interest and hold on women. His charisma is what draws them in. His marketing is targeted at them. His messaging doesn't work as well on men, I've studied the attendance of his talks and workshops. Most attendees are female. He's playing the same game a lot of misogynists already play and using his sexual energy on vulnerable women. That's my theory, and that is why I find him fascinating. He's a predator that's out in the open. Out in broad daylight.”

"I'm no lawyer,” Hailey added, “but I don't think we can prove he solely markets to women to control them."

"I'm not sure what the best legal angle is at this point, we'd have to do more digging. But some of the language, like writer, writee, it's meant to control people. Giving a false promise of publication, that's another way to control people. What would be the icing on the cake is if we could prove women were also sleeping with him as some sort of quid pro quo agreement."

"I cannot imagine him sleeping with Writer Marie, she's haggard, but I question how she advanced so quickly."

"Listen, ladies," Gwyneth clapped her hands together, "We're getting off track. Let me finish. Hailey, we will vet you on what to say and which questions to ask. You'll meet Dr. Loering at a fancy restaurant. Dr. Loering is partial about where he eats, as we know. We will pick one of the best places in town, somewhere he cares more about his appearance."

"This whole thing is already making me nervous," Hailey interjected, "I don't know, even though I don't know a ton of people what if I run into someone I know?" Hailey was grasping at this point. She was trying to find any excuse she could to get out of what seemed an impossible task, or a task she felt Jenna was much more capable of accomplishing.

Jenna looked over at Hailey, leaning towards her, she took her hands on her own. "I know this plan sounds crazy, but I've been trying to take him down for years. If we can pull this off, maybe we can bring him down. Then we help millions of women avoid going down the same path as you. We don't know that he hasn't been stealing other people's work. This is larger than your story, Hailey, this is the story of millions of vulnerable, well-meaning women who simply want to create. Gwyneth," she said turning away from Hailey, "What will you do for Hailey's costume? A wig and a fake mustache? I'm not sure that's enough. Dr. Loering isn't the smartest man, but he isn't stupid either. I worry about sending Hailey into a situation that she can't handle. If Dr. Loering catches on I'm not sure what he would do, but it won't be good."

Gwyneth looked at Jenna, "I think I have just the thing to calm your fears. Come this way."

Hailey nodded at Jenna as Jenna got up to follow Gwyneth to her spare room. As Gwyneth opened the door and they walked in, Jenna exclaimed loudly. "This is yours?" She walked around the room, looking at the shelves of wigs. She brushed her hand on the racks of costumes, holding up a sparkly blue evening gown.

"Yes. Ever since I was a little girl, I wanted to be a costume and makeup artist."

Hailey popped in after Jenna. "You need to see this," she said as she handed Jenna the photo album of Gwyneth's work.

Jenna flipped through the before and after pictures of actors. "I'm impressed." Jenna laughed. "You did Wicked?"

"That was one of my first theater productions."

"You're talented. But Hailey cannot look at all like herself. She also can't look like someone with 50 pounds of make-up on their face, if Dr. Loering suspects that something is off who knows what he will do or how he will react. Remember, not only does he have money, but he also has a huge following. He could ruin Hailey."

"He already has," Hailey said as she looked through various wigs on a rack.

Gwyneth and Jenna looked over to Hailey as she tried on a short haired brunette wig.

"Listen to my plan, I haven't even finished. I promise this could work."

Hailey nodded for her to continue.

"While you are interviewing him, Jenna and I will sneak into his house and take his hard drive."

"Are you serious? Breaking and entering? Just how do you plan to get in there? And how do we know where he lives?"

"I know that your assistant can figure out his home address Jenna."

"She can..." Jenna said cautiously.

"Before the interview, I deliver a fake order of sushi to Dr. Loering's house. Dr. Loering will be confused, and I will insist that the order was called in for him. I'll have a beverage, like a Coke or Iced Tea. When I'm handing him the beverage, I'll trip and spill all over him."

Jenna and Hailey were silent. Hailey wasn't sure if Gwyneth was joking at this point. She searched Jenna's face to see if she felt the same way, as Gwyneth continued.

"This is where it gets tricky because we are counting on the fact that Dr. Loering will not be able to handle a stain on his shirt for even a second. I am hoping that he will insist on changing his shirt before he's finished dealing with me. While he does that Jenna sneaks inside the house. "

Hailey and Jenna looked at each other again.

"And when Jenna's inside the house? Then what?" Hailey asked. "He calls the cops and gets us all arrested?"

"No, he leaves for dinner to meet you. Then she lets me in, and we find evidence that he stole your work. Or evidence about drugging participants in his workshop. Maybe we find evidence that he stole other women's work. I know he is hiding something. Don't you agree Jenna?" Gwyneth asked looking with anticipation at Jenna.

"I have a strong feeling he's up to something. I always have. But it will be better if we are specific about what we are trying to find. Plagiarism is a serious accusation, and we are going to need the best proof we can find. Did you email him your writing?"

"No, I mailed it to him."

"You mailed it to him?"

Hailey nodded back at Jenna, "Now I wonder if it's because he was thinking he might steal it? It would be more difficult to trace that way."

"Listen, Hailey, gather all the evidence you have that you wrote the story. Everything. Notes, ideas, any writing whatsoever. I can hand it in to my editor with the published piece to see what we can do. But having physical evidence that you gave your story to him is also what we need. The issue is he has money and power. Gwyneth's plan might work. And we will have a case if we are able to get his hard drive, I agree he is hiding something. It's just a matter of whether we get caught in the process."

"What then? What if he figures out I'm not who I say I am?" Hailey asked.

"Honestly, I don't know. We will have to cross that bridge when we get there. Do you care though? You said he stole your livelihood. If he figures out it's you and thinks it's a prank, let us know immediately and stall him as much as you can."

"He won't know it's her. Not with my work. There's no way." Gwyneth said.

"What about her voice?" Jenna asked.

"We can work on that, but I doubt he will recognize Hailey's voice from the few times he spoke with her. Even if he does my makeup and hair will be so good, he will feel like an idiot trying to make it seem like she isn't a man."

"What kind of man will I be?" Hailey said

"A nice clean-shaven man look; I have some ideas in mind." Gwyneth said brushing her hand on Hailey's cheek. "A nice suit, you'll look sharp and put together."

Jenna added in, " Facial hair would piss Dr. Loering off."

"Why?" Hailey asked.

"Because everything that is not tidy is a threat to him. Even facial hair. You need to dress sharply, in a suit and have your background story down. Obviously, Dr. Loering reads the Herald so he will wonder why he hasn't seen your name. That's because you are a up and coming journalist. We'll make a back story for you, I have ideas."

"Yeah," Gwyneth chimed in, "Maybe he..." Gwyneth said emphasizing he, "...Got his job at the Herald because his father is a wealthy man in the oil business. He's never known a day of hard work in his life. His dad got him the job because someone owed him a favor."

Jenna looked over at Gwyneth with a hint of amusement in her eyes. "That's in the right direction but let's keep it as mysterious as possible. Except of course for details that might intimidate Dr. Loering."

Jenna looked at Hailey. "What school did you go to?"

"Penn State?" Hailey said, attempting to lower her voice a few octaves.

"We'll have to work on that voice more than her physical appearance," Gwyneth said.

Hailey started to feel the weight of the past few days on her. Since she took the drugs from the workshop it didn't weigh her down as much as it would have in the past. Things seemed more possible. With Gwyneth and Jenna behind her, anything seemed possible. They walked back into Gwyneth's living room, plopping on various chairs.

As Hailey started to say, "I don't know."
Gwyneth interrupted and said, "I got it! She'll have a fake British accent. Dr. Loering won't catch onto that. Even if he does Hailey, or should I say, Tyler, will just say he's from London."

Jenna added, “I don’t know about the accent, that would be tricky. What if you casually mention your family comes from wealth? I’ll let you work out those details but if he knows you come from money it will humble him. I don't want to give you too many details, I think it will make you more nervous. I don't think Dr. Loering will catch onto you because of details like that, I think you could expose yourself with the questions you ask him. You will have to be careful. The most important part will be holding his attention. If he comes home before we are out of that apartment, we're all busted."

"I’ll talk about how great his work is and how effective his methods are. That will keep him captivated," Hailey said joking. She grabbed her phone to take a glance at the time and saw that she had a text message from her mother.

MOTHER: Hailey we are waiting for you, your dad is extremely hungry, are you nearby?

Did you use my credit card for some sort of workshop?

"Shit, I forgot I had dinner with my parents." she said to nobody and everybody at the same time.

Chapter 16

Bella was fifteen minutes late. Hailey took the time to respond to her mother who was becoming increasingly difficult when she didn't respond immediately to missing the mandatory dinner. Hailey didn't have it in her to respond. She felt exhausted from trying to make her parents happy. She was sick of being someone they'd never appreciate. Yet, she felt a tender love for them. They were her parents. She'd apologize and make it up to them. Maybe she'd go to church.

3:13 PM
MOTHER: we thought something bad happened to you. your father is talking about how inconsiderate you are. We asked two things, church, and dinner with us in exchange for rent, if you can't keep your part of the commitment, we may have to reconsider ours

9:15 PM

MOTHER: Are YOU ok? Your father and I are worried about you

10:00 AM
MOTHER: I TRIED calling and it rings and rings

10:01
MOTHER: Are you ignoring me?

10:05
?????????????????

11:30
Hailey: I don't know what to say Mom, I've had a crazy week. Can I make it up with another dinner this week? I'm sorry

11:31
MOTHER: Come tomorrow night and we can talk

11:45
Hailey: I can't, can I come the following evening?

11:46
MOTHER: The sooner the better, your father is upset

Hailey was so distracted by the texting that she didn't notice Bella's arrival.

"Hailey?" She stood above her, smiling. Hailey smiled back. She noticed that Bella had deep brown eyes. She looked casual but professional wearing a pair of nice jeans and a button-down shirt.

She stood, "Bella, I am so sorry, I was texting my mother about dinner plans, I didn't see you there."

She motioned for her to sit, "I should be the one to apologize, sorry I'm late, traffic was horrible coming from O'Hare."

"Were you working?" Hailey said as she sat down across from her, thankful that the place wasn't super busy. It made their meeting feel intimate. Like they were the only people on this planet. She didn't know what to expect from this meeting, but it wasn't the feeling she expected, rising in her.

"I wasn't supposed to work today, but I have a hard time saying no to making money," she said flashing what Hailey categorized as a kind smile. Her face had a healthy glow. Like someone who drank water and got the right amount of sleep. She eats healthily too, Hailey thought, thinking of the greasy pizza she often succumbed to.

"Me too," Hailey said returning her kind smile. She hoped Bella wouldn't notice the dark circles under her eyes. Or her wrinkled blouse. Or that she was super nervous.

"Are you going to order any food?" She asked as she looked at the menu, "I heard this place has great pizza."

"Not right now," Hailey thought again of the greasy leftover pizza she'd eaten for dinner the night before. "Just drinks for me, but if you're hungry go ahead."

"I'll order a drink," she said waving over the waiter.

Once she ordered her drink Hailey felt the impending doom of what was to come. She thought about canceling a million times. She was terrified that Bella had seen the article, if she had, if she knew, she would think Hailey plagiarized. She'd shown up regardless, mostly because she thought she was cute. Besides, maybe she hadn't seen the article. She was busy driving so maybe she didn't look at the paper. Maybe she knew it wasn't Dr. Loering's work. Maybe she hated Dr. Loering. Maybe she thought Hailey was cute and wanted to know her more. These were all the thoughts that were consuming her over the past day.

"Do you live around here Hailey?" She asked, snapping Hailey out of her thoughts.

"Oh, me, no, I live in Wicker Park, near the Damen stop. I chose this place because they have good pizza, and I wasn't sure where you lived so I picked something that was somewhat near to where you dropped me off." There was a slight pause, and she asked,

"Where do you live?"

"Lincoln Square, so I guess this is somewhat nearby,"

"Not really," Hailey said.

"No, not really," Bella said in response and they both started laughing. It felt easy to laugh with her, natural.

"Are you from Chicago?" Hailey asked.

"I am. I grew up in Lakeview."

"I'm ashamed to say that I'm from the burbs."

"Nothing wrong with the burbs, if you don't mind being bored."

They both laughed.

"You mentioned your mom was sick. What's wrong with her? Sorry, I mean, is she ok? You don't have to tell me if you're uncomfortable..."

"No, its fine. She has cancer. Ovarian Cancer, and it's bad. I'm not sure how long she has left."

"I am so sorry. I cannot imagine." Hailey thought of her own mom and how devastating it would be to lose her.

“And your father? I’m sorry, I’m being super nosy.”

“I don’t know my father. Never have. My mom said I was a “surprise baby.” I’m pretty sure it was a one-night stand. I know it sounds morbid, but once she’s gone, I really want to find him.”

“I don’t think that sounds morbid. Even though my dad can be a jackass I still love him. I think you should find him.”

They sat for a moment in silence.

"Well, now that I have my drink," she said shortly after the waitress delivered her beer, "Do you want to hear what I think about your story?"

"I guess it depends on what you have to say."

They both laughed again.

"I know, getting feedback as a writer is hard. But this is valuable feedback, trust me. Listen, you have a lot of talent. Is this one of the first stories you've written?"

"I've been writing for years but mostly auto fiction and the occasional poem. This is the first story I've written, the first piece of writing I put a lot of work into. The first piece of work I hope to publish."

Bella nodded and Hailey noticed her hands as they reached for her beer. They were strong, slender fingers, neatly trimmed. They looked soft and strong at the same time.

"Listen, the pacing is good, you write beautiful prose. The story is too simple, but your use of tension keeps me wanting more and more, until bam, that ending. It moved me. Your description of the falling out between the aunt and her niece was terrific. Where are you thinking of publishing this?"

Hailey was ecstatic that Bella hadn't seen her story in the Herald.

"I don't know, honestly I hadn't thought much of it until now. I was trying to workshop it and get feedback and direction, but I am still at a loss on what to do."

"Sometimes workshops can make the process even more confusing. Listen, there are a million ways to get published. Would you like me to run it by one of my professors? I think it's worth a shot and I know someone that might be interested in this style of literature."

"Oh, wow, that is unbelievably kind of you." Hailey felt despair inside of her knowing that she couldn't possibly let her show it to her professor right now. The odds of that person knowing about Dr. Loering or reading the Herald were too great.

"Can I think about it and let you know?"

Looking deep into her eyes Bella responded, "Yeah, let me know. I know it can be intimidating giving your work to other people. I trust this person. My credentials of Medill initially impressed you but now you've changed your mind?" She touched her lightly on the arm, "You can trust me. I only want to help you."

"Why?" Hailey asked, feeling a rush of warmth come over her from her touch. It was an electric feeling.

"Maybe because I have a feeling about you. Maybe I think you are the most beautiful woman I've ever seen in my life, and I haven't been able to stop thinking about you since I met you. Or maybe it's because I think you have raw talent..." Those were the words Hailey wanted to hear.

"Hailey? You there?" Bella asked waving her hand in front of her face.

"Sorry, I've been through a rough past few days, really, why do you want to help me?"

"I like your writing. And I like to help writers with promise get noticed."

"So I'm not your first?"

"That's an intimate question," she said melting her heart once again with the warmth of her smile.

– – –

Hailey was sitting on the sheik red couch in Gwyneth's apartment.

"My butt's numb, I need to stand up," Hailey said standing, stretching out.

"We need to do this Hailey. Let's get it over with, you've been practicing for hours. It's going to be about as perfect as it will ever be." Gwyneth dramatically sighed, stood and grabbed Hailey by the shoulders. "Let's do this. Let's bring him down. And then let's get some dinner. I'm starving."

"Shouldn't we run it by Jenna once to see what she thinks?

"No. We should not. You're not even talking to him tonight anyway. You're speaking with that twerp assistant of his, what's her name?"

"Annabelle."

"Right. Annabelle. She must be nuts to work for him. Besides, Jenna is doing enough. She's risking a lot for this story. Also, we don't know if anything will come of it," Gwyneth walked into the kitchen.

"Isn't that the same as any of her investigations?" Hailey mumbled quietly "Where are you going?" Hailey called, having a moment where the nervousness she felt dissipated.

"Just a minute," She yelled back. Hailey flopped back onto the couch and took a deep breath. Relaxation washed over her. A notepad sat on Gwyneth's coffee table. Hailey picked up a pen, "

"This is what friendship felt like, constantly being surrounded by butterflies...

Love always,

Hailey

She knew Gwyneth would see it and that thought made her smile.

On the coffee table before her was a glass of water and a joint. Hailey discovered that weed could help calm her anxiety. She picked her phone up. It was time. She lit the joint and dialed the number Jenna had given them.

After a few rings, "Hello". There could only be one voice tart and sweet at the same time.

Annabelle continued. Dr. Loering's assistant, can I help you?"

With a longer than normal pause Hailey started, "Hi, my name is Tyler, I'm a writer with the New York Herald."

"Who are you?" With an edgy on the border irritated tone.

"My name is Tyler, and I'm with the New York Herald." Shit, Hailey thought, my voice is too sultry sounding.

She cleared her throat. Trying to be more confident in a I went to Penn State, watched the stock reports, and own plenty of suit's kind of tone began her plea. "I happen to be in Chicago and was wondering if Dr. Loering was around for an interview. The thing is I only have Monday night. I'm finishing another assignment and I need to be back in New York on Tuesday. I begged my Editor to let me stay."

So far deafening silence from Annabelle.

I can do this, Hailey thought.
"I went to journalism school to get a chance to interview Dr. Loering. He's a personal hero. And I thought it'd be great timing considering the release of his new short story. I'm sure he already knows, but it's a masterpiece."

Still silence on the other end.

Hailey was running out of things to ask. "Monday night is it though, that's the only day I have."

"What's your name again"

"Tyler"

"Tyler what?"

Hailey was not prepared for a last name. She looked around Gwyneth's living room frantically. Pink, there was a lot of pink. No, I can't be Tyler Pink. Pink plush pillows, lilac accent throws. She saw the glass of water on the table. Outside an impatient car blared their horn The sound grew louder, until it passed.

"Tyler Carglass".

Another pause. "Huh, I haven't heard that name before. Are you new with the Herald?"
Good, Hailey thought. She sounds more curious than skeptical.

"Yes, I was an intern last year. I just started going out on my own assignments. My beat is environmental issues, but I'm a huge fan of Dr. Loering. I've read all his work, been to a bunch of his talks. I've even considered attending one of his famous workshops."

"Interesting. You have a press card you can email me with your credentials?"

"Sure, I can send it over after we get off the phone".

"Oh, well let me see. Dr. Loering never turns down an interview with the Herald. I'll check his schedule, hold on for a minute."

"Sure. A minute or two passed. Hailey couldn't be sure as she tried to anticipate any other questions that might come her way. Gwyneth made her way back into the room with a bowl of popcorn and a bottle of wine. Hailey glanced over at her and nodded.

She wished she had come up with a better name while she'd been waiting. Carglass? Annabelle popped back on the phone just as Hailey started to relax.

"I think he's available, I'll need to double check with him, but it looks like he's free that evening. Where are you and where did you want to meet him?"

"I'm in the Streeterville area and I'd like to meet him at a sushi restaurant in the area, Mira."

"Oh, well perfect. He isn't too far from there. Good choice, he'll be happy with that location."

"Great. Ok, after I get off the phone, I'll text my email. I need you to send the name and address of the place you want Dr. Loering to meet you. Also, send your credentials. Dr. Loering wouldn't mind seeing a recent article you have written. He likes to know who is interviewing him prior to the interview.

"Of course, he does" Hailey unintentionally said out loud.

"Excuse me?"

"I'm sorry, no problem. I'll send along all the requested materials. I'm happy he's available, it will be such an honor to sit down with the man."

"Alright, I'll send a confirmation once I speak to Dr. Loering. Before I let you go, we need to go over Dr. Loering's two rules. We tell this to all journalists. Rule number one: don't ever bring up Dr. Loering's past work. He doesn't want to talk about it. If you break this rule, you get only one more chance before he walks.

Rule number two: Don't call him by his first name unless he tells you it's ok. It's a respect thing. Can I trust you to follow these rules? Like you said, it's an honor to interview him."

Hailey struggled not to gag. Two stupid rules she wished she would have broken. It's not too late, she thought.

"Like I said, I've done my research on the man. I know all of this already. You're safe with me." Tyler was feeling more and more natural.

"Good. Be on the lookout for my confirmation and I'll be waiting for your information."

"You never told me your name."

"Annabelle."

"Pretty name Annabelle." There was a pause.

"Thank you, Mr. Carglass."

Hailey started to ask "Who?" But Annabelle had already hung up.

Gwyneth squealed, "You were amazing!" She ran over to Hailey throwing her arms around her.

"I think the secret to my success was smoking the joint," Hailey said smiling.

"Well, if that's the case we will no doubt have you ready for when you meet up with Dr. Loering."

Jenna walked up to her apartment, stood for a moment before turning the key. Self-doubt lingered in her mind. That was always there though, she thought. She loved her work because part of it was overcoming the doubt. Would this plan work? And really, how could they be sure they'd find anything? But she knew Dr. Loering had a lot to hide. She felt it in her gut. Her gut rarely proved her wrong. She walked inside and decided to make coffee and take a shower. The hot water felt surprisingly good on her body after walking in the cold, windy, city. She stood for a moment letting the water run over her body. The shower was a place where she felt like she could just be. There was no performance in the shower, nobody to catch. She was dreading checking in with her Editor. She knew she had to run this idea by him. She knew he would hate it. It was a lie, her being here. She said she needed time off to rest and get back on track. That was true. Before she left for her mental health which was not good. Maybe it was never good, but it was right at the sweet level where basic functioning was tough. She was suffering from burn out, she knew it. Yet, if she could just prove this one thing, she promised herself she would take a break. Maybe she'd take more time off, write a book. This time she felt serious about it. It was all talk before. She heard her phone vibrating as the water rushed around her. The spell was broken, and the familiar rush of anxiety crept up her body. Jenna turned off the water and stepped out of the shower drying off. She walked over to where she put her phone on the sink. There was a text from Hailey.

Meeting confirmed, I need credentials.

Jenna knew Annabelle would ask for that. She'd asked one of the assistants in her office she trusted to photoshop her credentials.

"What's your name?"

Jenna typed back.

Hailey: Tyler Carglass, we'll send a picture of him tonight.

Interesting name, Jenna thought. She called her assistant.

"Hello," he said, sounding tired. He was the least enthusiastic intern, it wasn't even clear why he was there, and for that reason, he was the most trustworthy. Jenna imagined him having two successful writers as parents who expected him to do the same. Or maybe he was doing this to piss his parents off.

"Hi Ronnie, I need some things from you. First, don't forget to check my mail when I'm out.

"Got it," he said with little enthusiasm.

"Next, I need you to look up some information and make something for me."

"Ok, what do you need?" Jenna could hear him eating what she knew was most likely an Italian beef.

Just as he was settling down to a hot cup of chamomile tea, Dr. Loering heard his phone. Since he was across the room from it, he pondered just letting it ring.

"Godamnit," he said quietly to himself.

"Why did I hire a goddamn assistant who can't pick up the goddamn phone."

Annabelle cleared out his schedule for a few days. He was tired. After 3 world tours in a row, he was tired. Tired of women, tired of hotel rooms, tired of talking. For months he dreamt about having the time to sit and read the New York Herald in peace. To have the choice of reading the Wall Street Journal sounded sublime. His life had been virtually nonstop since the first book became a hit. It was beginning to take a toll on him. He needed a break. After his new short story blossomed into a hit, he decided he needed a few days before facing what would inevitably be another round of readings, talks, and signings. He would enjoy a few days in his condo on the Gold Coast reading. Maybe he'd call up one of his lady friends in the area if he got bored and go out to dinner. The phone was still ringing, it paused for a moment and restarted. Then he remembered he told Annabelle to go home, he didn't want any distractions. This could be important; this could be Annabelle. With a loud sigh, he got up and moved across the room to the ringing phone. His dark brown corduroy pants made his movements feel stiff and restricted. Annabelle's name appeared on the screen.

“Yes, Annabelle" his voice answered in pure frustration

“Sorry to bother you on your time off Dr. Loering.

“Go ahead, what is it?”

“There is a New York Herald reporter who would like to interview you tomorrow evening. I know it's the last minute, but he finished an assignment in the area early and he had an extra night. He said it's been a dream of his to interview you."

"What's the guy's name?"

"Tyler Carglass. I received his credentials; he's legit although he doesn't have an online presence. I did receive a few of his articles though, he's good. Rising talent." Annabelle paused. She couldn't tell if he was pissed off or happy.

"I know you never turn down an opportunity to talk to the Herald."

Dr. Loering sighed. Annabelle was right, he never turned down an interview from the Herald. Yet, this guy was a no name. He straightened his turtleneck. Anyone who was writing for the Herald would eventually establish a name. Anyone writing for the Herald most likely had connections in high places or was especially talented. The guy probably wanted to interview Dr. Loering to rise in the ranks.

"You know I don't like being bothered on my off time." Dr. Loering grumbled.

"I know Dr. Loering. But I did this because I know it could work nicely for you to establish a relationship with a journalist earlier in their career. Then we can remind them, how they got their big start through you."

Still more pausing accompanied by a loud cough. Annabelle imagined him crouched on his paisley couch wearing one of his infamous brown turtlenecks.

"I promise, I vetted him enough that he won't be a stalker fangirl accusing you of all sorts of ridiculousness like Jenna Janders."

"Annabelle, does this kid know I don't want to talk about any of my past projects?"

"Of course, Dr. Loering".

And with that it was decided. "Send a car for me at 7 pm tomorrow. Make sure it's a Red SUV. You got me a blue one last time, and I like red. Also make sure you get a slow driver. I don't like going fast, especially on my time off. And you remind this NY Hearld guy, no talking about my past work. I will only talk about future projects. No goldarned questions about my family or personal life He needs to understand that we will talk about what I want and only what I want. If he needs pointers I would like to talk about my new story or my methods."

"The car will be there at 7."

Dr. Loering hung up. He was annoyed and excited. He hadn't planned an interview during his time off. This better be worth it. People were knocking non-stop on his door ever since all of his success. He walked over to the copy of the Herald with his new story in it. He picked it up, looking at his name in print, with the glowing review. That's what this was, success. That's what he was, success.

There were talks by HBO of it turning into a series. Maybe he'd get that young girl who gave him the idea to help him out with it, he thought as he walked to his bar and poured a glass of scotch. Hopefully she'd seen how he'd changed it and would learn from her own mistakes.

He set his paper down and poured a neat glass of Basil Hayden. The appeal of a younger, male reporter was too great. He needed the younger, male demographic. So far, his message was only resonating with a certain kind of female. Vulnerable, he thought. It's all the ones that were vulnerable. He seemed to attract that. He saw weakness all around him in the audiences he brought. He saw weakness everywhere. He looked at his Rolex. It was 5:30 PM. Time to go to the pub to read the Herald, he thought as he went to grab his large overcoat. Then he'd have a quiet dinner, alone. Being alone sounded more and more appealing these days. Maybe it was time to settle down, Dr. Loering thought as he stepped out into the cold, foggy evening.

Chapter 17

"Can I speak with you for a second? Kevin paused, "In my office."

"Sure," Hailey responded, thinking the worst. Maybe he caught her looking up personal things on her computer. Or Brock tattled on her. Brock seemed to take on an air of indifference to her this morning. Coworkers curiously looked at Hailey as she walked with Kevin back to his office. Gwyneth wasn't at her desk, which wasn't odd. Sometimes she didn't get in until 9:30. Kevin opened his door and motioned for Hailey to sit.

Hailey didn't come into his office often, gladly. His desk was a mess. There were papers everywhere. Piles of bills strewn around. Orange peels, and what looked like glasses that once held smoothies but now looked like a collection of green hairs. He sat down across from her and put his hands on the desk. She sat, trying to keep as neutral of a facial expression as she could.

"Let's get right to it. You know that I've been giving you more work."

"Oh really, I haven't noticed..." Hailey tried as hard as she could to sound authentic.

"Good. I like what you're doing. Your dad raised one smart girl. You must get your brains from him."

"I never really thought about it..."

"Well, you may need to plan on staying longer from now, because you're going to have more work."

Hailey felt sick to her stomach. She hated her work so much already.

"I'm giving you a promotion."

There was a pause while Hailey processed the information. "A promotion?" she asked in disbelief.

"Yes, effective tomorrow. You'll be Senior Level Three Manager Technical Assistant Secretary. You'll see the raise in your paycheck next pay period. Gwyneth will be transferring over files to you whenever she gets in today. Congratulations Hailey, you've done a good job."

"Thanks Kevin", she said, almost with suspicion. She knew she should be happy, but her job was joyless, the thought of more work seemed joyless, but it was an impossible situation. If she turned it down, she had no idea how he would retaliate. And no matter how little the raise was, it was money she needed. It was worth the fake enthusiasm.

"I suppose you can call me by my first name, since you're now Senior Level Three Manager Tech Secretary. Now off you go," he said in a way that Hailey couldn’t tell whether he was joking or not. She had been calling him Kevin the entire time she worked there.

"Will I be working with Gwyneth?" Hailey asked, standing, and walking toward the door as she heard his phone start ringing. He picked it up and she heard the first of a conversation with someone named Larry as he motioned for her to shut the door.

Hailey stood outside his door for a second. Not knowing how much her raise was made it hard to gauge how excited she should be, but it didn't matter. She never received a raise at work before. She took a deep breath and walked back to her desk and almost ran into Gwyneth who just arrived.

"Gwyneth," Hailey said, feeling uneasy. What would she think of this promotion? Hailey was certain that Gwyneth's title was the exact same thing. Hailey could feel her face coloring. It seemed unlikely Kevin would give them both the same job. Maybe Gwyneth was getting promoted too?

"Hailey," Gwyneth said, the warmth in her voice making Hailey forget any awkwardness that she might have felt in the moment. "So nice to see you, were you coming from the bathroom? My gosh, I fell asleep on the couch last night with a tub of Nutella, woke up and had no idea where I was. Did you ever see that documentary about that guy who killed every single one of his girlfriends? Then he'd dress in their clothes to be like them. He said he did it because he couldn't stand their success."

"Sorry I left so early," Hailey stammered.

"Oh, don't worry about it dear, I was so tired from doing your make up. You know, all this has me thinking again about what I want to do." She said as she put her jacket away and organized a few things on her desk.

"Gwyneth," Kevin, called from his office, "When you get settled, I need you to come in here."

'Right, I'll be just a minute." Gwyneth looked at Hailey and rolled her eyes. "I think he's mad at me for leaving early the other day," she whispered.

"Can we get lunch today? I have some news and we can discuss our plan,"

"Sure darling, I gotta get going." She blew a kiss to Hailey as she walked away. Hailey blushed as she walked back to her desk. For the first time since she bought the ticket to go to lunch with Dr. Loering she felt elation and a lightness to her step. She could really use the money this promotion was going to bring. Her parents' generosity always felt like the only way out of poverty. Writing seemed to be the only way out of her depression. Now she saw another path. The promotion could help her finances, friendship was the best kind of antidepressant.

"Yet," Hailey said under her breath sitting down in her cubicle, "I still hate my job."

"You hate what?" Brock said, standing behind Hailey, the usual smell of mothballs floating from his green and yellow argyle vest.

"Oh, um, I hate not getting these invoices in before they are due," she said knowing that even though Brock wasn't the brightest she probably wasn't convincing.

"You should always have your invoices in on time. It's important." Brock said in a confidence that disgusted Hailey.

"Did you hear about Gwyneth?" He asked and Hailey could smell coffee on his breath.

"Hear about what?" Hailey asked, uninterested anymore in whatever false rumor was going around.

"She's getting fired. She lied about where she was going the other day. I think Kevin's doing it right now."

"Shit." Hailey said, grabbing her jacket and walking back to Gwyneth's desk, thinking of how her feeling was opposite of how it used to be. For once she was looking for Gwyneth.

As she approached Gwyneth, she quickly saw that something was wrong. Gwyneth was gathering items on her desk.

"Should we go now?" Hailey said with caution, even though it was only 10 AM.

"Yes," she said grabbing her jacket and throwing a few of her things into her oversized purse. "More ready than I've been in a long time. It's time to leave this ivory tower of Kevin and his small pen"

"Do you want to talk about it?" Hailey asked as they walked to the elevator. Brock was staring them down with curiosity.

"Not right now."

"Hailey," Brock called, "I need to give you a new key card for your promotion..." The elevator door shut.

Gwyneth looked at Hailey.

"He's a real piece of work that Kevin. Years of harassing me and then he fired me. And you get a promotion?"

"Gwyneth, I had no idea, otherwise I wouldn't have taken it,"

Gwyneth interrupted, "I don't care. I'm out." She said, walking fast enough out of the building that Hailey struggled to keep up.

Hailey followed her from a safe distance, realizing the hurried pace was intentional.

"What did he say to you?" Hailey called after her, getting a few looks from a passerby.

"I was fired for lying to him and not taking my job seriously."

Hailey was stunned but she managed to mutter, "How? Why?"

The elevator came to a jolt at the 5th floor. An older man with a beard, dressed in jeans and a Grateful Dead t-shirt walked by holding a pizza.

"How did he come to that conclusion? That's a great fucking question. I thought I was a better actress. I could have won an Oscar for the compliments I gave that man's ego."

They both stopped, the sounds of blaring horns, ambulances in the distance enveloping them.

The man in the Grateful Dead T-shirt stood quietly eating a piece of pizza as Gwyneth continued, "Kevin told me I wasn't able to handle the workload of my current position. He was going to demote me. He also told me he found someone else to do my job for less money. I should have been recording him." Gwyneth said digging in her purse for what Hailey knew would be a joint.

Hailey also knew this situation was fragile. "What are you going to do?" She asked not knowing what else she could say. The Grateful Dead man turned to Gwyneth and said," How about a slice?"

"Don't mind if I do," Gwyneth said grabbing a slice of pepperoni pizza from his box.

"I don't know if you should eat that," Hailey nodded at him as she followed Gwyneth and her pizza. It was a warm, sunny Chicago day. Hailey was thankful for that, less complications for the evening tonight. Gwyneth was walking too fast for her to keep up.

"Gwyneth wait up," she called breaking into a small run.

Gwyneth turned around, "You haven't even asked how I am? You jumped right into what am I going to do rather than asking me how I am. Sometimes I think you don't give a shit about me at all. And I wonder why you even want to be around me, "Gwyneth said as Hailey watched the Grateful Dead man pass by them on the other side of the road.

"See," She said, "You're not even paying attention to me right now." She turned around and started to run away."

Hailey hadn't seen Gwyneth run before. She looked unnatural, her heels clacking on the pavement, barely avoiding all the cracks. Her arms were flailing. Hailey's first instinct was to run after her, but all the sudden the old man in the Grateful Dead T shirt was standing before Hailey with his pizza.

"You want a slice? I was going to ask you before, but you ran off before I could."

Hailey grabbed a slice and started stuffing it in her mouth. Maybe this was her defiance, against Kevin, Gwyneth's poor opinion of her. It tasted like the perfect distraction.

"I think she threw hers out in the trash when she was running away from you," Grateful Dead Man said as he grabbed what was the last slice out of the box and set the empty box on top of a trash can.

"Walk with me for a minute," I know where she's going, I see her often around here."

Hailey considered how crazy this guy was, but she didn't have a plan. If she couldn't find Gwyneth, her best plan was to go back to work.

"How do I know you aren't a murderer?" Hailey said as she started to follow him. Being murdered seemed like a decent alternative then going back to the office so Brock could gloat all day.

"How do I know you're not a murderer?" He responded back, not turning to look at her.

That was a good point, Hailey thought. He probably hadn't shaped an elaborate plan to disguise himself and break into a man's house to steal something. But Dr. Loering had stolen from other people, people like herself who lived with so little hope in world where nepotism and generational wealth were the most common markers of success. They were walking north towards what looked like a new-age Irish Pub. The kind with sleek bar tables, lots of Television screens and fancy versions of pub fare.

"This is it," The man pointed at the Irish Pub. "If you love her and cherish her friendship then do the right thing. There is nothing more important than family, nothing." He said walking away.

"Thank you," Hailey called after him, watching him as he disappeared around the corner. She paused for a moment before going in. She felt conflicted. Even though Gwyneth was fired Hailey was still hopeful that her promotion meant more money. But Gwyneth said that whoever was taking over this position made less than Gwyneth. Since Kevin hadn't mentioned a raise, Hailey wondered what the promotion really meant. Had she been duped? She walked in the door and Gwyneth was one of two people sitting at the bar, already drinking what looked like a vodka martini.

Hailey came behind her, "Gwyneth," she said softly. Gwyneth didn't turn around. "Gwyneth," she said loud enough that she knew she could hear her. Still, she didn't turn around. "Gwyneth," she yelled.

Gwyneth turned around, "Finally, that's the first time I've seen you put yourself out there in a real way."

"What is that supposed to mean?" Hailey said moving to sit down.

Gwyneth blocked her. "Seat taken," she said motioning to the door.

"I'm not interested anymore in someone who is self-absorbed. No matter what I feel, or how hard I try to be your friend, it doesn't matter because you don't think of anyone but yourself."

"Listen," Hailey said, trying to reach for Gwyneth's shoulder without any luck as Gwyneth pulled away, "I'm sorry. I'm sorry you got roped into helping me. I'm sorry that Kevin is such an asshole. I'm sorry you got fired. Please, I'm here and I'm going to listen."

"There's nothing to say about it," she snapped. "He fired me because I said I wouldn't take a lesser position. He's mad because he asked me out a few times and I said no."

Hailey touched her hand, noticing the bright red polish, immaculately done on her hands, "I am so sorry."

"It doesn't matter. I wanted an excuse to leave this job anyway, to start back into makeup. This is my chance and I'm going to take it, even if it means I'm going to be broke."

The bartender, who clearly knew Gwyneth, passed by Hailey several times, ignoring her presence. Probably all for the better, the drinking she had done as of late was catching up to her. She felt exhausted.

"I have some news, but I think it will... " Hailey said, knowing that she couldn't bring up Bella and their conversation the previous evening right now.

"You know what Hailey, I don't care about your plan, your story, your writing, or whatever it is you want from me or think you can get from me. Good luck with your new position and have fun working with Kevin."

"I don't care about Kevin..." She called after Gwyneth to no avail.

Gwyneth stormed out, leaving her drink half finished.

For a moment Hailey thought she might come back. Maybe she'd just gone out to smoke. But then, after several long pauses, Hailey realized that she was gone for good. Gwyneth, the only person she cared about was gone. The only person that could make her laugh. The only person she loved making laugh. She needed to fix things, but she didn't know how.

The phone rang five times before Kevin picked up.

"Kevin, who is this?

"Hi Kevin, it's Hailey"

"Hailey, where are you, I need you back here immediately to go buy notebooks for the whole office."

"Um, yeah don't we have someone else that can do that?"

"I'm asking you to do it."

"Ok, well, I'm calling to say that I don't feel good. It's something I ate at lunch, I'm sick and I need to go home and rest."

"Make sure to mark it on your timesheet Hailey. I'll see you tomorrow?"

"Kevin, before you hang up, you. never told me how much my raise would be?"

"Raise? I never said anything about a raise. I gave you a promotion. In your next paycheck you'll see that I'm not taking out money for office supplies. That should be enough, shouldn't it? Your old man covers your expenses anyway, doesn't he? At least that's what he told me the last time we met to drink."

"Enough, right. Thanks..." but before she could say anything else he hung up.

Hailey tried texting and calling Gwyneth over and over to no avail. She felt too heartbroken to be at work. But even with the heartbreak, Hailey felt somewhat refreshed after playing hooky and what she felt like was just enough energy remaining to deal with her parents.

She arrived earlier, hoping it would win some points from her mother who was clearly upset with her.

As she entered her suburban childhood home, the immaculate paint, absence of dust, sterile feeling, clean carpeting, neatly placed ornaments that were seasonally appropriate, pictures featuring her family and their forced smiles, a part of her felt like a foreigner walking into someone's home for the first time. This scene was far from what she experienced recently. She wondered if Bella would approve of her parents, and then quickly wondered why she cared if Bella would approve. With her streak of luck lately Bella would be best not knowing anything about her.

"Hailey," her mom called stepping into the foyer. "You're early," she said with more judgement than surprise.

Hailey followed her mom into the living room. "Well, your father won't be home for another hour, why don't you sit and relax. I'll brew some tea," she said walking away. Her mother was always doing something, Hailey thought as she went to sit down on the new leather couch her parents were overly excited to purchase. Her mom entered the living room holding a tray with cookies and tea. She sat the tray down and Hailey noted how even that was done with grace and thoughtfulness. Hailey imagined a life where she had the time to think of serving tea with grace as her mom settled into a leather armchair across from her.

"So, here you are. Your father won't be home for a while."

"You said that already Mom."

"Oh, did I? I suppose I have a lot on my mind. Your father and I have been extremely worried about you. In addition to that we've had a heck of a time with the contractor who is replacing our cabinets. I tell you; these days people just don't treat you with respect..."

"Mom, again, I'm sorry I missed dinner last week. I was busy and I completely forgot."

"Well, we weren't too busy to pay your bills. Your dad wasn't too busy either to have a conversation with your boss to smooth things over. Seems like you've been too busy to work as well."

Hailey was shocked. And although she hadn't read the Emily Post book her mom gave her, or had even forgotten about it, she was certain there was a chapter her mom was drawing her contempt from.

"Why is dad getting involved in my job? I don't need his help. And how would he know that I didn't work?"

"Your father got involved because Kevin reached out to him. I guess that some gentleman informed Mr. Kevin that you and a woman who is referred to as the "office slut" or something of that nature skipped out on work and lied about it. He wanted to let your father know he was going to have to fire you, but your dad worked out a deal with him. I don't know what's worse Hailey, you playing hooky or hanging out with the office slut. We are both very worried about you and..."

"First, the guy that told Mr. Kevin," Hailey said in condescending tone, "Is a boot licking ass kissing, sexually harassing, moth ball smelling, idiot," to which Hailey's mother gasped.

"Second, I'd rather be fired than have the promotion Kevin just gave me which includes more work with less pay."

"Third, Emily Post was a divorcee who became famous for her career in writing about etiquette."

Hailey's mother remained still, her face ashen, as the afternoon sun shone into the bay windows of the living room.

"I better leave now," Hailey said, realizing for the first time she'd rather be broke and jobless than have to sit through another one of her parent's awkward dinners discussing her broken love life and her dismal career prospects.

Hailey exited as quickly as she could, her mom still sitting, silent as she closed the door behind her gently.

There was only one place to go now, home. She felt exhausted as she climbed the stairs to her apartment. She got inside and threw her purse and keys on the table and went at once to the couch and laid down. She needed to contact Jenna, but she didn't have the energy right then. She felt so exhausted over the past week, anger, her fight with Gwyneth, the stress of work. She was sick of the dead ends of her life. Just as she was drifting off on her couch her phone buzzed. She slowly got up, dreading telling Jenna that all the work she put into their ruse was going to nothing. She rolled over and grabbed her phone.

Jenna: WHERE ARE YOU?

Hailey grabbed her phone and started to type that their scheme was off. It was over. Her life would remain in Kevin's hands doing three jobs for the price of one. Apparently, she'd also have to flirt with him and fluff his ego as well. As she was typing her phone started ringing. It was Gwyneth.

"Hello?" Hailey answered, trying not to sound too excited.

"Howdy," her voice came over the line. The sweet voice that smoothed everything over in an instant with its sweetness.

"I was just about to let Jenna know that the plan is off..."

Gwyneth interrupted her, "Hailey, I was really mad at you, I really was. I don't need shitty people in my life. But then I realized, you aren't really shitty, you're just a loner, an only child, you're kind of pathetic you know?"

Hailey laughed, "Yeah, I know... Listen Gwyneth, I hope you know that I care more about you than I do about any of this. I was empty when you met me, devoid of really caring about anything, maybe because I didn't know what it felt like to have a real friendship. I've had so few of them. Our friendship is more important than anything at this point in my life. Writing, my fake promotion..."

“I told you he wouldn’t give you a raise.”

“You were right. Listen, why don’t we skip the plan, maybe the best revenge is no revenge, we can move on with our lives...”

"Absolutely not. You're not taking away my chance to turn you into a hot male journalist. Come down to The Drake, I got us a room to prepare."

"I love you too Gwyneth, you're like the sister I never had.

"I love you too girl."

“So the Drake, huh?" Hailey asked.

“Yeah, it's close to where you're having dinner with Dr. Loering and if I'm doing your makeup and costume, I don't want any of the elements messing with it. It's supposed to rain later."

"Gwyneth, you didn't have to," but she was immediately interrupted by Gwyneth again. "Listen, I forgive you. I want to help you do this, if not for you, for all the others he might fuck over. Plus, I'm certain with my skills we can trick him, we can do this. Hurry up Sugar, we have a lot to do before dinner. Jenna just got here. Room 809, just come up." With that she hung up.

Hailey didn't waste time, grabbed her purse, jacket, and left for The Drake.

Chapter 18

Gwyneth painstakingly put makeup on Hailey for dinner with Dr. Loering. An outfit was picked out especially for the occasion of being a journalist meeting a famous author out for dinner.

"Where did you get this suit?" Hailey asked, pointing to the grey Kenneth Cole suit hanging up.

"One of my exes was a skinny hipster. I broke up with him because he wouldn't shave off his mustache. He listened to Bright Eyes. That and the fact he couldn't fit into my jeans was too much. He left in a hurry, leaving his suit and a bunch of his records behind in an emotional outburst.

"That doesn't sound like your type," Jenna observed as she watched Gwyneth adjusting the wig onto Hailey's head.

"That's because he wasn't my type, I bought the wig at Macy's on my way here. I decided you are going to have a Shepard Smith kind of look."

"Good choice," Jenna said.

Gwyneth pinned up Hailey's hair and was struggling to put the wig in place so it would cover her face and look natural.

"Fancy, but not too fancy for a skinny hipster," she said looking over at the suit. Hailey and Jenna looked at each other and started laughing.

"No laughing right now honey," Gwyneth said to Hailey. "You'll mess up my work." She glanced at Hailey in the mirror. The hotel suite had a bigger bathroom than Hailey had ever seen in her life, complete with a golden footed tub.

"Good thing you don't have to worry about facial hair," Gwyneth brushing her hands down Hailey's cheeks.

"I've heard Dr. Loering criticize facial hair on more than one occasion, clean shaven will come off as credible to him," Jenna said.

"Credibility," Hailey said, "let's practice my story. I was a journalist major at Northwestern's Medill School of Journalism."

"What else do you do in journalism?" Jenna said in a condescending tone, noticed the look of dismay on Hailey's face, "I'm not going to be easy on you, because he won't be either."

Hailey started off in her normal voice, "The subjects that have interested me are communities around UFOs...oh, excuse me," she said lowering her voice.

"Evangelical Christians, CraigsList and country-rock music (think Hank Williams III)," Hailey rolled out.

Gwyneth paused and stared, stunned at Hailey. "Where did you come up with all that?"

"Oh, and here's the final one," Hailey continued, I have a podcast on unsolved crimes on the Northside that is in post-production. I'm here to follow up on some leads before heading back to the place I live now, New York."

"Do you have a girlfriend? Or boyfriend?" Jenna asked with a slight smile.

"I'm into women. With work I haven't had much time. The last girl I dated cheated on me, so I don't have much faith in love now. I had a hard time recovering, I spent all last summer drinking beer, wondering what to do with my life. Then, when I went back to school, I realized I didn't need a woman, I started my internship at the New York Herald, and I haven't looked back since."

Hailey realized she enjoyed being Tyler the journalist. She never thought of becoming a journalist, but she started to realize it was a career that could suit her.

Gwyneth chimed in," Who do you admire as a journalist?"

"Well Jenna Janders of course. Her writing has helped millions of abuse victims. She's always working on groundbreaking cases. And she isn't too bad to look at either," Hailey said winking.

Jenna was laughing as she said," I trust you know not to say that."

"Finished," Gwyneth let out a sigh of relief as she put a final pin to hold Hailey's wig in place.

Hailey didn't recognize herself in the mirror. She looked like a young, handsome, professional journalist. If Dr. Loering wanted to press her on her gender, she could tell him that it was a topic that she wasn't comfortable discussing and leave the guessing up to him.

Hailey glanced at the clock. It was getting close to the time that Jenna and Gwyneth needed to leave to perform their part of the plan.

"You two better leave," she said looking around for a glass of wine to loosen her nerves.

"Jenna, I need to change quickly into my outfit but then I'm ready," Gwyneth called as she walked into the bedroom.

She emerged a few minutes later wearing a black shirt, skirt, and jacket. Only Gwyneth could make what was supposed to be a delivery costume look stylish.

"I'll grab the sushi and drinks and let's go."

"I'll go get my car out of the garage."

"Hailey, I mean Tyler Carglass," she said taking Hailey by the shoulders, when you are interviewing him don't forget who you are. You're an accomplished journalist that went to Northwestern, a school that Dr. Loering couldn't get into."

"Where did he go to school?"

"DePaul, although that's information he likes to keep secret."

"I'm scared he'll ask questions about New York, the only time I've ever been there was when my grandma took me to see Phantom of the Opera."

"While you're waiting to meet him look up more information about New York. I doubt he'll ask you anything about your knowledge of the city. He'll want to know about your writing and how you will help his image. Keep calm and try to keep him for at least an hour. That should give us plenty of time to get in and out. Well, plenty of time for me to get in and out. Gwyneth will be waiting and watching. Good luck, and like I said, don't forget who you are. You're a writer."

Hailey smiled nervously at her, "Good luck to you too. I hope you get that hard drive. I hope we can take down the lying, cheating, bastard."

Jenna nodded, "Gwyneth, I'm leaving, are you coming?"

She looked at Hailey and grabbed her by the shoulders. "You can do this. I believe in you."

"Thank you, Gwyneth." Hailey wanted to say more but she needed to be Tyler. Tyler Carglass. An up-and-coming journalist who was about to interview one of the most famous men in the world.

As she gave one final glance in the mirror, she thought about her change in luck. Meeting Jenna had turned around her summer. She was everything Hailey wasn't. She never thought about being a journalist, but the rush she was getting from this was more exciting than anything she felt before. Hailey wanted to be as cool as Jenna was under pressure. Jenna was the opposite of her.

She dedicated her life to a higher purpose, finding truth and justice. Hailey was starting to realize that finding the truth was her drug as well.

Then there was Gwyneth, who Hailey realized was a friend who would always stand in her corner. Hailey knew enough to know how rare that was. How special. She smiled thinking of all Gwyneth's endearing quirks, realizing how far she had come from believing that Gwyneth was the office floozy, to a strong, talented person, looking to find her own way in the world.

It was time to head to the restaurant. Hailey exited the bathroom.

Tyler entered the room. He didn't want anything to throw his credibility to Dr. Loering off. He had credibility. He was an intern for the Herald... He had a podcast in the works. He smoothed his shirt. Thankfully his suit fit and didn't look ridiculous, even with his skinny somewhat curvy frame.

Tyler turned around, he looked good. His hair looked professional, he just needed to shine up the scuffs on his shoes and find a notepad and pen. He lit up a joint (for relaxation) then grabbed a Kleenex to polish and a pen a notepad that was left on a table. Glancing at the clock he knew that he was getting close to being late. With relative urgency he wiped and shined his shoes. He wanted to arrive earlier than Dr. Loering feeling it was a power move. It would give him an edge to know his surroundings. There was a beautiful view from the room, the sun was lowering in the sky and reflecting long drawn-out shadows to people walking to their fates below. He zoned out for a moment, forgetting the joint in his hand, then left the hotel room, looking one last time to soak in his newly formed lifestyle.

He exited the hotel and scanned the street to make sure Dr. Loering hadn't arrived. Tyler figured he'd get a car service. It looked clear so he ran inside the restaurant. His tried ignoring his overexcited nerves. He walked inside. He was here to interview the famous Dr. Loering, his idol.

Gwyneth was nervous as she pulled up to Dr. Loering's front door. She thought to herself, all I'm doing is delivering sushi to a man. She'd be happy to see Dr. Loering go down. As someone who worked in the arts Gwyneth knew how hard it was to put yourself out there, and to have your work stolen like he stole Hailey's was her worst nightmare. She had a hunch this guy was a creep the first time he saw a video of him giving a talk. The audience was full of insecure, vulnerable women. Maybe she noticed it because that was what she had been before she started to pursue her dreams.

She parked her car. Jenna was busy typing away on her phone. Sitting for a moment she looked down at her outfit. Different from her usual dresses, a drab one. Luckily this was a one-off outfit she thought. She took a long hit from her pen. It calmed her nerves. Gwyneth glanced in the mirror to make sure her hair wasn't all over the place. Feeling good about her appearance and state of mind she opened the car door and grabbed the paper bag of food sitting in the passenger side seat. She looked over and nodded at Jenna.

"Wish me luck."

"Good luck, remember, you're only delivering sushi. Pretend it's just a customer."

"I got this darling," she said to Jenna, flashing a smile.

When she went to grab the paper bag containing the food the bag ripped. One of the food containers poured out all over her car seat.

“Shit, that’s a big fucking mess”.

She scanned the area all around her.

"Do you have napkins in there?" Jenna said frantically.

They began to pick up the mess of sushi. Little bits of rice were stuck to the seat. They did the best they could to make the rest of the order look ok.

"If the plan goes right, you won't get as far as showing the sushi to him anyway," Jenna said dabbing at a stain of soy sauce on her seat.

"We need to let Hailey, or Tyler, know that we are here."

"You can call her Hailey, since we know the plan" Jenna said as she started to get out of the car.

“Right, "Gwyneth grabbed her phone and texted her,

“here”

The plan was on.

"I'm going to run into the gate and hide behind some bushes nearby. Don’t look for me though, he might be watching.” Jenna said and with that she was gone.

“Ok,” Gwyneth said to herself.

She grabbed the containers of food putting the appetizer of edamame on the top. The edamame looked a little soggy and brown. Hopefully Dr. Loering wouldn't notice that either. Gwyneth said out loud as she shut her car door, glancing one last time at the rice now embedded into her passenger seat

"Hey Dr. Loering, here is your brown edamame with a side of car seat sushi," Gwyneth said out loud as she shut her car door.

Her heart was thumping in her chest as she approached the front door. There was an ornate knocker on the door. Dr. Loering's home wasn't the sprawling mansion she imagined. A little larger than the other homes in the neighborhood, it was basic looking. Probably a few bedrooms but nothing fancy. Gwyneth wondered why Dr. Loering would choose such a basic place when he obviously had a ton of money. It was almost like Dr. Loering didn't want to stand out or be noticed.

She took a deep breath and reached up for the ornate knocker and knocked. There was no movement. No door to answer. She knocked again, trying to make it louder. After a minute she heard movement coming towards the door. Gwyneth took a moment to take stock in the moment. She was at some famous guy's house, delivering sushi he didn't want, higher than she should be, with a reporter hiding in the bushes ready. She saw the doorknob turn, she took one last time to straighten her hair and shirt with the hand that wasn't holding the food.

As she straightened her hair, she lost her balance and began to fall towards the ground. She lost grip on all the food she was holding in one hand, and it slipped from her hand, the flimsy plastic containers landing and spilling all over her pants. As Dr. Loering opened the door, she was covered in a mediocre four course sushi dinner.

"Well, it's not every day you open your door to some girl covered in sushi. What are you doing here?"

“No sir, I was ordering, I mean I was delivering your food," Gwyneth said in the sweetest voice she could conjure.

“Food, what food? What is this some kind of practical joke? He looked like a powerful troll standing over her. His power in person made Gwyneth feel like she could crumble, something typically no man had the power to do.

"No, sir, it’s not a joke, I have an order to deliver this sushi (as she pointed to her body) to this address.

"What is this address?" Dr. Loering said in an irritated voice.

Dr. Loering was much shorter than Gwyneth had imagined. He had a turtleneck on which showed his muscles. She was close enough that she could smell Dr. Loering’s cologne. His teeth were less than perfect, his eyes brown, beady, and darting around angrily. This was the man that millions of women were obsessed with?

"65 East Goethe Street" Gwyneth said, hoping that was an address nearby.

“You’ve got the wrong house. You look sort of pathetic standing there covered in all this food and I wouldn't be surprised if you get fired for making this kind of mistake.”

Dr. Loering stood for a moment scanning the mess on Gwyneth. She could see that deep inside a small speck of empathy was churning in Dr. Loering. The guy had a heart however small it might be, and she needed to play on it. She looked as pathetic as she could, trying to wipe some of the embedded soy source off her black blouse.

With a loud sigh Dr. Loering gave in to what might have been the last remaining speck of empathy within him, “Hold on, I’ll go get you some paper towels to wipe off that junk all over you. Then I want you out of here, this is private property.”

As Dr. Loering walked away he could hear him swearing.

"Goddamn son of a bitch girl coming onto my property trying to pull some sort of joke about sushi on me…"

His ranting faded as he walked further into the house. The door was slightly ajar. Gwyneth looked around frantically. This was the only opportunity for Jenna. Suddenly she saw her emerge from the bushes and start sprinting towards the door. She was dressed in all black, and unrecognizable, which was good. They expected security cameras on the premises. As she got closer, she put her finger up to her mouth.

"Be careful" she mouthed brushing by her and entering his house.

Gwyneth nodded, she wasn't sure what she was nodding for, but she knew he would go to great lengths to make sure Jenna was ok. She wouldn't let this short, turtlenecked, man hurt her.

Now with Jenna inside, Gwyneth couldn't hear where she went, and still no sign of Dr. Loering. She had lost the audibility of Dr. Loering's cussing. It was chilly outside, and the soy sauce had started to mingle with the sweat accumulating on Gwyneth's forehead and back. She stood soaked in soysweat. As she stood there, waiting for the jagged toothed man to return she recalled the one hitter in her pocket. She looked down, there were bits of crushed tuna roll, dragon roll and a California roll laying all around him. "Fishy", she said out loud as she reached into her pocket and grabbed her pen. She inhaled, pulling the smoke into her lungs, and holding it for a moment. Exhaling slowly a huge puff of smoke, she looked up and Dr. Loering was standing right in front of her.

"Now you're smoking up on my property stoner girl? Get the hell out of here before I call the cops on you" he said as he threw one single paper towel at him.

One paper towel? Gwyneth said as she scrambled towards her car. “I’m sorry” she called. "I use weed for anxiety." He was watching Gwyneth get into her car as he ranted, loud enough for Gwyneth to catch, “God damn kids these days just want to smoke up and cause trouble, get out of here before I do something I regret.”

Gwyneth heard Dr. Loering’s voice increase in volume as he said, “something I regret." He got into his car fumbling around for his keys. Where are my keys? “Shit. I’m high and I lost my keys.” It’s the situation that every stoner fears, she thought. She started to search for the car seats, looked above under his mirrors even though he never left them there. Dr. Loering was still standing at his door yelling at him.

“Lady, I swear, if you aren’t off my property in 10 seconds, I’m going to go get my gun and escort you off.”

Dr. Loering was getting serious with his gun talk. Or presumably he had a gun, which sent chills down her spine. She frantically looked around the glovebox, backseat... She was just about to give up and start running when she realized that the keys were in the ignition already. Without time to even feel relief she started the car, put it in reverse, and slammed the accelerator. She pulled into the street without even looking to see if there were any cars coming. She was out, Jenna was in. She reached into her center console to grab a joint. At a stop sign she scanned the labels. Franz’s Nightmare (Sativa, Indica Blend), Sizzle’s Junkyard (high THC Sativa), or Louis CK’s Comeback (Indica, lower THC). She chose the Comeback. Taking a giant she turned onto LSD, the orange sun sinking in the sky as she trolled the neighborhood looking for a place she could park.

Chapter 19

Jenna was crouching inside of the closet in Dr. Loering's house. Her heart was pounding so loud she worried that Dr. Loering might hear it. There was nothing she could do about it. Breathe she thought, breathe. That's all you need to do, air in the lungs, air out. You will survive this. Awhile back she had heard Dr. Loering cussing out Gwyneth. He came back swearing to himself.

"Piece of shit godamn no good son of a bitch woman. Where do these people come from? Why do women always harass me? I'm so fucking sick of these godamned crazed females trying to get into my space."

Then complete silence for a minute.

“Godamnit. Where's the turtleneck for tonight? I thought Annabelle left it out. And where are the paper towels?”

Clearly Dr. Loering was in a mood and anxious about his upcoming interview. Jenna wished she had more time to prep Hailey. She was a smart, but Dr. Loering was a tough interview even for the most seasoned reporter.

It had been a while since Dr. Loering had come back in the hallway and it seemed he was somewhere on the opposite end of the house from the diminished sound of his swearing and complaining. It was time for her to move. Hiding in his jacket closet was too much of a risk. It as Chicago, most people would wear a jacket. But here was a man who lived in turtlenecks. Jenna wouldn’t be surprised if he slept in them. She had never seen Dr. Loering without a turtleneck. Not once. Every picture of him on the internet was in a turtleneck. She wasn’t sure of the layout of his house, but the next time he swore she would run in a direction that would hopefully keep a distance. A minute or two passed and Jenna heard a bang.

“Godamnit. Fuck. Fuck. Fuck, my foot...” He howled like a wolf.

She left the closet and ran towards the middle of the house. As she was running, she noticed portrait after portrait of Dr. Loering on the wall. He's so full of himself, she thought as she entered what looked like his kitchen. There was a walk-in pantry, without much thought, she ran inside, quietly shutting the wicker door. The odds of him having a snack before he went to eat were lower than him grabbing a jacket, hopefully. She could hear his swearing growing in distance. Safe for now, she thought. As her eyes adjusted to dark in the pantry the slits of light shone onto what were cans on the shelves. Looking closer she realized they were kidney beans. Cans and cans of different assortments of beans. Kidneys, pinto, Lima, garbanzo. The man liked beans.

His swearing paused. Silence rang throughout the house. After what seemed like an eternity, she heard footsteps coming in her direction. Would he want a can of beans before he went to dinner, she thought frantically, cowering back as far as she could into the pantry. He came into the kitchen humming a song. Jenna recognized Phil Collins, *Invisible Touch*, and then felt fear creep into her skin. Holding her breath, she stood still as she could without her limbs going numb. She wanted to be prepared to run if she had to.

He searched around the kitchen drawer, opening drawer after drawer, humming away. He stopped right in front of the pantry. He was so close she could hear him taking breaths while he continued to hum *Invisible Touch*. Pins and needles were shooting into her limbs, she needed to move soon.

If she moved, she took the chance of hitting something and making noise. He continued opening other drawers. Finally, it seemed he found whatever he was looking for and left the kitchen. She heard *Invisible Touch* fade away into another area of the house.

Even though it seemed he was in a different area of the house Jenna still waited a moment before shifting her body. Fear was begging to overtake her. She reminded herself why she was here in the first place. It wasn't just about Dr. Loering's stealing Hailey's work. It was about women being consumed by his message. Wasting their money on his phony methods, being drugged, and brainwashed to think he was a god. This was her life's work.

All the sudden Jenna heard the front door open. A few moments later she heard a car door. Then nothing. It seemed like he left. She would wait a few minutes longer to make sure he didn't forget anything, then she would begin the search for his hard drive.

Tyler looked around the restaurant. He wanted a table away from other people, he didn't want Dr. Loering to be recognized. There was a large main room in the place, then a side room that seemed empty. A guy approached Tyler, tall and muscular, maybe a guy Tyler would notice, and think was attractive if he wasn't so damn nervous. His name tag said Jeff.

“Hey man, how are you doing? Do you have a reservation this evening?"

"Yes," Tyler said, wondering if his voice would throw him off. "Under Tyler Carglass".

Seeming unfazed Jeff looked on a piece of paper at the front stand, "Right here, we have a table for two," he said grabbing menus.

"Could we have something private? My companion is hard of hearing."

Jeff looked around, "I've got the perfect spot for you, follow me."

Jeff was dressed all in black, his black shirt undersized. Tyler had a hunch it was to show off his muscular upper body. His dark hair was heavily gelled back. He reeked of cologne and Old Spice deodorant. He led Tyler to the back of the restaurant which was entirely empty.

"Here you go dude, hope this works," he said laying the menus on the table. Then he paused as Tyler settled into his seat. "You look like a dude who knows what's up. Can I share something with you?"

The Hailey inside of Tyler couldn't believe it. It was rare that anyone would randomly strike up a conversation with her in this way.

"Sure bro," Tyler said in a tone that seemed unconvincing but seemed to work on Jeff.

“Bro, look at this guy, Dan Bilzerian, dude, he is the man. You've heard of him, right? I want more than anything to be this guy someday” He took his phone out and was scrolling through pictures of a muscular douchebag who had a lifestyle of a muscular douchebag. Dan Bilzerian, the tall, dark haired, white man, with a beard that you can't tell is ironic or not, built of pure muscle. A lifestyle influencer for the white privileged man to see what the opus could be. Lots of thin waisted, perfectly bronzed, big breasted women. These idyllic douchebag trophies holding guns, posing in exotic looking places. Mostly tropical places. But there was a string of photos where he was surrounded by beautiful looking girls dressed in Christmas attire, standing in the middle of the street in a city somewhere European looking.

"Wow, yeah this guy is pretty amazing." Tyler said, feeling conflicted and a freedom in her character at the same time.

“It looks cold though, like put some clothing on, right?” Tyler said, immediately realizing that it wasn't something. Tyler wouldn't have necessarily said. Jeff's face fell. "Yeah, I guess you know, being out in the cold, that would kind of suck. But look at the tits on those women. And look at this, Jeff said as he scrolled through pictures. There were five pictures in a row of hot women watching Dan as he wrote what he tagged as his autobiography.

“Yeah, the manosphere is pretty entertaining but it's not really my thing. Could I order...” Jeff interrupted Tyler scrolling through another series of posts.

“Did you see Candyman's new post? Man, that guy is so rad..."

“Jeff," Tyler said, hoping to gain control of the conversation, "Tonight, if possible, can you keep our table under a low profile? I'm meeting this guy for an interview, and he is a little skittish. I don't want to scare him off."

“Yeah, no problem, man, I get it. I 100% get it. One time we had Rahm Emmanuel come in here and everyone was freaking out, he's real short in person, did you know that? He's gotta use his mouth to make up for his size I bet,” Jeff said laughing at his own joke.

Hoping to reign in the conversation again, Tyler responded with a slight hint of irritation, “No, I didn't know that. Thank you, Jeff, listen, I appreciate the extra effort. I'll make sure that extra effort is reflected at the end of the night.”

“I got you man”.

Tyler looked around nervously. Dr. Loering would be there any moment. Jeff was so loud and obnoxious; he didn’t want him to repel Dr. Loering.

“What can I get you to drink man?”

“Jameson neat.” It was the most masculine drink he could think of something Uncle Frank loved to drink on Christmas morning.

“Jameson neat coming up sir,” Jeff said as he whisked away.

Tyler rolled his eyes at the “sir”. There was a high probability Jeff was going to piss of Dr. Loering. Tyler took a deep breath, settling into his chair. Even though it was cool out, with all the makeup and his increasingly itchy wig he felt moist with sweat. He hoped to be cool and collected by the time Dr. Loering got there. He started studying the menu and. As he was adjusting himself to get comfortable the rubber cushion on his chair made what sounded like a loud fart. Tyler looked up, embarrassed. Dr. Loering was standing in front of him.

“Tyler Carglass?”

Tyler stood up, eyes wide, face most likely beet red under all the makeup, and shook Dr. Loering’s hand. He was surprised again at how short the man was. He was wearing a brown turtleneck with black corduroy pants. Never one for fashion, he thought.

“Yes, excuse me, I was just adjusting my chair, there. Dr. Loering, the one and the only, he said, motioning at the seat across from him. What a pleasure. Please, take a seat, he said as he sat down himself, eyeing him with suspicion. Tyler hoped the chair wouldn't make another uncouth noise again as she sat herself.

"Thank you so much for joining me this evening. As Annabelle probably told you I am a huge fan of your work."

"Yes, she did mention that." Dr. Loering settled into his chair, staring intensely at him. He picked up the wine menu. Tell me Tyler, what assignment brought you into this area? And how did you find out I was around?"

Inwardly, Tyler rolled his eyes. He was already starting with the tough questions.

Tyler cleared his throat. "A murder. A murder and kidnapping brought me down here. Unfortunately, I can't share the details yet. You'll have to read about them when my piece comes out."

"Where can I read that? Because that is the interesting thing, Mr. Carglass, I looked for your name online and I couldn't find one single piece that you have written."

"Oh, you wouldn't be able to," he said in the most confident male tone he could muster. "This is my first assignment as a reporter. I was recently hired by the New York Herald. I have been an intern for about two years now."

"I see. Well, you must work with other journalists on assignment. Who did they have you under?"

"As an intern I'm not at liberty to talk about which journalists I helped out. I am under an NDA," Tyler offered, hoping that would suffice, "So unfortunately I can't disclose that information."

"Ok. Between me and you, who is your favorite writer?"

Jeff appeared, ready to take the drink order. Tyler felt overjoyed to see Jeff in all his muscular, manosphere glory.

“How are you two doing this evening?”

“Fine, just fine,” Tyler said quickly.

“Can I get you anything to drink, Sir? Jeff said looking at Dr. Loering.

“I will have a glass of the Petrus, oh heck, why not bring a bottle. You’ll have some, won’t you? Dr. Loeing said glancing over at Tyler.

"I ordered a whiskey, but I'll take a glass with my dinner."

Jeff nodded. “Very well then, a bottle of Petrus. I’ll be right back with that.”

Tyler was impressed with Jeff's professionalism and thankful that he had played it cool even though he most likely had recognized Dr. Loering. He was also thankful that he hadn't gone into different idols he had in the Manosphere.

“Back to our conversation, please do, enlighten me on who your favorite writer is at the New York Herald? Surely there was someone who inspired you to work there. Someone you looked up to.”

“I suppose." (Hailey didn't read the Herald. She didn't really watch the news). Tyler stalled a moment, taking a sip of his whiskey, trying to look mysterious and confident. "But the person who has inspired me most is sitting right in front of me. And that is who I want to talk about this evening.”

“Oh well, Annabelle did mention to you that I do not speak of any of my past work, right?”

Tyler flashed what he hoped was a winning smile. “I’m not here to talk about your past work Dr. Loering. I’m here to get to know you.”

“For what reason?”

“I’ve read every article about you and every book by you Dr. Loering. It’s no secret that I am a huge fan. But I know nothing about the real Dr. Loering. What your day to day looks like for example. Do you drink coffee when you wake up? What does your process look like?”

“I’ll stop you right there. I don’t talk about my process because it is my process. I don’t share personal details with others.”

“Is that right? Are you afraid someone will steal your success?” Tyler responded, restraining himself as much as possible. (It was the exact trite answer Hailey expected from him. He was entirely predictable with his spindly little ego).

“Not at all. The success I have speaks for itself. I don’t feel comfortable speaking about my process because it’s *my process*. Mine.” He cleared his throat loudly as if to make the final point.

“I just find it odd there is virtually nothing about your personal life. With such a high profile, it’s a little odd...”

Thankfully Jeff came up to the table and began his wine presentation. Sensing the uncomfortable atmosphere, he began to list the specials of the evening. Tyler wasn’t listening. He was thinking of how to steer the conversation away from his job at the New York Herald and to keep it on a man who could qualify as the most elusive member of the Manosphere. He now understood Jenna’s fascination with interviewing him. He hid everything and gave very little. It was suspicious. What harm could it do to share his process?

Jeff had finished opening the bottle and giving Dr. Loering a taste. He began to pour wine into Hailey's glass, then Dr. Loering's.

“Could we please hear the specials for this evening? I feel indecisive." Tyler asked again abruptly before Jeff walked away.

Jeff started rattling off a bunch of overpriced items that sounded embellished as Tyler felt satisfied in his efforts to bide time.

“Classy”, Dr. Loering mumbled under his breath.

“Thank you, Jeff. I think we need a moment to look over the menu.”

“Of course, sir. I'll give you a few minutes.

As Dr. Loering swirled his wine, “Tyler Carglass. Interesting name by the way. So, I really am dying to know, who is your favorite writer at the New York Herald? Perhaps you have just about as much knowledge about your fellow colleagues as you do about dining out."

“Excuse me?”

“Your choice of this place? Why did you choose this spot? Did you do any research? At least they have decent wine, I bet this bottle is worth more than your apartment.”

Tyler knew this comment was meant to get under his skin, but it didn't matter. Tonight, was on his “company”. Payment had already been arranged by Jenna knowing ultimately that Tyler would be stuck with the bill.

“I looked up places that were close to the hotel I'm staying at, but as a matter of fact, Annabelle suggested this.”

“Annabelle, yes. Indecisive and forgetful, she sounds a little like you. You see," Dr. Loering said, moving his body closer to Tyler to a point where it felt uncomfortable..." It’s just that, for being an up-and-coming journalist you seem to fall short on your research. Except, perhaps when it comes to knowing the server’s name.”

“He introduced himself to me before you arrived.”

“Interesting, he didn’t feel the urge to tell me his name. I suppose I come off as intimidating. I’m not sure why." He tapped his fingers on the table.

“I don’t seem intimidating do I, Tyler?”

Tyler felt that this interview was wildly spiraling out his control. Dr. Loering was suspicious, and they hadn’t even ordered their entrees yet. He needed to diffuse the conversation, take him off the subject of his experience.

“Let’s cheers to being here, together in Chicago, me, an up-and-coming writer, sitting with you, a world-renowned genius. Your methods inspired so many women. Dr. Loering. It is an honor.”

Dr. Loering held up his glass, not breaking eye contact with Tyler for one moment.

“Well thank you Tyler. I aim to inspire *people,”* he said with an emphasis. “But cheers, thank you for inviting me out. You know I’m weary of interviews, but when Annabelle mentioned that you were newer at the New York Herald I made an exception. I thought perhaps you could be someone that would finally get my story,” he paused to take a drink of wine, “right.”

“Why don’t we start with how your story is wrong?” Tyler asked, feeling relief, if he was getting somewhere or at the very least preventing him from walking out the door.

Dr. Loering cleared his throat loudly again. A woman from a nearby table looked over in his direction. Tyler was hoping this woman wouldn't notice Dr. Loering.

"The wrong story about me. The wrong story. I'll start with this. Nobody knows how to interview anymore. They think that it's interesting to talk about what made me famous. They want to know how I got where I am. They want a piece of my fancy writer lifestyle. Traveling the world, several houses, cars, all the money one could imagine. For simply using my brain. For once, for once, I'd like someone to ask me questions that dig into unrealized projects of mine. I get so sick and tired of talking about what made me, rich. I am just doing my life's work. I don't want to talk about it. I want to talk about what's next, what I can do, not what I have done."

Dr. Loering took another large drink of his wine. Tyler noticed a faint red stain forming on his lips.

"That's fascinating. You don't want to revisit past work because you are searching for your future work, is that what I am hearing? Are you struggling with ideas for a new book? It has been a while, hasn't it? What, seven, ten years? Or has it been longer?" Tyler hoped to bait him into talking about the story he stole. If Hailey couldn't face Dr. Loering Tyler was the second-best person to do so.

Dr. Loering was looking at him with something that resembled hatred or disgust or both. Either way, Tyler knew then the interview wasn't going to last the duration of dinner.

"You know what," he said, "I'll let you think about that, I need to use the men's room. Please excuse me."

"Take your time." he said scowling.

Tyler started walking to the bathroom. It dawned on him then that he would need to use a men's bathroom. As he was worrying about the logistics of a men's bathroom, he lost his footing and fell backwards, hard, in front of the entire restaurant, which had an open concept. The wind knocked out of him for a moment. While sitting he got his bearings, realizing that the entire place had gone quiet. Jeff came running up to him.

EXIT TYLER/ENTER HAILEY

She felt her head, her wig was off center, she thought in horror.

“Are you ok man? Shit, that looked rough. Seems like someone spilled some spaghetti sauce there," The look of alarm on Jeff's face let Hailey knew that even if Dr. Loering hadn't seen the fall, her ruse was up with Jeff.

As Jeff helped Hailey up, Dr. Loering had come up behind him.

“You, ok? He said, seeming genuine. "I saw that fall from over there, looked rough, you must be hurt.”

“I’m fine. Go sit back down, I'll join you shortly.” Hailey, surprised at his unpredictable kindness, was about to head to the bathroom when she heard her name being called from the bar area.

“Hailey? Hailey? Is that you? " Hailey felt a new rush of dread as she turned and saw Brock approach her. Dr. Loering was still within earshot and Hailey watched as he stopped when he heard her name.

"I saw you fall, why are you dressed like that? The makeup, the wig, the whole outfit? Are you in a theater production or something? I knew that Gwyneth was rubbing off on you."

Hailey froze, she either needed to deny who she really was or deny tell Brock to get the hell out of there.

Chapter 20

As soon as she was certain Dr. Loering was gone Jenna left the pantry. Her muscles were completely numb. Taking a big sigh of relief, she made her way out of the kitchen. It was hard to believe he had been inside just a moment ago, so close that she could smell his overpriced cologne that smelled like a mix of wood and nail polish. But she was safe, he was gone, for now. She entered what looked like a living room, halting for a moment to observe his horrible color schemes.

There were bright pink couches with pea green throw pillows strewn across them. The wallpaper was a bright yellow, with matching curtains that had fringe hanging from them.

She continued walking past two wooden framed chairs with pink felt cushioning and a grey rug into the hallway. The colors almost made her nauseous. Jenna was looking for Dr. Loering's bedroom. She left his horrific color scheme back to what appeared to be a hallway going to the bedroom. Dr. Loering gazed at her from both sides of the hallway. There were more portraits of himself in the hallway. It looked like he had them commissioned by different painters. But they were all the same picture, him in his trademark turtleneck and told-you-so expression. There were no pictures of anyone else. No parents, sister, family dog, friends, spouses, nothing. Just himself.

She wandered into the bathroom figuring she had enough time to relieve herself. Realizing that any proof of her break-in could jeopardize her reporting if nothing came of it, she thought better not. But what about the medicine cabinet? There was always something in the medicine cabinet. Jenna pressed on the mirror to open it. Prescription bottles and the usual assortment of ibuprofen, aspirin, and vitamins. She picked up the bottles, finding an erectile dysfunction medication.

"I knew it," she said out loud. Jenna continued. She was relying on Hailey to keep Dr. Loering for at least an hour. But she knew there was a high likelihood that Hailey would push his buttons. He was entirely made of push able buttons, so it was easy. Anyone who questioned him offended him. She made her way back into the hall of Dr. Loering's portraits, it looked like the master bedroom was at the end of the hallway. Jenna entered. His bedroom was just as hideous as his living room. His bed had a comforter with pink and purple flowers and there was a green chaise lounge with multicolored throw pillows.

Without thinking she went straight to his closet. It was likely there were secrets there. It was a walk-in closet with walls of brown turtlenecks, slacks, and suit jackets. Shiny brown shoes were neatly stacked below his clothing. Everything was neatly organized, not one piece of clothing out of place. She opened a drawer from his nightstand, and it had tissue, vics vapo rub, a nightlight, and what looked like a notepad.

She grabbed the notepad and ran to the other side of the bed. It was difficult to know how much time had passed, but she was certain that it was possible that he could be home at any moment. She threw open another drawer. Inside was what looked like a faded picture of a woman who looked pregnant. Jenna snapped a picture of it and replaced it. Scanning the bedroom one last time she decided to find his office, that's where his laptop would be, that's where she could find his hard drive.

Not far from Dr. Loering's house Gwyneth parked by the lake. She sucked in a hit and exhaled, blowing it out the window. She was debating whether to get out and walk to the beach, knowing it was important to stick near the car. Jenna or Hailey could call at any moment needing help. A group of four teenagers pulled up. Four teenagers in what was probably their dad's BMW. She looked at them laughing and teasing one another as she took another hit. They looked at her with curiosity as they got out of their car and headed to the beach.

There was a time when she would be going to the beach in her dad's BMW, she thought as she snubbed out the rest of her joint and lit up a cigarette, turning up the music in her car. Gwyneth decided to step out, she needed fresh air. She had been sitting in the car for almost forty-five minutes waiting for any news. Checking her makeup in the mirror quickly, she got out and took in the view of the Lake Michigan. She never came down here anymore. She wasn't exactly a lake person.

Looking out at the water always made her feel better, reminding her that her dreams were possible. She used to walk with her dad down to the lake when she was younger. The only thing that was missing was the joint that she had left in the car. As she grabbed it one of the teenage boys walked towards her. She ran her fingers through her long hair, looking up, knowing what the kid wanted. Clean cut, with perfect beach blonde hair, the kid was wearing designer board shorts. He had the look of the star high school football player.

"What's up kid?"

"Kid? I can't be much younger than you?"

"I look young for my age."

"What do you want?"

"I was wondering if you had any more of that stuff we smelled when we pulled up next to you?"

"Nah, no, I've got nothing on me."

"Aw, come on, I know you have some…"

Gwyneth huffed and walked away. How dare this kid? She looked for a bench that wasn't too far from her car but far away enough from the teenage boy who was now walking back to his friends in defeat.

With that Gwyneth got up and started to head back to her car. When she got back, she turned it on, grabbed the other joint and turned up *I Get Wild/Wild Gravity* by the Talking Heads and at the same time wondered what time it was, all the clocks in her car were off. She grabbed his phone out of the center console, there were several missed calls from an unknown number. Her phone never rang unless it was someone already in her contacts.

"Shit," she said as she hit the unknown number to call back. As the phone rang and rang she hit the joint. Finally it went to voicemail.

"This is Jeff, you know what to do."

Jeff? Who the hell is Jeff? She said out loud. A pit of anxiety started to form in her, what if something had gone wrong, she texted the number,

Jeff what's up, why do I have a bunch of missed calls from you, all good?

It occurred to Gwyneth in that moment that something might be wrong. Maybe Hailey was trying to get a hold of her. Gwyneth tried to call Hailey and it went straight to voicemail, no ringing. Odd, she thought. She knew that Hailey was with Dr. Loering but it was odd her phone was entirely off. Maybe she should go check in on Hailey to see if things were all right. But Jenna might need her.

"Shit" she said out loud. She was high and felt conflicted. She should go to Jenna. There was more potential for danger in that situation. She started her car and tailed it back, her tires screeching as she pulled into traffic. Something was off.

Now Hailey was in a situation.

"I have no idea who you are talking about, my name is Tyler," she said running off to the men's bathroom. She'd deal with Brock later. Dr. Loering was already suspicious, she didn't have a lot of time. She took out her phone and started to text Gwyneth and Jenna.

Dinner gone bad Loering could be on his way soon, 20 minutes tops

Before she hit send the door burst open. Dr. Loering walked in.

“Tyler? Tyler Carglass. Carglass. I should have known” Dr. Loering said stepping up closer to Hailey's face than she was comfortable with.

“What’s your real name Tyler? Or should I ask what your real last name is? You don’t work for the Herald do you? How did you get the credentials then? Those are hard to copy. I guess you are good at doing some research. Just not all of it. You know Tyler,” he said with a sneer. “I’ve had some bad interviews in my day. Ones that ended, let’s say, with a bang.”

He stepped closer to Hailey with his eyes on her phone.

“But this, as he snatched Hailey's phone from her hand, is by far the worst of them all," he said as he walked to a toilet and threw her phone inside.

“Hey, what the fuck! That’s my phone.” There was no point in hiding her voice anymore.

Dr. Loering towered over her, spraying spittle on her as he talked. Sweat had started to form under his armpits. Hailey realized the one question she should have asked Dr. Loering was why he dressed like he was in Siberia all of the time.

"And your career you piece of shit, you will never be anything once word gets out about this. Do yourself a favor, pick up a shift tonight at the bar. You'll need it." With that he walked out of the door.

Hailey stood for a moment stunned, then ran to the bathroom stall to retrieve her phone from the toilet. She was in wonder he hadn't figured it out, that it was her. Ok, he knew that she wasn't Tyler, but Gwyneth's makeup had worked enough that he still didn't recognize her.

"Please let it be flushed please let it be flushed," she pleaded to herself as she ran forward. As she got to the toilet, she could see that in classic fashion for the kind of place it was, the toilet was not flushed. It was bright yellow, the kind of pee from someone who was highly dehydrated.

"Fuck!" Hailey yelled, just as Jeff came rushing into the bathroom.

"Everything all right? I just saw that weird guy beeline out of the place. I hope you weren't counting on him paying for that bottle of wine, because he didn't leave any money on the table. First thing I checked before I ran in here."

"Jeff, give me your phone. It's an emergency, I have to get a hold of someone, now."

Jeff paused, looking at Hailey like she was crazy.

"Now Jeff!"

Jeff threw his phone at her. Hailey turned it on, racking her brain for Gwyneth's number. The first thing that pulled up on Jeff's phone was the Instagram feed of Joe Brazilian, a Dan Blizerian wannabe.

“Oh man, yeah, let me see. Yeah, I just found that guy Joe Brazilian the other day. He’s pretty rad man. He like hangs out with all these hot Asian chicks.

“I don’t give a fuck about Joe Brazilian,” Hailey said running out to the bar with the only idea she could think of. There he was, sitting at the bar, her only chance to get a hold of Gwyneth immediately.

"Brock," she said struggling to pull off her wig entirely.

"I knew it was you," he said in the know-it-all tone that Hailey hated, she felt so much disgust towards him and his tattling on her and Gwyneth, his righteous office attitude, men like Brock were what made the world stalled, stagnant, and colorless. She needed to put it aside and put on a performance.

Hailey started before he could get another word in, "Listen, I need your help immediately and I can't explain why. But I promise you, if you help me now, I'll go on a date with you tomorrow night."

"You think you can bribe me with a date?" He said clearly enjoying his newly found power. "What makes you think I'm interested in you anymore anyway; you've blown me off however many times, and why are you dressed like that?"

"Brock, I'm serious, Gwyneth could be in danger. I know you have your work phone with you. Can you please, please let me use your phone to call her? I know you have her number."

"Why would I have Gwyneth's number? The office slut? I guess not anymore because she was canned," He said laughing and looking to a man to his left who wasn't paying attention.

"Because you asked her out when she did work there, and I know, because she told me. Listen, Brock, I don't care, this situation is more important than that. Please help me."

Brock looked Hailey up and down, letting his eyes settle on her taped down chest before moving down her body.

"Tomorrow night then?"

"Tomorrow night, I promise."

"It better be a promise," he said as he started to scroll through his phone.

"You know," he said as he handed her the phone with his clammy hands, "She is a bad influence on a good girl like you. That's why she needed to go."

Hailey hit send, ignoring his comment. The phone rang and rang.

"Shit, she probably sees it's you and isn't picking up." As soon as the words came out of Hailey's mouth, she knew she had made a mistake by not appealing to Brock's fragile ego.

Hailey had just enough time to text Gwyneth

"YOU NEED TO GET JENNA OUT..." before Brock snatched the phone back from her.

There was no way for her to warn Jenna or Gwyneth that Dr. Loering was on his way home.

Chapter 21

“Shit,” she said as she hit the unknown number to call back. As the phone rang and rang, he hit the joint. Finally, it went to voicemail.

“This is Brock Pogie, you know what to do.”

Brock? Brock from work? Why in the hell would he be calling?" She said out loud. The nerve of that guy, she thought, he had asked her out relentlessly for a year. Gwyneth noticed that he had moved onto Hailey and was thankful but also felt Hailey's pain. He probably wanted to try asking her out again seeing she got fired.

"In his dreams," she mumbled, as she pulled up to Dr. Loering's place. Thankfully it didn't look like anyone was there. As she got out of the car she heard her phone buzz,

YOU NEED TO GET JENNA OUT

Gwyneth started running toward the house.

Hailey didn't know what to do other than to try and go to Dr. Loering's house. She ran out into the street where she knew a cab stand was and jumped into the next cab in line. She told the cab drive the address,

"Fast please, it's an emergency" she said with fear in her voice. What if it was too late?

Jenna had entered into his office; his laptop was sitting right on his desk. She opened the drawers, shuffling through various notepads. Finally, she found a drawer of hard drives. One part of the plan Jenna hadn't anticipated was the fact that he had about 10 hard drives. She hadn't thought to bring a bag in. There wasn't enough time to look at all of them. As she was considering how to stuff them all into her pants and bra, she heard a door open, then silence.

"Jenna?"

It was Gwyneth. "Thank fucking Elvis" she said under her breath

"Gwyneth, I'm back here, hurry, I need your help."

"Jenna, we need to get the fuck out of here, like now, I can't explain right now, we don't have time, but I think he's on his way back,"

"Ok, be calm, listen I found his hard drives but there's a bunch of them. Help me..."

Gwyneth walked over, "But won't he notice if every single one of his hard drives is gone and get suspicious? Remember we weren't supposed to leave a trace, he has security cameras."

Jenna was surprised by the insight from Gwyneth, how had she failed to think about this?

"You're right. We need the most recent one, that one probably has Hailey's story on it."

"Plug a few in, that's all we have time for, I'll try and dig around for a paper copy of her story,"

Gwyneth shoveled through cabinets. There were mostly photo albums, out of curiosity she opened one. Photos and photos of Dr. Loering posing in magenta colored banana slings.

"Oh God," she said taking one of the photos out. "I don't want to look but I can't help it."

Meanwhile Jenna had opened one hard drive and saw that it was from ten years ago. Another one, five, then, she looked below his laptop and saw a smaller drawer on his desk. She threw it open and there was a hard drive, "Gwyneth, this might be it."

"Good," Gwyneth said walking over.

Jenna plugged in the hard drive and saw today's date on a document. "This is it, this is fucking it, Ok Gwyneth," she said closing out of the hard drive and slamming his laptop shut.

"Let's get out of here, now." They were about to head to the room when they heard the door open and shortly after heard Dr. Loering yelling at Annabelle.

The cab driver was doing his best, but the traffic had stalled them. Hailey impatiently sat in the back, praying that Dr. Loering had been stuck in even worse traffic.

They pulled up to his house. Hailey felt a sinking feeling in her stomach as she realized Gwyneth's car was there and it looked like Dr. Loering had beat her to the house, the porch light was on. She thanked the driver, getting out, her wig was entirely off, and she had taken the pins out that were holding her hair up.

There was only one thing she could do, she thought as she ran to the door hoping that Dr. Loering wasn't a gun owner.

She rang the doorbell.

"Who the hell is it now," she could Dr. Loering yell as he approached the door.

"Are you kidding me? Now you?" He looked her up and down. "Wait, you have to be kidding me, you were that dipshit at the restaurant?" He said with a maniacal laugh. "You? The timid little squirrel girl?"

"Timid squirrel girl?" Hailey said feeling anger stirring up inside of her. "Apparently my timidity yields good writing results, wouldn't you say, Dr. Loering?"

"I don't know what you're talking about," he said, "But I don't allow fans on my property and I'm going to have to ask you to leave. You're lucky I don't press charges for the stunt you pulled today. What did you think you'd achieve anyway?"

"I achieved fooling you."

"Oh yeah, how so?"

"You believed I was Tyler at first. I know you did."

"The second I saw you I knew you weren't who you said you were. Journalists don't wear suits to meet with people at a restaurant. You looked overdressed and under confident. Kind of like you did at lunch as a matter of fact."

"Why did you steal my work?" Hailey said ignoring him. She knew she needed to buy as much time as she could for them to get out. But she also genuinely wanted to know.

He stood glaring at her; his arms crossed.

"I didn't steal anything from you. And what does it matter, you're a writtee, remember, and you're supposed to do anything a writer asks of you. If you don't follow the rules, then you pay the consequences. I'll make sure your name is ruined in this town, in this country, in this world if you ever try and accuse me of such a thing as stealing your work," he said emphasizing the word *your*.

"It makes me wonder how much other work you've stolen in your career. Is all of it stolen Dr. Loering? All your methods, all your ideas? Who did you get them from?"

"Now listen little lady..."

"No, you can listen to me. That story took me years to write, hours and hours of work and sacrifice. It may seem small to you, or like just because I've taken your workshops you have the right to tell me what to do and what not to do with my writing, but I'm not in your world anymore Dr. Loering. I could give two fucks about your writing methods. I've realized that I never needed them anyway." Hailey had his attention, so she decided to keep going. She needed to keep him occupied but she was hoping to hell she'd keep him long enough for them to get out.

"What I realized, is I have my own process, my own way. And I don't need you or anyone else to tell me how and when to write. Or that I"m less than because I haven't reached some golden standard of society that is gross with classism and obstacles that have nothing to do with how talented I am, but how much money I have in the bank and who I know and what's swinging between my legs. Why don't you just tell the truth, and say something like you put it out in your name so I would get attention? It would make you look selfless, like a hero. And you wouldn't lose anything..." as soon as Hailey said anything out of the corner of her eye, she saw Gwyneth and Jenna crouched by the side of his house.

Dr. Loering was still standing there, "I don't need to tell the truth because there is no truth of me stealing anything."

From the corner of Hailey's eye Jenna and Gwyneth were waving frantically.

"You're pathetic," Hailey said, feeling like it was the best thing she could come up with, but it wasn't enough, it didn't serve the justice she had hoped.

"I think you should leave and get off my property before I call the cops."

"Gladly," Hailey said and with that Dr. Loering slammed the door in her face. She stood for a moment, looking at his ornate wooden carved door. A door that probably would have been the cost of her college tuition for a year. She waved at Gwyneth and Jenna, and they ran to the car.

"We got it, we got his most recent hard drive," Jenna said getting into the backseat. "Back to the hotel, let's see what we can find."

Gwyneth looked over at Hailey, "Why the hell was Brock involved with this?"

"Valid question, I bartered a date with him so I could use his phone. Thank goodness he's a big enough dope that he hangs out at places like that bar."

"The kind of place where he might be noticed by the right people," Gwyneth said snickering.

"Exactly."

"I'm so glad you're safe Hailey, when I saw that message, I thought the worst."

"I'm glad you're safe too, Gwyneth, now we just need to see if we have any evidence."

Jenna sat in the back seat, hard drive clutched in her hand, smiling, because at the very least a strong friendship had been formed out of this mess, and Dr. Loering's poison hadn't been able to stop that from happening or stop it from strengthening.

They arrived at the hotel and got Gwyneth's laptop out to hook up the hard drive. While it was booting up, they laughed about Hailey's performance at the restaurant.

"I can't believe your wig fell off!! If only I had predicted spaghetti sauce on the floor. I'll have to keep that in mind going forward, "Gwyneth said laughing.

"The wig was still on, it just moved, I had to rip it off, trust me, under any other circumstance short of a hurricane that piece of hair wasn't moving."

Jenna was pacing back and forth until she saw his device pop up on Gwyneth's screen.

"There it is, she loudly exclaimed, "Let's see what we got," she said as she clicked on the drive. There were several folders in there. One labeled "Cats", "For Later" and "Art". Jenna clicked on the

"Cats" folder first. There were several video clips. Jenna clicked on one and a clip of what looked like anime porn pulled up.

"Are those tentacles?" Hailey said, leaning over Jenna.

"Hentai Tentacle Porn," Gwyneth said. "He has Hentai Tentacle Porn on his hard drive. Figures."

"What the hell is that? Hailey said as Jenna clicked through the rest of the videos which were all the same.

"I'll explain later, Jenna what about the "For Later" folder, that sounds promising. Jenna clicked on it and there were several other videos. The first one was of Dr. Loering sitting in a chair, laughing hysterically. Jenna fast forwarded through it; it was several minutes of him laughing. "This is fucking weird," she said.

"What about the other ones?" They went through the other videos, and it was different shots of Dr. Loering laughing.

"I don't see any word files, just movie files. We have one last folder, she said clicking into the "Art" folder. This folder had several jpeg files and one video file. Pictures of dirty socks and a few videos of cats sleeping.

"I didn't even see a cat in his house," Jenna said. Hope was beginning to wane in the room. It was starting to hit all 3 of them that there was no proof in the hard drive. Nothing, not even anything they could blackmail him with. It was a bunch of weird, innocuous videos. Nothing they could use.

"Nothing," Hailey had repeatedly said as she slumped into a chair. "All of that for nothing. I couldn't even get him to admit that he stole anything. When you two were hiding and I confronted him, he still wouldn't admit he stole my story. It was like he felt that I owed it to him, that it was his work even though it came from me.

Jenna stood up and put her hand on Hailey's shoulder. "It was a good try Hailey, sometimes you don't always find what you're looking for."

"Sometimes you find jack shit, "Gwyneth said pouring herself a shot of whiskey. "Now what?" She said downing the shot. "We can't pull this off again, he was already suspicious."

"I don't know ladies," Jenna said picking up her bag and heading to the door. "Listen, we gave it all we had, but I think for now we need to recoup and figure out what to do next, if anything. I'm sorry Hailey, I know it sucks. I'm going to head home, you take care of her alright, "she said looking at Gwyneth.

"You know I will. Wait Jenna," Gwyneth said running up to her and wrapping her arms around her. "Thank you. You didn't have to do all this. I know it's your job, but it means so much to Hailey and I."

"You don't have to thank me; I should be thanking you two. Usually I'm solo, it was nice working with you two. You know," she said looking at Hailey, "You could have a future in journalism, I know it isn't what you envisioned, but I think you have the talent for it."

Hailey was on the verge of tears and could barely muster a thank you, as Jenna left them to both face their uncertain futures.

Chapter 22

Hailey stepped into the cozy, low lit, pub from the cold, bare-tree street. Barely anyone was at the bar, and she took advantage of finding a seat at the far end of the bar. As she entered there was a burst of warm air, a reprieve from the cold, windy, drops of rain outside. She walked up to the bar and took a seat. Setting her black vintage Coach purse on the wooden bar she settled in. She was too cold to take her jacket off. The bartender, a younger looking woman dressed in a black blouse and pants walked by, acknowledging Hailey with a nod. As she settled in, grabbing her notebook and pen to jot down some notes for an idea she had, the bartender came back, and she ordered a glass of Pinot Noir. A moment she set it in front of Hailey.

People were trickling into the bar. It was happy hour in the Loop. The bar was a small, cozy, intimate space nearby work. Hailey had to keep her word to Brock, if even to save face.

Hailey took sips of her wine and started to fantasize about Bella locking eyes with her, a dreamy look that Hailey could get lost in. The reality was that Bella hadn't reached out to her since an uncomfortable conversation. She had finally seen the story in the Herald and called Hailey. She seemed curious when she explained the story to her but ended the conversation abruptly. It was another blow in the aftermath of everything that had happened with Dr. Loering.

Hailey saw Brock approaching her, he nodded.

"You're here," he said smiling at Hailey. "I thought you'd cancel," he said turning to order, "Can I get a peanut Greegio?" He said loudly next to her as he sat down, bumping her arm in the process.

Hailey felt no motivation to correct him. She had decided she would sit for one drink and exit.

“What are you writing there? Is that your diary?” He asked her in a way that expected an answer.

“Not quite.” She replied with a tiny, fake laugh.

“What’s so funny?” He asked in a tone that suggested he was clearly offended.

Confused at his tone she looked around to her to see if he was talking to her.

“Are you talking to me?”

“Oh sorry." He said doing a double take, examining her up and down. "Sometimes I come off a little harsh when I'm reminded of my ex-wife."

"You were married?" Hailey said not trying to hide her disbelief.

"Ha, yeah, don't try to hide your surprise. I see a woman like yourself, writing, and that reminds me of her, I guess I kind of lose it, or lost it there. I apologize. Really, it’s a compliment I loved my Dolores."

"It's ok." Hailey said, intrigued enough and happy to keep the conversation off of her.

Brock's head shined in the light, he was bald, and that day wearing a maroon sweater and khaki pants.

“Well Hailey,” he said moving closer to her, you don’t see people writing nowadays.”

This was going to be a long night if he was going to blabber on about writing and his ex-wife, but what else did she expect?

He took a sip from his drink and kept on going, even though Hailey was visibly annoyed.

“Most people are sitting on their phones looking at that social media stuff. I don’t use that stuff. I think it’s a waste of..."

"Brock," Hailey said, "Listen I hate to be rude, but I don't want to talk about writing..." Hailey's thoughts trailed off as she watched Kevin, and a crew of what looked like three spitting images of him with their button-down shirts and business wear dress pants enter the bar. They settled at the opposite end of the bar from Hailey and Brock, slapping one another on each other's backs and trying to get the bartender's attention. She had no idea that Kevin came to this bar, but most likely because she was always at work late while he was here.

"So, what, are you a writer or something?" Brock asked, looking over at her like she was a big shot.

Hailey turned her body towards Brock, trying to block out Kevin so he wouldn't see her, "Um, yeah, I don't know if I would classify myself as that, but I write, yes."

"What do you write?"

It was the last thing she wanted to talk about, but she was severely concerned about Kevin seeing her for several reasons, "Oh, all kinds of stuff. Poetry, essays, things like that," she said nervously rubbing her hands.

"Well good for you." He continued either not noticing or ignoring the nervous tone of her voice.

"I like to watch those detective shows and figure them out before the conclusion, "he said as he took another big drink, finishing his glass.

Hailey's thoughts were racing about how she was going to get by Kevin without him seeing her as Brock rambled on, "You know, I'm so glad you took over Gwyneth's position. She never took her job seriously. I hate people at work who don't take their jobs seriously. Like Florence today, she was blatantly texting all morning…"

As Brock continued rambling on, Hailey saw Kevin and his friend's downing shots. She needed to buy time. "You know," She offered, "I can't stand Florence either, her spreadsheets are sloppy, and she has coffee stains all over her shirt."

"Ah," he said, impatiently waving at the bartender for another round. "Yeah, I excel at excel, don't I?" He said laughing brushing his hand upon her hand. The feeling of his hand sent chills up and down Hailey's spine.

"You know, I do know a little about writing, my ex-wife was into that Dr. Loering all you ladies fantasize about." Hailey was displeased at the subject change, but she didn't care if Kevin didn't see her. At this point, Brock was so close that Hailey could smell his breath. It smelled faintly of stale whiskey. Kevin would have to go to the bathroom to see her and even if he passed, she could easily turn around.

"My ex-wife absolutely loves his book, what's the title of it? I'm blanking, something like, "I Know What to Think More Than You". She's read it a million times and used to quote it to me. Yep. I've heard all about Dr. Loering."

"Interesting," she responded loudly over what was now Kevin and his friends laughing.

"Hailey," he said, tapping the bar with his hand. Hailey sat wishing she had just gone to a cafe before the event.

"I'm trying to think of one of the more profound examples my ex-wife gave me. Oh, I remember, here is something, it was something like, "It's actually hilarious noticing people totally piss away the one solid opportunity to do their life's work on something absolutely stupid". I remember that one because she wrote it down and put it on the bathroom mirror. Boy did she look up to Dr. Loering. She *really* screwed herself believing his words."

The bartender had brought him another glass of wine and set it down, making eye contact with Hailey knowingly as she walked away.

“You see, Dolores worked as an administrative assistant.” He continued, staring straight ahead. "She had the whole world in front of her. I tried to get her to apply at our company several times, but she insisted on keeping her own job."

Even though the last thing Hailey wanted to do was listen to Brock's perspective on Dr. Loering and his failure of an ex-wife she knew she had to endure because she was hoping that Kevin and his friends would leave before she had to.

“She was trying to save up for college." Brock continued on, consistent with his lack of awareness. "

"She wanted to better herself. I told her, “Honey, I want you to stay home and take care of the kids we are going have, I’m the one who should be working.” She wouldn’t have it, damn determined that woman was. Anyway, it would have taken her half her adult life to pay for school with how expensive it is. We wanted to four children, what about their needs? What about my needs? She didn’t have any help or support and wasn’t the sharpest tool in the shed if you know what I’m saying. I said, “Tootz, I know you like them books but that kind of paper ain’t going to pay the bills. After reading Dr. Loering’s book she changed. Went nutty if you ask me. Quit her job against all logic, we had four hypothetical mouths to feed! Of course, at that point I was chopped liver. She stopped being the wife that I first married, my needs came last. Applied to community college, took out loans. Went and got her “writing” degree or whatever they call it and not much changed. She had a piece of fancy paper, but she ended up working a job that pays about the same as before. Dolores has a ton of debt now. And she isn’t satisfied. Now she wants more, she wants to pay off her debt and become a full-time writer. I said, “Honey, you could have done that before without all the debt. What about the kids we wanted?" I think that man Dr. Loering should be held responsible for his words. My wife guzzled his poisonous words down like a glass of cold water on a hot day. He ruined my marriage. Ripped apart my chance at having a family. Not everyone gets to do what they want in life. There is a balance. Take me for example, I'm good at what I do, but is being Kevin's right-hand man my Dream? No. But you don't see me complaining."

"Dr. Loering's message isn't for everyone I suppose" she said half-heartedly in response. She was exhausted hearing about Dr. Loering and could care less about Brock's ex-wife. She would be happy if she never heard his name again. Hailey's listening had gone in and out while taking large drinks of wine.

Everything seemed frustrating and pointless right then, men were always in the way, they'd always be there.

Her glass almost empty, now was time for action. She could go to the bathroom, stay in there for a while, then leave. Kevin wasn't going anywhere by the look of it, they had ordered food and another round of shots while Brock rambled on about his hopeless ex-wife. She felt ashamed of herself for fearing Kevin, but he was a bully and was certain to notice her if she tried to leave, she would never hear the end of it. She'd be the office slut. She glanced at the time. She'd have to try and run by Kevin.

Brock was rambling on about an array of topics, consistently unaware she wasn't fully listening.

"You know they don't make cortisone cream the way they used to. You need a gallon of it to relieve yourself these days and even then, it doesn't fully take care of the itch. I've got all the skin problems…"

Hailey frantically rummaged through her cluttered purse full of items she didn't really need but didn't want to waste to find cash.

He stopped his monologue and looked at her, "How's Gwyneth doing?"

Hailey looked him dead in the eye," She's great or at least I hear."

"You know, I did my best to get you away from her, such a bad influence, a dirty girl too. I'm glad I spoke up and had her canned, you know that she hooked up with Kevin..."

Finally, at the very bottom beneath her various notebooks, sunglasses case, and lipstick she found a few loose bills.

She threw down cash on the bar for the wine and a small tip and quickly gathered her jacket without fully knowing what she was about to do.

"Brock, you are an asshole. But I think the best thing you could have ever done for Gwyneth was to have her fired. So, thank you for that."

“Have a good evening,” she called as she walked as fast as she could to the exit. Thankfully Kevin was facing the bar in what looked like an in-depth conversation. Hailey was about to open the door when she heard someone yell, "Hey you, girl about to leave" from the bar.

Hailey stopped cold in her tracks.

"You, about to leave..." the bartender called, "You didn't leave enough for your wine."

Hailey heard Kevin, "Is that Hailey?"

"You didn't leave enough, you left $12, and the glass was $15, pay up." The bartender motioned for her to come to the bar. The bar was right where Kevin and all his friends were.

Now Kevin was fully aware it was Hailey. She fumbled again in her purse as she approached the bar, her face beet red.

"What, don't they pay you enough where you work?" Kevin laughed as he came up and slapped her on the back.

"It's dark in here and I couldn't see," Hailey mumbled as she grabbed her emergency cash out of her wallet and set it on the bar.

"I didn't see you in here," Kevin said, blocking her into the bar. "Ditched out early for a drink, huh? Something got you stressed?" He guffawed with his full beer in his hand as Hailey moved back, trying to dodge getting his mess all over her clothing. Hailey was praying Brock was too humiliated to make an appearance.

"Hey guys, this is one of my employees, Hailey, " he said, nudging his friends who were busy flirting with a pair of girls waiting for their drinks. They glanced over, all in with their neat hair, gelled, touting their button ups, their eyes getting glazed with what Hailey figured was the combination of booze and the hope of getting one of these girls.

"Nice to meet you," Hailey said in a meek voice, hoping he would leave her alone.

"Well not that I busted you, how about I buy you a drink?"

"I'm late already to an event Kevin, another time?"

"I'll take you up on that, as long as Brock doesn't mind," he said, nudging her.

"Mind what?" Brock was now standing in a circle of her two least favorite people.

"Hailey just enlightened me on how I did Gwyneth a favor by firing her, maybe we should do the same kind of favor for Hailey,"

Kevin gawked, "Brock you can be such a dick. Hailey's off, come over with the guys and get a beer, we can talk shop..."

"No, really, " Brock said, clearly doubling down on heckling Hailey. "I've heard her talking shit about you a number of times Kevin, you really going to let her get away with that?"

Hailey looked at Brock's determination and the dumbfounded look on Kevin's face and realized she didn't give a shit what either of them thought.

"You two can figure the whole thing out by yourselves because I quit. I'm done. One of these assholes will pay for my bill," Hailey screamed to the bartender. She walked as fast as she could to the door. Right as she was leaving, she could hear Kevin say while guffawing "Only reason she got the job in the first place is because I owe her dad a favor..."

Chapter 23

Jenna was back in the office trying to chase another potential lead. She'd had a break, a short break at least, one that satisfied her editor. There was too much going on, too many stories. She had a serious talk with her editor about taking a sabbatical to write a book in the next year or two. She'd been thinking of it for a while and felt it would give her time to reassess her life and satisfy her editor. He was on board. She was about to leave to follow up on a source when her office phone rang. A rare occasion, which she usually ignored, made her think twice to answer it.

"Jenna Janders" she said into what seemed like an ancient device, her cell phone was her real office phone. This was almost for show at this point.

"Jenna? I'm so happy I got you; I've been trying another number and it goes straight to voicemail."

"Do you have information for me?" Jenna asked, thinking he sounded like a potential source for one of her current stories. "What's your name?"

"My name is Bella, Bella Wicken. I'm a student at Medill."

"I don't take student interns Bella, so if that..."

"I'm not looking for an internship. I have information on Dr. Loering that I want to give to you, what you want to do with it is up to you. But I thought long and hard about it and you're the one that should have it. I've seen the work you've done on him over the years, and it inspired me to go to Medill for investigative journalism."

"Uh huh, well tell me Bella, what do you have?" She was skeptical as she always was, and she had never heard of this lady.

"I'm Dr. Loering's daughter. And I have proof that my mom developed all of his methods."

"How do I know you aren't full of shit, Bella? Do you have a paternity test?"

"No, not. yet. But I have my mom, she passed away a while ago, breast cancer, but she left an account of her relationship with Dr. Loering in addition to a bunch of records she had of their meetings. My mom dumped him and their program when she found out she was pregnant with me. She said she didn't want to deal with him when she was alive, I guess he's a real asshole. But she wanted me to have the information in case I ever wanted to reach out or pursue the story."

The thought of the pregnant woman picture flashed in Jenna's mind. There could be truth to this story, and if so, it would cause a huge controversy. Bella would be owed half of whatever the profits were that Dr. Loering was making. The implications were huge.

"Bella, let's meet. I want to see your proof if you're willing."

"Now?"

"Now's better than never."

Hailey had spent the last week applying for jobs and moping around her apartment. Her life was decidedly less busy without Writer Marie constantly texting her. She pictured the struggle Writer Marie would be having without her and wondered momentarily if she'd been assigned a new writee. Not my problem, Hailey thought. Hailey didn't miss the workshops, but she felt emptiness. She hadn't written a word in almost a week.

Gwyneth had been incessantly texting her about big news she had, but Hailey couldn't muster the enthusiasm or energy to respond fully or go see her. It was all too much. After applying for almost 50 jobs, she realized that finding a new position wasn't going to be an easy task. Her rent was due, she had enough for this month, but the next month she would not. Her parents weren't talking to her and had officially cut her off, although her mom had mentioned she was expected to attend holidays.

Even with the constant fear she was living with of not being able to survive and pay her bills, she felt a sense of freedom that she had never felt before. All of it was over. Her shitty job, her chance at publishing her story, but now the future laid ahead of her. She didn't have to deal with her parents, Dr. Loering, Kevin, Brock, none of them, they were all gone. After a few threatening texts from Kevin, she had to go hand in her name badge and security badge to get in the office. It was a quick transaction, with a weak apology, in hopes that maybe a consideration would be given to say something decent about her if anyone called for a reference. Hailey figured she could always use Gwyneth.

Hailey knew she needed a job and waiting wasn't a possibility, so she decided to apply to a local bar. She had spent enough time there, it couldn't be so bad, she thought as she tried her best to clean up and make herself look like a bartender versus an office person.

She was about to head out the door when her phone rang. She fished around in her purse, figuring it was Gwyneth again bothering her to go get a drink. It was Jenna.

"Hello? Jenna" Hailey said questioning why Jenna would call her. Jenna didn't seem like the type to call to catch up or check in.

"Hailey. I need to talk to you. Where are you?"

"I'm at my apartment but I was about to head out to The Local to apply for a job."

"A job? Like a part time job?"

Hailey started to respond but Jenna interrupted her, "Listen, lets meet and we can talk then. I'm headed there, give me 15."

"Ok," Hailey said and then the phone was dead.

Hailey had time to grab an application for the restaurant before Jenna arrived. She was searching her purse for her pen when Jenna showed up.

"It's so good to see you," Hailey said, embracing Jenna, an act that surprised them both. Jenna's returned the gesture with a warm smile.

"I'm so happy you could meet me. I needed to tell you this in person. Well, I have two things to tell you. I think I'll start with the one about Dr. Loering first."

Hailey's heart began to race.

"It's not about your story," Jenna said, "But it will hurt him. This woman called me the other day and told me she is Dr. Loering's daughter. I thought she was full of shit at first, but she convinced me enough to go check out some of the so-called evidence. Turns out she wasn't so full of shit, she had documents dated and signed by her mom, who basically developed Dr. Loering's entire writing program. She also wrote a lot of the material he later sold under his own name. Of course, she had more of a feminist view, and it his methods make a lot more sense coming from her, but it's good news."

"Does Dr. Loering know about his daughter? Or any of this? Why did she come out right now?

"All good questions. Bella that's her name, the daughter's name, she came out after her mom died, which was recent. I guess Bella's mom didn't want to have anything to do with it while she was alive. I'm not sure why Bella is doing it, she didn't tell me. I know that she goes to Medill, so maybe she wants it as her first big story, although she gave the story to me.

Hailey was silent. This had to be her Bella, the Bella whose eyes she could get lost in. Bella who she had thought about every day since she last spoke to her but figured she would never see her again. Bella who had seemed so sweet when she first met her.

"Do you have her number?"

"Why aren't we the investigative journalist," Jenna said jokingly pulling out her phone. "I do, but I want to ask you something."

"Shoot," Hailey said, all she cared about now was getting a hold of Bella. She wanted to see her again, right then. And it would be different from her, none of her usual reservedness, she would run up to her and throw her arms around her. She'd always dreamed of doing that, of being someone who could announce their love to someone in a romantic scene.

"Why are you applying to a bar? I thought you had a job at that plastics shipping company or whatever."

"I quit. Now I'm broke and I need a job before I get evicted."

"I see. Well, I wanted to talk to you. With your writing skills I could see you fitting in at the paper, you know it'd be a starting position, but I think it'd be enough to pay your rent. You wouldn't be working under me, but I know the person you'd be helping out and she's just as sharp as me, if not more."

"Are you offering me a job? Like as a writer?"

"I am offering you a chance to write as a journalist. You won't make much money, but it's a surefire way to improve your writing and find a story worth telling."

"I'm in." Hailey said excitedly even though she knew the salary would be barely enough to survive. It didn't matter. She would make it work. She was free.

After

Chicago 2018

Henry went bankrupt. He stopped teaching workshops. He didn't have any credibility after everyone found out he had stolen all his ideas from a brilliant woman. I think the worst thing for him was finding out he had a daughter. A daughter who wanted nothing to do with him.

I never heard from Writer Marie again. I heard there are still a few followers of Dr. Loering but they are discreet.

I found out that the pain I felt growing up of never following my own dream caused me to fall prey to someone like Dr. Loering. He was the ultimate dream maker to me. His message was opposite of the practicality that had been bestowed upon me during childhood. Yet, that very same practicality I saw as a prison in my earlier years helped me to see through Henry. The values instilled in me helped me to recognize a good friend when I saw one. Those same values helped me to be a good friend. Henry promised me something larger and in a way he delivered. He helped me see the most valuable gift, friendship. He helped me to find my own voice, my own power. I only had to stand up to him to find it.

Each word felt like an anchor pulling her fingers down. Each sentence begged to be complete, fighting for the ending to come, to arrive. She was close to being finished with her first book and the finish line seemed even further away than it had in the beginning. It was a cloudy day, helping her to feel less guilty about the fact she'd been in her office for 9 hours straight trying to finish.

Nevertheless, she needed to get up and walk around, a walk sounded like the perfect activity for a short break before finishing her last chapter. 10 years had passed since Jenna had given her the job, so much had happened since then, but the biggest thing was being able to write her first novel. And because of all her hard work at the paper, she'd been able to land a deal on her book. She stepped out into the grey day onto a somewhat deserted sidewalk and started to head towards one of her favorite bookstores. One she went to on a regular basis just to sift through the Beat Collection.

She entered and said hello to the owner who knew her by her first name.

"Hailey, how are you doing? Got this one in today I thought you'd appreciate, only because I know about your past" he said handing her a book. Hailey studied the title, "What I Got Wrong" by Dr. Loering.

"It's no good. The guy's a hack," a voice said behind her. She turned around and saw an older man wearing a brown turtleneck with slacks. He was bald with a thin ponytail trailing down his back. It was only noticeable when he turned his head. His breath smelled like coffee and moth balls. She studied his face, "Do I know you?"

"I think you do Hailey, but I understand if you don't recognize me. I don't get out much these days, not after all the commotion."

"Dr. Loering?"

"You do recognize me, even after all the hair loss. That happened after I found out about my daughter, then the media, the loss of money, everything gone you know, the way I had imagined life all changed when Bella came out. You knew her, didn't you?"

"I did know Bella," Hailey said, in disbelief. She had a short-lived relationship with Bella, but their work lives didn't allow the relationship to grow. She had loved her in that short time though, she was her first love, the one she'd always remember. She had moved to D.C. years ago so she could be a political reporter. She had no idea where she was now, but she thought of her from time to time.

"You really fucked me you know," Hailey said. "After all these years, you still haven't come out with the truth about my story."

"Read this," he said turning away. "Maybe it will help, maybe it won't. I tried to help people write, I tried to get women to stop being the second sex, ha the second sex in the second city, I wanted them to be the first, to beat the odds."

"You were the wrong person to want that. I could sue you now for my work. I could have done it years ago."

"Then why didn't you?"

"Because you looked so fucking pathetic, when your teeth got knocked out in by some random attacker. Every time I read something about you it was negative. I guess the right people always knew the truth about my work and that was enough for me, I didn't need to take away the only piece of your work that was considered original just to prove something to myself. Also, that story wasn't even that great, it just had your name on it, that's why the Herald published it."

"Read this." He said patting the book. "It's one of my best works," and with that he walked out of the store. Hailey watched him cross the street, he looked so old, diminished, a ghost of his former self. Hailey stood for a moment wondering what to do. She was curious but she didn't want to give this man one more cent. She chuckled at the title, "What I Got Wrong", how original she thought as she opened the book. There was a dedication.

"To Bella and to that girl I had lunch with, I'm sorry. I hope this serves as my penance."

She flipped to the first chapter. The word "For Everything" repeated itself for the first page. Maybe it's a mistake, she thought flipping to the second. "For Everything, for everything, for everything, for everything... the entire book was “for everything”. Hailey put the book on the shelf and walked out the door, it was time to get back to writing.

About the Author:

Jane Kirsling lives and works in Maine with her fiancé, their 2 dogs and cat. This is her debut novel.

Made in the USA
Las Vegas, NV
18 January 2026